MURDER ON THE TRANS-SIBERIAN EXPRESS

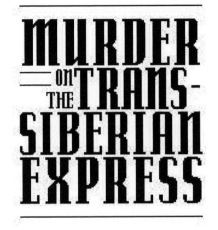

Also by Stuart M. Kaminsky
in Large Print:

The Big Silence
The Devil Met a Lady
The Dog Who Bit a Policeman
Hard Currency
Poor Butterfly
The Rockford Files: The Green Bottle
Rostnikov's Vacation

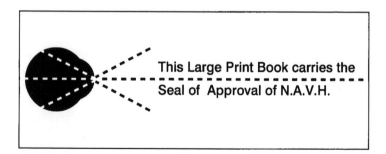

This Large Print Book carries the
Seal of Approval of N.A.V.H.

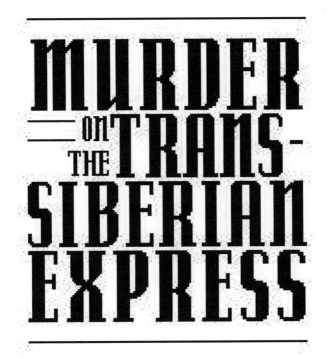

MURDER ON THE TRANS-SIBERIAN EXPRESS

Stuart M. Kaminsky

Thorndike Press • Waterville, Maine

Published in 2002 by arrangement with Warner Books, Inc.

Thorndike Press Large Print Basic Series.

The tree indicium is a trademark of Thorndike Press.

The text of this Large Print edition is unabridged.
Other aspects of the book may vary from the original edition.

Set in 16 pt. Plantin by Rick Gundberg.

Printed in the United States on permanent paper.

Library of Congress Cataloging-in-Publication Data

Kaminsky, Stuart M.
   Murder on the trans-Siberian express / Stuart M.
Kaminsky.
     p. cm.
   ISBN 0-7862-3814-3 (lg. print : hc : alk. paper)
   1. Rostnikov, Porfiry Petrovich (Fictitious character) —
Fiction. 2. Police — Russia (Federation) — Moscow —
Fiction. 3. Siberia (Russia) — Fiction. 4. Moscow (Russia)
— Fiction. 5. Railroad travel — Fiction. 6. Large type books.
I. Title.
PS3561.A43 M75 2002
  813′.54—dc21   2001054449

This one is for Momus with thanks
for his inspiration.

Prologue

Catch a train direct to death
Glide where wheels and rails caress
Hear the last taboos expressed
In language looted and compressed
Abandon this world for the next
Cross the great plain of forgetfulness
Trans-Siberian Express

Siberia: 1894

The six men trudged into a thick forest of birch and aspen trees so dense that this gray morning had the feel of oncoming night.

The permafrost had started its slow thaw and their ragged boots cracked through the glassy upper layer and sunk an inch or so into the earth. Had they not each been carrying a body they would probably not have broken the steamy surface.

Boris Antonovich Dermanski kept walking when he heard the blast of dynamite no more than three miles away. The blast was followed by the distant sound of raining rocks from the wounded mountain. It was a familiar sound. Boris had lost track of how many mountains they had ripped through, how much frozen ground had been torn up with dynamite, how many bridges they had built.

He walked on, shifting the nearly frozen naked body on his shoulder. Boris was the biggest of the group and the only one who was not a convict. Though it had not been specified by the section leader, it was assumed that Boris was the leader of this burial detail. It had also been assumed that he would carry the heaviest corpse.

He grunted softly and watched the men move slowly through morning mist in no particular formation.

Boris estimated that they had moved about two hundred yards from the temporary camp next to the end of the train tracks. Every foot of track had been laid by hand by men like and unlike Boris with picks, axes, and hammers; men in lines of six or more carrying lengths of steel and men in twos carrying wooden cross-ties which were laid quickly under the unnecessary guidance of a series of men introduced only as Engineer Kornokov, Engineer Sveldonovich, Engineer Prerskanski.

They were told that they had laid over two thousand miles of track. They were told that they had more than three thousand miles more to put down.

The best way to think about it, Boris had long ago decided, was not to see it as a project that had an end. He had quickly decided that this was his life's work and that he would probably not live to see the last tracks laid down in the city of Moscow.

One of the men, a lean convict known as Stem, looked over his shoulder at Boris.

"Here?" Stem asked.

"Keep going," said Boris, again shifting the body on his shoulder. Boris's dead man had died the night before, gasping for air, eyes wide in horror, looking from face to face for help, for air. Boris did not know his dead man's last name, but he did know his first, Yakov, and his approximate weight, heavy.

Stem stopped and turned. The others stopped too. One of them, a dark little bull named Hantov, rasped, "What's wrong with here?"

Boris strode on, moving through the scattering of men. Here would have been fine. It really didn't matter where they dropped the bodies, but Boris was in charge. He had to make the decision. There were thousands of miles to go, and his survival and reputation might well depend on how resolute he was.

Many had died, from the plague, disease,

landslides, floods, anthrax, tigers, a wide variety of accidents and fights. The engineers and bosses who died were boxed and shipped to Vladivostok or back to Moscow to be buried as heroes of the czar's grand plan to unite Moscow with all of Siberia, right to the coast, only a few hundred miles from Japan.

It was to be the longest railroad in history. It was to be the most expensive railroad in history. It was to be a tribute to the royal family, to the memory of Alexander, to the triumph of Nicholas.

Boris cared nothing for the royal family. He cared only for his own family in Irkutsk, for warm clothes and enough food to eat.

He had been among those in the crowd two years earlier on May 31, 1891, when the Vladivostok station had been declared open and the construction of the Trans-Siberian Railway had officially begun. Czarevitch Nicolya Alexandrovitch, the heir to Emperor Alexander III, laid a stone-and-silver plate to commemorate the undertaking. There had been applause. The white gloves that Nicholas had worn to lay the stone had been taken off ceremoniously and placed in a jeweled box, which was carried away by the mayor of the city to be displayed in a place of honor to be determined.

"What's wrong with here?" asked Stem.

Boris kept walking. He did not turn around. They would either follow him or kill him, drop the bodies, and go back saying he had fallen in a hole or been attacked by a bear. No one would know. No one would check. There were more than eighty thousand men working on the railroad. Hundreds died every week.

"I said, What's wrong with here?" Stem repeated.

Stem had been in a St. Petersburg prison for theft. He had also committed two murders but had not been caught for those crimes. The other convicts had come from all over Russia. None had been asked if they wanted to die building a railroad. None had been promised anything more than food and work and time, perhaps years, away from prison.

Boris walked on.

"These corpses are diseased," another man called to Boris's back. "We're breathing in their death."

Actually, only four of the dead bodies had been superficially diagnosed as diseased. Two had died in accidents.

A second blast, louder than the first, shattered the morning. Birds went silent to listen.

"There," said Boris, continuing forward toward an opening before him.

He moved slowly to a trio of rocks, large, almost black, each the height of a man. He dropped the corpse he was carrying in a small clearing next to the rocks and looked around. Silence. Streaks of sunlight, not many, came down like narrow lantern beams through the tree branches. It was the right place, a natural cathedral. Boris had imagination and intelligence he kept hidden. There was nothing to be gained by the revelation of either, and much to be lost.

He was big Boris, good-natured, a loner, not to be crossed. When he fought he was ruthless and violent. When he talked, which was seldom, he kept it brief.

Boris turned to face the five men, who moved toward him and followed his lead, dropping the bodies not far from the dark rocks. One man shivered with the loss of his burden. Another tried to rub death from his shoulder.

There was no talk of burial. The wolves and other animals would come quickly. There would be only bones before a week was out.

Stem looked at the jigsaw pile of bodies, made a *V* with the filthy fingers of his left hand, and spat between them in a gesture of peasant superstition which Boris ignored.

"A prayer," said Boris.

Some of the convicts laughed. One turned into a paroxysm of coughing, a hacking cough which suggested to the others that he might be among those on the next pile of the dead.

"Go back, then," Boris said.

"I have a message for the dead," Stem said. "Save a warm place for me. May there be large women in hell. May there be a hell to welcome us."

"Stem's a poet," called a man named David, who had a large lower lip and the look of an idiot.

"Go back," Boris repeated softly, knowing that their show of false courage in the face of lonely death needed punctuation. "I'll join you."

The men started back through the forest. Boris remained behind. No one looked back at him. Let him say a prayer. He wasn't one of them. He wasn't going to run away, hide, try to find a village or a hunter to take him in. None of the five convicts even considered escape. They knew better.

Boris did not pray. He watched till the men were no longer slodging ghosts in the mist. Then he quickly removed the package from his pocket.

The package was narrow, small, animal-skin-bound with strips of leather covering a metal box. Boris moved quickly behind the three rocks, searching for some safe place, some protected niche. He spotted it quickly.

Luck was with him, though he had been prepared to make his own luck.

There was a thin opening in the rock on his right, a little above eye level. Boris knew his package would fit. It would be tight, but it would fit. He had a good eye for such things. He wedged the package into the space as far as it would go and then found a handful of small stones to cover the opening. He cracked through the permafrost with the heel of his boot and scooped up cold mud, filling in the cracks. He worked quickly and stepped back to assess his work. It was close to perfect. He knew it would be. He had planned, practiced.

He stepped away from the three rocks and the white corpses without saying a prayer. The dead needed no prayers. If there was a God, he would take those he deemed worthy. No entreaties from the living would make a difference. If there was no God, then prayers were only for the living who believed or wanted to protect themselves in case they might someday believe.

He moved quickly, straight, his boots no longer cracking the icy surface now that he had relieved himself of Yakov's corpse. Boris knew exactly, within feet, the number of miles they were from the next planned station. He knew the range of hills and low mountains and had chosen this spot and this moment be-

14

cause of the distinct shape of one of those nearby mountains. He had seen the mountain the day before when there had been some sun and the mist had drifted away.

He had missed one opportunity a week earlier. There had been another burial detail scheduled. Boris could not volunteer. No one volunteered for corpse carrying, but he had known the detail was coming and had stayed near the weary section boss who usually simply looked up and pointed to the nearest men, assigning them the duty. The section boss, through dull heavy eyes, had simply missed Boris in spite of his proximity and size. So Boris, his dangerous package tucked deeply and safely inside the lining of his jacket, had to wait.

And then this morning's chance had come and the signs had been there, the mountain, the location. He committed distance and signs to memory. They were not complicated. Later, if he lived, he would return. If he did not, he would give directions to his wife or his brother or whoever remained of his family, though he doubted anyone but he could find the place again.

Boris moved back toward the train quickly. He caught up with the five convicts, whose pace had slowed once they had left the dead comfortably behind in the clearing.

"You said your prayers?" asked Stem.

Boris nodded and grunted.

"If you have to carry me someday," Stem said, suddenly solemn and very softly, "say the same one for me."

"I will," Boris said. "You have my promise."

When they got back to the camp, they smelled something cooking. It was familiar and not welcoming — a huge vat of soup or gruel made from whatever stock might be on hand and whatever animals, if any, the hunters had found.

Boris had once found a whole mouse in his bowl. Others had claimed to find even worse.

There was a stir of activity among the men both outside the railroad cars and within. People were shouting. Armed soldiers, rifles in hand, hurried in pairs and trios alongside the tracks. Through the frosted windows Boris could see men being stripped naked, uniformed soldiers watching over them. He saw one man bent over, spreading the cheeks of his behind so a teeth-clenched soldier could examine his opening.

"What's going on?" one of the convicts who had been on the burial detail asked.

"Search," said a cook's assistant with a big belly. The assistant was smoking a cigarette and glancing back. "Something's missing.

They won't say what. They've torn the camp apart, gone through the train, everything. They decided I haven't hidden whatever it is up my ass. Now it's your turn."

"Shit," said one of the convicts. "I'm going to hide till they're finished."

"You cannot hide. Better get it over," the cook's assistant said. "Can't serve food till they're done. And they give you a red card when they finish with you. When they've gone over everything, we all stand in line and return the red cards."

"What the hell is missing," asked Stem, "the crown jewels?"

"How would the crown jewels get on a track-laying train in Siberia?" answered the cook's assistant.

"Then . . ."

"Who knows?" said the cook irritably. "Maybe some government official or a general just went crazy, lost his wallet or his pocket watch. Just get it over."

Boris stepped ahead of the group and moved toward a trio of soldiers who stood before a shivering quartet of naked men. One of the soldiers went through the pile of clothing. The other two soldiers were giving careful examinations of the naked men.

Boris looked up at the frosted window of the train car a few feet away. Inside the car, a thin naked man was dangling from a bar by a rope tied around his wrists. At his side stood a very short man in a heavy black-wool sweater. The short man was whispering to the dangling man, who struggled to keep his head upright. Boris's eyes met those of the dangling man and Boris gave a small nod.

By the time the short man had turned to look out the window, Boris was but one of a group of more than a dozen men.

"You," called one of the soldiers, pointing at Boris. "You are next."

Boris moved dutifully forward.

Part I

Day One

Chapter One

Chief Inspector Porfiry Petrovich Rostnikov stood at the window of his office with a reasonably hot cup of strong Turkish coffee warming the palms of his hands. The sun glowed like a dying bulb through gray clouds that hinted at a first snow of the season.

He looked at the two pine trees in the courtyard of Petrovka, the central police headquarters in Moscow. Petrovka was named for Petrovka Street, which runs in front of the six-story U-shaped white building, just as Scotland Yard in London and One Police Plaza in New York were named for their addresses.

He had ten minutes before the morning meeting with Igor Yaklovev, director of the Office of Special Investigation. He took a sip of coffee. It was strong, and that was good, because the cold gray winter sky of early morning suggested not even a hint of warmth.

The biggest unit of the Moscow Criminal Investigation Division is the Investigative Directorate, which includes fourteen investigative divisions, including theft, plunder, and murder. The fifteenth unit, the Office of Special Investigation, exists for one thing only, to deal with those cases which no one else wants because they are politically sensitive, unlikely to be solved, or offer little promise and much potential grief.

The young man seated in front of Porfiry Petrovich's desk looked down at the sheet of paper in front of him. A name was written on the sheet. Rostnikov had not spoken the name aloud. His office was wired. Everything said within its walls was recorded on tape in the office of the director of the Office of Special Investigation. Rostnikov knew this, and Yaklovev, known as the Yak, knew that his chief inspector was aware of the recordings.

The Yak had survived the reshuffling of the former KGB, the fall of the Soviet Union, enemies, both political and personal, and had come out with information that could embarrass many leaders in government, the military, intelligence, and business.

The Yak had worked with and knew Vladimir Putin from the days when they had both been with the KGB in Leningrad, which was now St. Petersburg.

The Yak could have insinuated himself into a higher office but he had judged that his time had not yet come. Leaders fell too quickly.

Patient and cautious bureaucrats survived.

And so he had asked for and been assigned the Office of Special Investigation which, under its former head, Colonel Snitkonoy, the Gray Wolfhound, had been largely ceremonial, that is before Rostnikov had been transferred to it from the Office of the Moscow Procurator.

The Wolfhound had been promoted to head of security at the Hermitage in St. Petersburg largely as a result of the success of the Special Investigation Office under Rostnikov. The Yak had stepped in with the goal of adding to his well-protected collection of incriminating tapes and documents while building his reputation as a man who could get things done without embarrassment.

Rostnikov and the Yak had a distinctly symbiotic relationship. The Yak protected Rostnikov — who often stepped on the boots or polished shoes of those in power — and Rostnikov and his team provided the Yak with a series of successes and connections to grateful victims and offenders.

And so, not wanting to put on tape the name that was before his son, Iosef, Rostnikov had written it out. Iosef Rostnikov, the most recent addition to Porfiry Petrovich's team, had understood.

"Find what you can about her," said

Rostnikov, looking out the window at a man in a knee-length leather jacket, briefcase in hand, hurrying through the guarded iron gates below.

"She doesn't want the children," Iosef said.

"She says that she does," Rostnikov said, turning from the window and moving to his desk. There was only so long that he could stand on his metal-and-plastic left leg. It was far better in many ways than the withered one he had dragged around since he was a boy, but the lost leg had been like a crippled child. He could talk to that leg, urge it on, cajole it. This piece of alien material had no soul. Sometimes Rostnikov admitted to himself that he missed the pain of the lost limb. He could, of course, visit the leg whenever he wished. It resided in a large jar in the second level under Petrovka in Paulinin's laboratory, a jungle of books, jars, metal containers, tables, and equipment that might well have been antiques salvaged after the fall of the castle of Baron Frankenstein. That was the way Paulinin liked it, Paulinin who talked to corpses and collected their spare parts and assorted objects of metal, wood, plastic, and bone. It was widely believed that he had Stalin's brain well hidden among the rubble. Rostnikov's leg was in good or bad company, depending on one's view of Stalin.

At one point in his youthful zeal, Porfiry Petrovich had (as had most Russians) seen Stalin as a near God, a father, a man who deserved the name Man of Steel. Porfiry Petrovich had named his only child in honor of Stalin. Not many years afterward Rostnikov had regretted his decision, but his son had by then worn the name well.

The name on the sheet of paper before Iosef Rostnikov was "Miriana Panishkoya Ivanovna." Miriana's two young daughters, Laura and Nina, along with their grandmother, Galina, were now living in the one-bedroom apartment of Rostnikov and his wife, Sarah, on Krasnikov Street.

It had come about like this. Miriana had simply walked out on her children, leaving them with her mother. The grandmother, who was sixty-four years old at the time, had done her best for them on an insignificant pension and odd jobs. Then one day in a state bakery she had been turned away by the manager, a petty tyrant. The grandmother had begged for bread. The manager had grown loud and foul. The grandmother, in a state of confusion, had shot him with his own gun. The grandmother had gone to prison, and Rostnikov and Sarah had taken in the two girls while she served her time.

Now the girls' mother was back.

"She wants money?" asked Iosef, pocketing the sheet of paper.

"That will be the next step," said Rostnikov, seated but not wanting to settle in because it was nearly time for the morning meeting.

"And you shall refuse?" said Iosef.

"I shall tell her that it is her right to take the children and that your mother and I will miss them."

"And she will walk away."

"Perhaps with some help provided by you. If that fails, I will employ the law."

Neither man needed to discuss what this meant. The laws of Russia were a shambles: a basis in old Soviet law, assumptions of common sense and vague precedents, smatterings of Western manipulations gleaned from reruns of "Law & Order," "L.A. Law," "Rumpole of the Bailey," and ancient black-and-white episodes of "Perry Mason."

The law, in short, was whatever the politically appointed and frequently corrupt judges wanted it to be. While corruption and politics pervaded the old Soviet system, there were still occasional Communist zealots on the bench who stood behind and believed in the oppressive laws in the books they seldom read.

Now the law was written by Kafka.

Rostnikov would know how to use that law to rid himself of the suddenly returned mother. His concern was less with getting rid of her than in not adding to the weight of the world the two girls and their grandmother were already carrying. It was only in the past few months that the girls had begun to come out, to talk, to begin to smile and ask for small things.

Rostnikov finished the last of his coffee and rose, saying, "Shall we go?"

Iosef rose and nodded.

Rostnikov picked up his notebook and with his coffee cup in hand followed his son to the door.

"Karpo and Zelach are not back?" Rostnikov asked as his son opened the door.

"No."

"Then," he said as they moved into the corridor, "perhaps it will be a short meeting."

"We can hope," said Iosef, walking next to his father.

"We're Russians. It's what we do best."

There were three of them, two young men and a young woman. They were nude from the waist up. They were in one bed, looking up sleepily at the two odd men who had awakened them at the insane hour of eight in the morning.

27

"Which one of you is Misha Lovski?" asked the lean pale apparition in black slacks, tieless shirt, and jacket.

Karpo and Zelach had knocked at the door. They had heard the sound of tired voices inside the apartment. No one had come. They knocked again and waited. When there had been no answer, Karpo had nodded to Zelach, who adjusted his glasses and threw his shoulder against the door. The door flew open with a spray of wood chips and splinters.

Karpo had his weapon in hand as Zelach stepped to the side. In front of him in the single room cluttered with clothes, compact disks, empty liquor bottles, and full ashtrays was the bed with the trio under a blanket covered with cartoon figures of a fat man with a flowing white beard and a mass of wild hair.

The three in the bed should have been frightened. Perhaps they were, but the fear did not fully surface. To Emil Karpo they looked drugged, sleepy, and less than aware that life was a fragile thing.

"Misha Lovski?" Karpo repeated, putting his weapon back in the holster under his jacket.

The young man on the right side of the bed ran his hand across his shaved head and said to the ghostly figure in front of him, "Cops?"

"We are the police," Karpo answered.

"We know no Misha Lovski," the young man said, touching his bald head.

"He pays for this apartment," Karpo said.

"The Naked Cossack pays for this apartment," the young man said.

"Who are you?"

"Yakov Mitsin," said Zelach. "Known as Acid. The Naked Cossack is the name of the lead singer and of the band. They are the Naked Cossacks."

Karpo glanced at his fellow officer. Zelach was a constant enigma, overweight, nearsighted, less than bright. He lived with his mother and blessed his luck at having been assigned to the Office of Special Investigation. He knew he was slow, but Zelach the Slouch was loyal and reliable. He was also a constant surprise to his fellow investigators in moments such as this.

"You've got it," said the literally nude young man, pointing a finger at Zelach, who was doing his best not to look at the full breasts of the girl in the middle of the two young men. "The Cossack's name is not Lovski. Lovski's a Jew name."

"What is his last name?" Karpo asked.

The three looked at each other for an answer. None came.

"We never asked. He never mentioned."

29

"And you two?" asked Karpo. "Your names?"

"Valery Postnov," said the other young man, the youngest of the group, frail, blond hair cropped bristle-close, blue-eyed.

"Pure Knuckles," said Zelach.

"Pure Knuckles," the young man confirmed.

The girl reached past Pure Knuckles, her breasts brushing against his chest. Her right hand grabbed a package of cigarettes and a matchbook. She jiggled as she sat upright, lit one of the cigarettes, and lay back. Her hair, cut short in a neat bob, was a flaming and artificial neon red.

"And you?" asked Karpo.

"Nina Aronskaya," she said.

Karpo hesitated for an instant, waiting for Zelach to reveal her colorful identity. Zelach said nothing. This one he did not know.

"Anarchista," she said, looking at Zelach and smiling.

"Steel Ladies," Zelach said.

"You know your metal," the girl said with a smile, pointing her cigarette at the bespectacled, rumpled detective who managed not to blush. "Now I'm with Naked Cossack."

"So," said Yakov Mitsin, who got out of the bed, revealing his full nakedness. "I will guess. Somebody doesn't like our music.

30

You're going to haul us in for treason or drugs or something. Okay. Then we get our lawyer. The newspapers, television, foreign journalists come. We get big coverage, free publicity. I'll get my pants on and be ready in a minute."

He moved across the room.

"Stop," said Karpo.

The young man halted, shook his head, and turned toward the pale figure in black. He met the man's eyes with an air of practiced indifference, but he saw something there that he had not seen before.

The pale detective did not blink. He neither smiled nor frowned.

"Turn around, sit down," said Karpo.

The young man considered a smirk but thought better of it. He sat on the edge of the bed and took an offered cigarette from the girl.

"What do you want?"

"We're looking for Misha," said Karpo.

"Naked Cossack," Zelach reminded him.

"What's he done?" asked the thin blond boy, looking at the girl for guidance.

"Nothing," said Karpo. "He is missing."

The nude Mitsin laughed and looked at the equally unclothed girl, who smiled.

"When he's gone for a month, we can worry," Mitsin said. "He could be . . ."

31

"He made a call to the police," said Karpo. "Said he was being held by someone. He sounded frightened."

"Bullshit," said the girl.

"The call is recorded," said Karpo. "It is his voice. He sounds genuinely frightened."

"Genuinely frightened," Mitsin mimicked.

"I am familiar with genuine fear," said Karpo.

And the three in the bed knew instantly that he was.

"We do not know where he is," said the blond boy. "Why come to us? Hell, what are we going to do? He's got a concert on Saturday. You think he is? . . ."

"I will ask questions," Karpo said. "You will answer them. If I am satisfied with your answers, we will leave. If I am not, you will come with us to Petrovka."

"Shit," said Mitsin. "Ask."

"What are you doing here in Misha Lovski's apartment?"

"We crash and burn here sometimes. Sometimes other places. Sometimes here. Places," said the girl, looking at Zelach and smiling. "And his name is not Lovski."

"When did you last see him?"

"Cossack? Yesterday maybe," Mitsin said.

"Day before," the girl corrected.

"Day before," the blond boy confirmed.

"Where did he go?"

"Go?" Mitsin shrugged. "I got to piss."

He got up and moved slowly, sleepily, toward the open door of the bathroom a few feet away. Zelach could see a melange of towels and a dented bar of soap on the floor.

"Could have gone lots of places," the girl took up, playing with her cigarette. "He hangs with the *skiny*, sometimes in Gorbushka. Sometimes at Loni's. Sometimes who knows where?"

Skiny, Karpo knew, were the young skinheads, not an organized gang but a teeming youth culture with no core but a shared belief in hatred of foreigners and nonwhite races, clad in neo-Nazi chic leather jackets decorated with swastikas and wearing highly polished black boots. Groups of skinheads routinely beat up blacks, Vietnamese, and Chechins and sprayed anti-Semitic graffiti on the walls of public buildings and in the dark underpasses beneath broad and crowded Moscow streets.

Their enemies were the *rappery*, with baggy pants, baseball caps worn backwards, puffy parka jackets, spiked hair, addicted to American rap and hip-hop and trying to sound African-American, which was particularly bizarre in street Russian.

Rappery and *skiny* clashed, often violently, the *skiny* going for bright, Phat Pharm rip-off clothing, and the *rappery* tearing off the treasured boots of a *skiny* caught alone and kicked to the ground.

Karpo had seen both groups, sometimes in the same *obyezannik,* the police-precinct cages designed for drunks and petty criminals, sitting in clusters across from each other, neither group moving, too weak from the beatings they had been given by each other and the police who picked them up.

Gorbushka was the open-air market in a wooded park at the northwest edge of the city. Not unlike the Paris flea market, Gorbushka was where ordinary citizens flocked to buy pirated videotapes, computer software, compact disks ranging from country-and-western to Frank Sinatra. But lately the market had become a mecca for *skinys,* and foreign visitors, particularly those who were not white, had been issued unofficial warnings to avoid the market. An African-American marine guard at the US Embassy had recently ignored the warning and wound up badly beaten. When one of his attackers was caught, he proudly told the television camera in his face, "Black people seem to be attracted to my fists like metal to a magnet. Everywhere I go they bite me on the fists."

In the market stands a low gray granite building where only the *skiny* dare enter.

Heavy-metal music promising death and celebrating hate booms while bald young patrons laugh and buy boots, CDs, American Confederate flags, leather jackets, Nazi flags and copies of Nazi medals, and pick up pamphlets preaching racism and rabid nationalism.

"Where is Loni's?" Karpo asked.

"Kropotkin Street," said Zelach.

The girl looked at Zelach with amusement and said, "You retro?"

Zelach looked at Karpo, who looked back and said nothing.

"Jefferson Starship, Aerosmith, Black Sabbath," Zelach muttered.

"Favorites?"

"Ozzy Osborne's 'Sabbath Bloody Sabbath' and 'Psycho Man.' Ted Nugent's 'Cat Scratch Fever.'"

"No," the blond kid said incredulously. "Heavy, really heavy. Russian?"

"Kruiz, 'Mental Home,'" Zelach said, taking off his glasses so he would not see the bare-breasted girl clearly.

"Favorite fem?"

"Diana Mangano," Zelach said softly, cleaning his glasses.

"*Total Chaos?*" the blond kid tested, showing teeth in need of serious dental work. "Latest album."

"*In God We Kill,*" said Zelach, putting his

glasses back on and glancing at Karpo in apology.

"Amazing," said the girl. "Old bastard like you."

Zelach was not yet forty.

The toilet flushed. The door had not been closed. There was no sound of running water. Acid had not washed his hands.

"This cop is plugged in," said the girl, bubbling out from under the blanket now, sitting cross-legged, totally and un-selfconsciously revealing herself. "Try him."

Mitsin stopped and said, "Best Latvian group."

"I think Skyforger," said Zelach.

The blond boy clapped and the girl laughed. Mitsin grinned.

"We'll talk to you," Mitsin said. "Not the slant."

Karpo considered. His primary nickname, never spoken to his face, was the Vampire. He was well aware of the appellation and did not consider it unflattering. He was also known as the Tatar because of his Asian eyes, earned through Tatar blood. His options were simple. He needed information. He had an assignment. Emil Karpo had no family, no religion — aside from his almost-forgotten mother, the only woman who had meant anything to him was dead, and the religion of

Communism in which he had fully believed and to which he had dedicated his existence was gone. There was only his duty, the universal hope of the policeman to keep the animals from taking over the jungle, the personal commitment to social order.

Karpo considered firing his weapon or breaking the arm of the strutting, chicken-breasted young man, not out of anger but because he knew the effort would be rewarded. Death, which Emil Karpo did not fear, turned young posturers and old criminals into cooperative babblers. These three held no beliefs or loyalties for which they would risk their lives. But instead of speaking he turned to Zelach and nodded.

Zelach did not want to speak. He did not want to look at the girl, who could have been no more than seventeen or eighteen. He wanted to leave but he had trapped himself into being the interpreter of a language that Emil Karpo did not understand.

"Loni's," Zelach said. "Where else? Politik, Ruint?"

"Bloody," the girl said. "Cross Ruint. Alloys now. Aluminum. Naked Cossack's pure iron. You know his grunt?"

" 'Clear the streets with my grandfather's scythe,' " said Zelach. " 'Cut the weeds that hide in the folds of slants and midnight faces taking root in dark places, breaking through the cracks and spaces we'll take back from spades with aces.' "

"Fucking amazing," said the girl. "Come back alone later and get skinny."

Zelach blushed and tried to catch his breath. He wanted to run from the room. "A name?" he asked.

"Time is it?"

"Early, early," said the blond boy.

"Boris 666 at Politik," the girl said.

"And?"

"No *and*," Mitsin said, getting back in bed.

Zelach looked at Karpo, who nodded. Zelach suppressed a sigh of relief.

"The Cossack is just playing games," the girl said. "He will turn up."

Karpo walked to the open broken door of the apartment with Zelach behind him.

"Name the cop in black," the girl said.

"Pure Death," said Mitsin.

"And specs," she added. "He's mine. Nine Millimeter."

Zelach couldn't help glancing back at the girl, who smiled at him as he followed Karpo into the hall. Zelach knew his nickname in the department as surely as Karpo knew his and Porfiry Petrovich knew he was the Washtub. Zelach was the Slouch. He far preferred Nine Millimeter.

On the street, Karpo turned to Zelach, who tried to suppress a twitch and meet the Tatar's eyes.

"You are an enigma, Zelach."

"I'm sorry."

"It was not a criticism. It was an observation. The music?"

"I . . . when, it was a year ago — no, it was two years ago. Sasha and I, a crime scene. The boy who killed his mother. I don't remember his name."

"Konstantin Perkovov," Karpo supplied.

"Yes, Perkovov. He had boxes of heavy-metal compact disks. He killed himself. No relatives. They would just be taken by neighbors, uniformed officers."

"You stole them," Karpo said.

Only to Karpo would it be considered stealing, Zelach thought. The police helped themselves in cases like the Perkovov killing. The police were barely paid a living existence. There were few advantages to the job. Minor pillage was an accepted perk. Zelach almost never took advantage of such opportunities, but when there was something for his mother, something small, a table lamp, a painting of flowers, a good cooking pot, he would tuck it under his arm, not trying to hide his small booty. The CDs had been a mistake. He had hoped they would be popular songs or classical music for his mother. He had not looked at the covers. The CDs had been crammed into a cardboard box and he had seen only their plastic edges.

When he got home and saw what he had taken, he considered selling them to his neighbor Tatoloy, who had a stall near Pushkin Square. But he had played one of the CDs, something by a group called Deep. The song, booming, beating, had moved through him like a jolt of straight caffeine. "The end is now," a raspy voice had croaked, and Zelach was fascinated.

Even his mother had listened, though she had told him to keep the volume low. She did not like the music but she saw what it did to her son. She sensed him vibrating with emotions he certainly did not understand. She did not discourage him.

None of this Zelach could explain to Karpo.

"I stole them," Zelach said simply.

Karpo nodded and moved toward the nearest metro station. Zelach knew they were going to search for someone named Boris 666 at Politik. He walked next to the Vampire quietly, trying not to think of the naked girl, saying to himself "Nine Millimeter," trying to hear her voice as she had said it, trying not to see her smile.

Chapter Two

"The subway attacks," said the Yak, opening the top file in front of him.

It was his first statement of the meeting, the first thing he had said since the detectives had filed into his office and taken their usual seats at the rectangular wooden conference table.

Rostnikov, sitting across from Igor Yaklovev, did not look up from the open notebook in front of him. Pencil in hand, moving on the page, he nodded in acceptance. The reason the subway attacks had been moved to the top of the agenda was the fact that the latest victim was an army colonel who had died on a busy train platform the night before.

The newspapers carried photographs of the dead man on the platform, wearing a black suit and tie. Television commentators spoke hurriedly while the screen showed photographs of the dead man in full uniform with a chest full of medals and a solemn look on his face befitting a veteran of both the Afghan and Chechin wars.

The clock on the wall, round, with a dark wooden frame, ticked softly.

The office was large, larger than Yaklovev would have wanted, but he had inherited it. To have asked for a smaller one would have been seen as a calculated move to appear humble. The Yak was not humble but he was cautious. He had changed little in the office when he moved in. The large desk with the Gray Wolfhound's high-backed chair behind it stood behind the conference table. Where a painting of Lenin had once hung over the high-backed chair there now hung a full-color photograph of the gate to the Kremlin. A large window, now behind the Yak's back as he sat, faced into the same courtyard Rostnikov could see from his own small office. The day was sunny. The parted curtains let in the light.

The Yak was alone on his side of the table. Across from him sat Rostnikov, flanked by Sasha Tkach, Elena Timofeyeva, and Iosef Rostnikov. At the end of the table, seated alone, pad open in front of him, a pile of files neatly stacked, sat Pankov, the diminutive assistant to the director. Pankov was a thin, nervous perspirer who, like the office, had been inherited by the Yak. Pankov's mission in life was to survive. He survived by pleasing the director, whoever the director might be. His fear was that he would displease the director. Nothing, not even a kind word from the Yak, which had not come in the two years Yaklovev had been the director, could give Pankov real pleasure. The little man lived simply and gratefully to continue to exist, eat an occasional sweet, avoid being scolded, and visit the zoo to calm himself in the presence of animals in cages even smaller than his office.

Rostnikov had already given his report explaining the absence of Karpo and Zelach. Since the director had given the order to find the missing musician, he asked no question about the absence of the two detectives.

Rostnikov knew why the task of finding a missing semipopular singer was of any importance. The young man's father was one of the most important men in all of Russia.

"Elena Timofeyeva," Rostnikov said without looking up.

Elena had her notes before her. These meetings were the low point of her day. She did not like the Yak. She was not alone in this, but she liked even less the sense of constant scrutiny, a scrutiny she was sure was far greater than that which the Yak gave the others.

True, the one least trusted by the Yak was Iosef, who clearly disapproved of the director's hidden agendas, which often served his own needs rather than Iosef's sense of justice.

Elena was sure that, had it not been for Porfiry Petrovich, Iosef would have been transferred to another criminal-investigation division long ago.

It did not help that Elena and Iosef were now, more or less, officially engaged. The shadow of distrust had now extended to her.

Elena had no illusions about herself. She was thirty-four, slightly plump like the other women in her family, and reasonably pretty. She kept her straight, dark-blond hair cut short and wore sensible dresses. She had been advised in this by her Aunt Anna, who had once been a senior procurator of Moscow and Rostnikov's superior. After a third heart attack, Anna Timofeyeva had been forced to retire. Elena owed her career to her aunt and she heeded her advice on most matters, including proper dress. Elena had a small wardrobe of dark, sensible dresses with long sleeves. She always wore some small piece of modest jewelry — a pin, a simple bracelet, occasionally an understated band of silver around her neck.

"Four attacks in three weeks," she said, passing a small stack of papers around the table. "The stations, as you can see, are all on the Tagansko-Krasnopresnenskaya line. She jumps around, doesn't select them in their order on the line. First, the Kuznetsky Most station. Then the Kuzminki, and then to the Krasnopresnenskaya station, and then back to Kuzminki."

The men looked down at the neatly printed computer-generated report before them.

"The first attack, on a Monday, was followed by another eight days later and another two days after that. Then the most recent was three days later. They occur at all hours of the day, a few more late at night but some in the morning, afternoon, or evening. And she jumps about, up and down the line. There are officers in civilian clothing working in shifts at all nineteen stations on the line."

"Forty-five officers drawn from the uniformed traffic division," said the Yak, with a small intake of air to show that he had no great faith in such a grab bag of new young police officers and tired veterans with no zeal for this or any other task that might offer the possibility of personal danger. "And what do we offer traffic division in exchange for their help?"

"I told Mihalovich that we would issue an official letter of thanks for his cooperation, personally citing his contribution, should we make an arrest."

"You mean I will write such a letter," the Yak said.

"It would be of little consequence if it did

not carry your signature," said Rostnikov.

Normally, Rostnikov would have consulted with the director before making such a decision, but the Yak had been missing for four days, unreachable, on a secret visit to Tbilisi. He had given Rostnikov the authority to make necessary decisions. The purpose of the Yak's visit to Tbilisi, which existed in another country, Georgia, was not revealed to Rostnikov and probably never would be.

Rostnikov had chosen not to speculate on the reason for his superior's mission. Indeed, he knew the destination only because he had been leaving the director's office when Pankov was in the process of arranging for the Yak's flight.

"Progress," said Yaklovev, sitting upright.

He bore a distinct resemblance, at least in his own mind and in his slight distortion of the image in his mirror, to Lenin. It was a resemblance he had cultivated before the fall of the Soviet Union. But the Yak had seen the signs, the attempts to overthrow Gorbachev, the increasing boldness of the drunken lout Yeltsin, the street gatherings and newspaper articles. Before the fall, Yaklovev had shaved, removed the painting of Lenin from his KGB office wall, and passed on information about the personal corruption of several high-ranking Communist *apparatchiks* to a journalist who was certain to be important in the new Russia.

"We have, as you see on the third page before you, a drawing of the woman. She has made little effort to hide."

"It could be anyone," the Yak said.

The drawing before him was of a wide-eyed female between thirty and fifty, with a thin face, large mouth, and dark straight hair.

"We do not actually know what color her hair is or if it is straight or curly," Elena said, speaking with a confidence she did not feel. "Her head is always covered by a hat, babushka, scarf. She is of medium height."

"Illuminating," the Yak said, with only the slightest touch of sarcasm.

Elena glanced at Iosef, who gave her an almost imperceptible nod of encouragement. Yaklovev continued to look directly at Elena but was well aware of the exchange.

"The knife has been described as a common wooden-handled kitchen knife," she said. "Very sharp. Each attack is sudden, a lunge, strokes to the face, neck, and stomach, no more than five. Then she runs, always up the stairs or escalator, to the street."

"And all the victims are men," said the Yak.

"That is correct. All between the ages of forty-five and sixty."

"Two are dead," said the Yak.

"Two are dead," Elena confirmed.

"What links them together besides the woman?"

"Their general age," said Elena. "Nothing else. One was a liquor inspector. Another a retired postal worker. The others, a suspected drug dealer, a furniture-factory foreman, a bank teller, and the army colonel who was on leave."

"On leave," Rostnikov said softly.

"Yes," said Elena.

"You find that significant?" the Yak asked.

"In the newspapers, the dead colonel is wearing a suit and not a uniform. What were these men wearing?" asked Rostnikov, continuing to make notes or drawings.

"I . . ." Elena began.

"Suits," said Iosef. "I believe they were all wearing dark suits."

"Check," said Rostnikov. "Be sure."

"Anything else on this?" the Yak asked.

"Paulinin has the body," said Elena. "He told us to come to him for a report at eleven."

That was two hours away.

"Report directly to me," the Yak said. "Chief Inspector Rostnikov will be on special assignment for a number of days."

The Yak watched Rostnikov for a reaction to this announcement. He got none other than a nod from his chief inspector, who looked up without raising his head.

Porfiry Petrovich had much on his mind. Among his thoughts were Nina's and Laura's mother and his wife Sarah's headaches, which they had been assured were a natural and probably lifelong effect of successful removal of a small tumor from her brain three years ago.

On a more immediate level, he was engaged in self-analysis. He had automatically drawn a man's suit jacket with a white dove peeking out of one pocket and a gray-white crow out of the other. Above the suit jacket were two wide eyes, one of which was closed. A knowing wink? An irritating eyelash? And behind all of that was the sun, with weak little lines of radiation bursting from it and a large dark cloud partially covering it. Rostnikov was a fair but not exceptional craftsman with pencil. His notebooks were filled with drawings and words. He never planned what would appear. He let something deep within him guide his hand. He was always most in contact with his muse when he was at the regular morning meeting.

He wrote the word *bahlotah*, "swamp," under the jacket and the word "sun" over it. Whatever it might mean, Rostnikov felt the mélange was complete. He looked up.

"The search for the musician," the Yak

said, wondering what Rostnikov was drawing or writing in that notebook. His curiosity had twice sent the frightened Pankov on missions into Rostnikov's office when the chief inspector was out on a case or home at night. Pankov had retrieved the notebook and brought it to the Yak.

The contents of the book were a puzzle to the director, who had concluded that Rostnikov's imagination might well be the key to his success as an investigator. But the answer was not to be found in the notebook. The book contained not careful notes taken at the morning meetings, or even fragments involving ongoing investigations. There were pictures and words of varying sizes, words that made little sense to the Yak.

"Karpo and Zelach are in search," said Rostnikov.

"There is some urgency," said the Yak.

Rostnikov nodded knowingly and felt a sudden urge to underline the words he had written. He did not resist.

Word that the son of Nikoli Lovski was missing would eventually begin to leak out. It would swell from minor rumor to major story within days if he were not found. The Office of Special Investigation had been given the case because all other divisions were well aware that any investigative body that took it on and failed to find the young man might well take a serious bite from their behind.

The reasons were many. Misha Lovski, the Naked Cossack, was a rising folk hero to the skinheads of the city. The Naked Cossack's blaring, angry music spewed hatred toward foreigners, Jews, the police, bankers, rappers, and the government. Lately, he had included a wide variety of Mafia organizations in his attacks. At the same time, the lyrics praised the tattooed independence and defiance of the law by Mafias consisting of former convicts.

The hate-spewing Naked Cossack had many enemies, but he had one thing that others who were exhorting hate and violence did not have. Misha Lovski had a father who owned five television stations, a newspaper, a construction company with major contracts with the city of Moscow and its mayor, and import deals for high-tech equipment from Japan, China, France, the United States, Sweden, and England.

The world was not aware that the Naked Cossack was the son of a wealthy man, a Jew. Misha had certainly hidden his heritage, but perhaps someone had discovered his secret, his wealthy Jewish father, perhaps one of those to whom he had sung of hate and Russian purity. Perhaps many things.

"There has been no more telephone contact with Misha Lovski?" asked the Yak.

"Other than the one phone call, none," Rostnikov said.

"So," said the Yak, looking at each person at the table. "We have made little progress on all fronts."

"Except the extortions," Rostnikov said.

"The extortions, yes," the Yak confirmed, as if it were a matter of little consequence. "Well?"

"Sasha," Rostnikov said.

Sasha Tkach, who until two years ago had still appeared boyish enough to pass as a university student, had changed greatly in appearance and attitude. He was lean and good-looking, with a lock of hair that fell boyishly in front of his eyes and had to be frequently brushed away. For some reason, this lock of hair attracted women of all ages. Sasha had proved frequently that he had great difficulty resisting the more serious advances.

His failure of mind and body had cost him his wife, Maya, and their two children. Well, there had been more to her resolute move to her brother in Kiev. Sasha had grown increasingly depressed and moody, had spoken little and touched Maya even less.

On this day, however, Sasha had the mote of hope. Maya had agreed to return with the children, but only for two weeks, a test. It was agreed that she would leave with the children after those two weeks. She had round-trip tickets from Kiev. If the test went well, she would return to Moscow, perhaps on a more permanent basis.

Such travel was beyond Sasha's means, which meant that he had to accept money from his mother. Lydia Tkach loved her son. Lydia Tkach was a not-inconsiderable contributor to his depressive state.

Having invested wisely in several very small businesses both before and after the fall of the Soviet Union, the former government employee and widow of a KGB major had grown more than just financially comfortable. Lydia was definitely well off and willing to help others. She had employed Galina, the grandmother of the two girls who lived with the Rostnikovs, in her bakery. She had supplemented her son's income. She brought food to the table, gifts for the children and her son and daughter-in-law. But there was a price to pay.

Lydia Tkach had strong opinions, which she voiced frequently and loudly, a result of the fact that she was nearly deaf and refused to wear a hearing aid. One of her strong opinions was that her only child should not be a policeman, and to this end she frequently petitioned Porfiry Petrovich.

Though his independence was under unrelenting attack by his mother, Sasha clung with determination to his identity as a police investigator. Without it, he felt, he had nothing. He was without skills other than fluency in French and a fair knowledge of computers. Maya had far more potential than he did. She worked for a Japanese import company and had risen quickly. The company had accepted her move to Kiev and given her an even more important office position there. In fact, the company had been very willing to cooperate with her decision to move.

In retaliation for Sasha's indiscretions, Maya had engaged in a brief affair with one of the Japanese vice-presidents of the company. The man was gentle, kind, and married.

"The report before you shows that two uniformed officers and a lieutenant in the plunder-investigation unit have been identified as the extortionists," Sasha said. "We have recorded statements from eight businessmen from whom they have been taking money. One of the two officers has confessed in the hope of receiving leniency, which I suggested she might receive."

"I will talk to the procurator's office," the Yak said, making a note. "The name of the cooperating officer?"

"Ludmilla Vianovna," said Sasha. "I was

fortunate enough to gain her confidence."

The Yak did not pursue the means by which Sasha had gained the female officer's confidence. He looked at his watch and declared, "Anything else?"

No one spoke. The goal of all around the table was escape from the room at the earliest possible moment.

"The meeting is ended. Porfiry Petrovich, please remain."

Sasha, Iosef, and Elena stood and headed for the door. Pankov remained in his seat, resisting the urge to wipe his moist brow.

"You, too," the Yak said.

Pankov nodded, gathered his papers, and followed the others out the door.

When they were gone, the Yak folded his hands and said, "Tonight you will be aboard the Trans-Siberian Express."

Chapter Three

For breakfast Inna Dalipovna had prepared buckwheat porridge with a large glob of butter and sour cream, a small bowl of *kyehfer* with sugar, and a glass of strong tea. When her father came in, fully dressed in dark suit and tie, he barely looked at the food. He was absorbed in his newspaper.

"Submarines," Viktor Dalipovna muttered, reaching for the mug of tea without looking up from the newspaper or at his daughter sitting across from him at the small table.

Viktor was fifty-five, brown hair neatly trimmed, gray temples, tall and lean. He was considered handsome, judging by the many women in his life since Inna's mother had died a decade earlier.

He drank, making a face at either the taste of the tea or his thoughts on submarines. "Who do they fool? I ask you. Who do they fool?"

Inna knew the question was not meant to

be answered, certainly not by her. She ate some porridge and listened to her father as he shook his head, turned the page, and put down his tea to pick up a spoon.

"The Americans, the British, even the Norwegians know everything that goes on inside of our submarines. And we spend millions, millions, millions. On what?"

Inna kept eating.

"Appearances," he said. "First the *Kursk* and now the latest one. They won't even tell us its name. I tell you, the way to deal with the Americans is not to rattle swords or shake sticks. They laugh at us. We must become capitalists, not a country of criminals and incompetents as we are now, but real capitalists. We have resources. Oil, gas, diamonds, sulphur, forests. Siberia is better than a vast gold mine."

He put the paper aside neatly on the table and began to attack his porridge.

"Well?" he asked.

This time the question was for her. "Appearances," she said.

"No, what did the doctor say yesterday?" he asked, eating as he spoke, a napkin tucked under his collar to protect his white shirt.

Viktor had come home to the apartment they shared late the night before. He had been out with a woman whom he had met at the

Up & Down Club. She said her name was Dorthea. She said she was the wife of a Roumanian watch manufacturer. She said her husband was away for the week, leaving her alone at the hotel. She said many things Viktor did not believe, but she did many things in the hotel room which pleased him and cost him nothing but dinner and a few drinks.

Viktor was in a good mood. Today he had a meeting with Anatoli and Versnikov about a deal with a department-store chain in Germany. Viktor would probably have to go to Bremen to seal the deal. That was fine with him. He knew a number of people in Bremen who could provide him with the company of engaging and willing women. The last time they had found him a very young woman who claimed to be a Kurd.

"The doctor?" he prompted his daughter.

"He said the medicine is working fine," she said.

Inna had not met her father's eyes. She could not when she lied, and she could not for periods longer than a few seconds when she did not lie.

"Good," said Viktor, moving to the *kyehfer* and adding more sugar.

He had heard what he wanted to hear. For an instant only, he glanced at his daughter before continuing to read the newspaper on the table.

Inna was thirty-two years old. She had inherited a few things from her father: his leanness, his deep, dark eyes. The rest was the gift or curse of her mother. Inna had suffered from panic and anxiety since childhood, just as her mother had done. While her mother complained, ranted, wept, Inna had learned to keep her sleepless nights and terror-filled waking dreams to herself. Her father did not like them. Her father had hated her mother for her weakness. Her father did not hate Inna. He did his best not to notice her or deal with her. Even when she had been twenty-two and was going to have the baby the gas-maintenance man had planted inside her, her father had not gotten angry. He had clearly been annoyed. He had other things, more important things, to deal with. He had called Inna's aunt, his sister, and asked her to take her to the clinic and get rid of the problem. He had not asked Inna's opinion on the matter. The baby was disposed of.

When he got home that night, he had asked, "Is it taken care of?"

Inna had said yes.

"No complications?" he had asked.

"I'm a little sore. I'm tired."

"Rest," he had said. "I'll get something to

eat at Rodyoki's. I'll bring back something for you."

And then he had gone. He had awakened her after midnight. Slightly drunk, he had handed her a jar of borscht, deep and green. She had told him she wasn't hungry.

"Sleep," he had said. "I'll put it in the refrigerator. You can have it in the morning."

And they had never again spoken of that day or of the baby.

Inna had inherited more from her mother: a dry, humorless look, washed-out blond hair, and a distinct lack of beauty. Her plump mother had looked more like a mother to Viktor than a wife. And now it was common for the few people they met together to assume that Inna and Viktor were husband and wife instead of father and daughter. Indeed, on one occasion, an old woman clearly assumed that Inna was older than Viktor.

Inna had learned how to please her father. The few times she had displeased him were the result of sudden outbreaks that seemed to have no specific cause. Perhaps a dozen times in the past ten years she had lost control, ranted, and wept about suicide.

Viktor's solution was to take her to the nearest state hospital. That was during the waning days of the Soviet Union when Viktor had been a Communist with a large *C* and a black-market capitalist with a small *c*. The Soviet solution to all mental ills was the same: drugs. Can't manage your child? Keep her drugged. Is she too agitated? Give her drugs. Is she depressed, angry, sullen, confused, annoying, too silent, too talkative, too anything? Drugs.

And it had worked. Inna had taken large doses of pills and a syrupy red-brown liquid. She was sleepy most of the time, moving in a tranquil dreamlike state, but she was docile. Then, several months ago, she had awakened from a night of sleep feeling as if she could stay in bed forever.

She stopped taking the medications. She did not tell her father. Anxiety returned. She welcomed it. She was awake. She had rejoined the living. She had searched for something to do, something to distract her besides keeping house for her father, watching television, and going to the park to sit and listen to her neighbors gossip.

"Good," Viktor said, pushing away his empty bowls and finishing his tea. "The shopping money is on the table near the door."

She acknowledged with a nod, though he did not look at her. She knew there would be enough to provide him with his favorite foods and delicacies, particularly *blyeeni sah smeetah-nigh,* pancakes filled with sour cream

61

and then baked. She planned to make that for his dinner tonight, along with a sausage thinly sliced just the way he liked it so he could place the pieces on a slice of bread.

"You will be home for dinner?" she asked.

"Who knows?" he said, reaching for his briefcase next to the front door of the apartment.

"I'll have something ready," she said.

But he was not listening. He was studying the contents of the closet door he had opened.

"It is supposed to snow today," he said, looking from his down jacket to his black wool coat.

"I think I'll kill someone today," Inna said softly, starting to gather the breakfast dishes.

"I think the jacket," Viktor said. "It comes down low enough to cover my suit jacket."

"On the subway," Inna said, across the room in the tiny kitchen, putting the dishes in the sink. She carried each dish in her left hand. The pain in her right wrist had subsided but she was afraid to put any pressure on it. Her father had not noticed that she had avoided using the hand. She had not expected him to notice even if she dropped a plate.

"Here," Viktor said, turning, jacket on, buttoning it. "How is this?"

"You look very handsome," she said. "Distinguished. Perfect."

Inna knew that if she looked in the mirror, which she seldom did, she would not see a distinguished, perfect person. She would put her face close to the glass, watch a small circle of steam appear and fade, and look at the permanent mask she did not want to wear.

"I'm going," he said. "Be good. Take your medication. Put on your coat if you go out."

"I'm going to take a ride on the metro," she said.

"Where?" he asked, a hand on the door.

"Shopping," she said.

He made a sound and left the apartment. The sound of the closing door remained in the room as Inna returned to the sink to finish cleaning the dishes.

Her mother, plump, resigned, appeared at her side as she carefully soaped and rinsed each plate, cup, knife, and fork. Her mother often reappeared to talk to her daughter, give her advice and support. Occasionally her mother preached, but generally she gave her approval to Inna's plans.

"You are going on the metro again?" her mother asked as Inna finished a cup, rinsing it with running water.

"Yes," Inna said.

"And you will try to kill him again?"

"Yes," Inna said. "For you and for me."

"I do not need him dead now," said her

mother, standing with folded arms, leaning close. "He will be dead soon enough. I am in no hurry."

"I must," Inna said, without looking at her mother.

"Your wrist?"

"It will be all right," Inna said, finishing the last dish and placing it in the metal rack next to the sink.

"You hate him that much," her mother said.

"No," said Inna. "I love him that much."

Inna looked at her mother now. She did not question whether her mother was a ghost or a creation of her imagination. Inna simply accepted.

"Wear something warm," her mother said. "It is supposed to snow tonight."

Inna dried the long, sharp carving knife.

"I will," Inna said.

For breakfast, Pavel Cherkasov ate a large platter of frankfurters and sliced tomato with three cups of coffee. The breakfast had been brought to his room at the Hotel Rossia. It cost the equivalent of twenty American dollars. Pavel didn't care. It wasn't his money.

He ate slowly, watching the television screen, on which a serious-looking American policeman with a mustache was giving orders in dubbed Russian to a pair of underlings, one of whom was black, the other a thin, pretty Chinese woman.

Pavel poured more salt on his tomatoes. His blood pressure was high, but what good was food without salt? What good was life without pleasures? Food was Pavel's principal pleasure but not his only one. He liked to make people laugh. He longed to be a comedian, to stand in front of a crowd of people and make them laugh with his stories and jokes. He had told one of his jokes to the man who had brought his breakfast.

"I should take my Vitamin B-1 pill for my memory with this meal," he had said in earnest deadpan, "but I forgot where I put the bottle."

The dour man in the white jacket and bow tie had smiled, a smile that could have indicated sympathy for Pavel's misfortune or quiet appreciation of the joke.

Pavel had given him only a moderate tip.

In his pocket Pavel carried small lined note cards on which he wrote jokes that he thought of, incidents he viewed that he thought were funny, humorous things said on television or in the occasional movie he attended.

Some of Pavel's best jokes he could never use except in particular company. They were not sexual in content but dealt with the comic aspects of the violent world with which he dealt. He had seen a humorless Mafia hit man park carefully and legally in a zoned area on Gorky Street when Pavel had pointed out the man's target. The hit man, known only as Krestyaneen, "the Peasant," had explained that there were too many accidents on the streets of Moscow and one had to obey the parking laws. The man had not been joking. The Peasant had gotten out of the car, crossed the street, shot one of two men who were deep in conversation. Three bullets to the head. Then the hit man had returned to the car and very carefully pulled out of the space, avoiding even the slightest touch to the rear of the Lada parked in front of him.

The story was funny, but only if you knew it was true.

Pavel had never performed the entire, ever-evolving stand-up routine he had been working on for more than five years for anyone but himself, though he regularly tried individual jokes on waiters, shopkeepers, clerks, and people he met in bars or restaurants. He had taped the routine and kept reworking the lines and delivery. He had tried copying the styles of various comics and settled on a mix of Yuri Obleniki and the American George Burns.

When he received his pay for this job, he would take a year off, go on stage in amateur clubs, work on his timing. Deep inside he yearned to be noticed, given a part in a movie, perhaps a role on a television series.

It was possible. Russia had become a land of opportunity for enterprising people like Pavel Cherkasov.

Pavel finished his breakfast and moved across the room to pull his suitcase from the shelf next to the bathroom. Later he would retrieve the blue duffel bag he had locked in a box at the train station. Now, however, he put the suitcase on the bed and opened the drawers of the small dresser on which the television sat. It was a day early, but he liked being prepared well in advance. There really wasn't much to pack. His clothes, already folded neatly, could be washed in a sink and dried on a hanger on the train.

Pavel had long ago discovered the American company TravelSmith, which provided clothes and gadgets for people who traveled a great deal, people who wanted to travel light and live out of one carry-on. Pavel was one of these people.

He spoke six languages, none of them but Russian particularly well, all quite passably. He had passports in a variety of names and nationalities. These he carried inside a box of expensive Dutch-chocolate candy, which he replaced frequently.

He selected the passport under which he

would be traveling the next day. The stamps were right. The photograph was good. It was under the name on this passport that Pavel Cherkasov had purchased his ticket on the Trans-Siberian Express.

One of the nice things about traveling by train was that it was so easy to carry a gun aboard. Of course he could smuggle a weapon onto an airplane. He knew employees, flight attendants, baggage handlers, people at the machines that checked the hand-held luggage, even airport janitors and concession workers at the major airports in Europe, Asia, and the Americas, who could be bribed to cooperate.

Tonight, before he headed for the Yarolslavskiy train terminal, Pavel thought as he finished packing, I shall eat at an Uzbekistani restaurant on Neglinnaya Street. *Tkhum-dulma*, a boiled egg inside a fried-meat patty, *shashlik* marinated over hot coals. No, wait. First he would have a *maniar*, a strong broth with rice and meat, with hot Uzbek bread. Everything would be served on and in the finest Uzbek porcelain and pottery. And the wine? He was particularly fond of the Aleatiko. A bit sweet but perfectly suited for the meal.

Moscow was a good place to be if one had money and knew the city. Pavel was very pleased with himself. He would finish packing, lie down, and play with some ideas he had for jokes.

He hoped that within the next week he would have enough material to put together a part of his routine about traveling on the Trans-Siberian Express.

He closed his suitcase, turned off the television, and got back on the bed to rest.

There was much to think about. Jokes, the relatively simple and safe job he had to do, and what he would do with the money he had already received and the rest that would be given to him when he had completed his task. Later he would get up for lunch. He would eat elegantly but lightly and perhaps treat himself to an early movie before dinner. For a resourceful man with a sense of humor, life could be very good indeed.

For breakfast, Misha Lovski received nothing.

He was hungry. He was angry. He was naked. Misha paced. He was in a cage. Literally. A cage with iron bars. There were no windows but there was a single ceiling light outside the cage, well beyond his reach.

The cage itself was empty except for a narrow mattress on the floor. Misha had grown cold during the night. He had wrapped himself in the mattress and awakened with a stiff neck, which he now massaged as he paced the ten-foot by ten-foot concrete floor.

"I'm hungry," he shouted.

No one answered.

"I'm cold," he shouted.

No one answered.

He could have been anywhere. He had only the slightest recollection of how he had gotten here. The night before last, two nights ago or was it three, he had been at Loni's. He had been drinking. He had taken a respectable dose of acid handed to him by a *skiny* whose name he couldn't quite remember. The *skiny* was big. He was with someone else who joined them when Misha was well into his trip. Misha couldn't remember who the other person had been.

He remembered voices, music, loud music even for him, smells, sweet for a moment and than as acrid as vomit the next. And he vaguely remembered someone handing him a telephone and telling him he was going to be caged and killed. Was that at Loni's? He had panicked, said something into the phone, called for help. And that was it. Or perhaps there had been no call. Perhaps he had dreamed or imagined it.

He had awakened in this cage. No watch. No windows.

He was not self-conscious about his nakedness, though he knew whoever had caged him might well be looking at him through some hole at this very moment. The Naked Cossack had torn off his clothes on stage more than once, more than a dozen times, maybe more than a hundred times. He had torn off his clothes in the beginning when the music and the smell of girls in the flashing lights in front and the deep darkness farther back had given him an erection. The audience had always gone wild as he shouted his signature line, "*Kher s nim*, I don't give a damn. Does anybody give a fucking damn?"

To which the audience always responded with a loud, cacophonous "Nobody."

"That's right," the Naked Cossack would answer and launch into a new song filled with anger and attack, love for those who hated, and hatred for those who loved. He sang of strength and sex and the rights of those who were strong. The stompers. The raised fists. The heavy polished boots.

Misha moved to the bars of his cage and shouted with a driving angry voice that was all performance, "I'm the Naked Cossack, you dumb shits. What the hell do you want?"

For most of the first day Misha had maintained an angry scowl, had muttered curses, had been afraid that he was going to be killed.

71

He had a dream the first night that he was a ritual sacrifice. There was an altar. He was tied down with ropes. The altar was outdoors, an uneven rock that scratched his back. A huge man with a bald head approached with an ax. On the blade of the ax was a swastika. The man who looked familiar had clearly said, "We know you are a Jew."

Misha had awakened, cold, sweating. The dream was the enactment of "Sacrifice the Son of God," in which a Jew is killed on such an altar. It was one of Misha's own songs. He had shivered. Not knowing if it was night or day, he looked at the ceiling light outside his cage, thinking for an instant that he was looking into the sun.

At that moment, Misha had lost some of his fear. If they had wanted him dead, he would already be dead. No, they wanted money, ransom. They were not *rappery* or rapists. They were not fans kidnapping their idol so they could have him for their own. They were simple kidnappers. They would keep him alive. If they had discovered who he was, they would go to his father for money. His father would pay. He hoped they would bleed him dry. If they did not know about his father, they would go to Acid, Anarchista, and Pure Knuckles. They would pay as long as it was not too much money. They needed the Naked Cossack. He was the band. He was the attraction.

All Misha had to do was to remain the Naked Cossack, the singer, guitarist, poet who didn't give a shit.

But he was hungry. He was thirsty. And he had to use a toilet. He couldn't imagine squatting in a corner and existing in the same space with his own feces. He had written about such things, sung of them, suggested that the weak enemies of all who heeded his word deserved the fate he was now enduring. But he didn't deserve it.

Misha shouted again.

"I need a toilet. I need food. I need something to wear."

He let out the yowl of a wolf. He laughed. His throat went dry. The lights went out. He was in total darkness, sudden total darkness. He stepped back. He could hear the door to the room outside the bars open, but no light came in.

There was a sound of footsteps on concrete.

Misha staggered back. Something clanked to the floor beyond the bars. The footsteps retreated. The door opened and closed. The lights came on again.

Outside the bars were a cracked metal pot, a roll of toilet paper, a metal platter with a half loaf of bread and a piece of sausage, and a metal cup of water.

Misha had trouble getting the pot through the bars. He had to force it. It was the single item he needed most.

Chapter Four

"It was a meaningless comment," Iosef Rostnikov said to Elena Timofeyeva as they headed slowly down the corridor two levels below Petrovka.

"It was not meaningless," Elena said, eyes forward, stride steady.

"So, I said what? That there is a resemblance between you and your aunt? That is meaningful? An insult?"

"My Aunt Anna and I are alike in only one way physically. We both have a tendency, as does my mother, to be overweight. You were suggesting that I am growing fat."

Iosef stopped walking. "I . . . your aunt is a shrewd, intelligent, highly capable person. See, I said *person*, not *woman*. That was the comparison I was making."

A pair of uniformed policemen walked past them, talking softly and emphatically, taking a quick step to the side to avoid collision with the couple who now stood facing each other.

"I am watching my weight," she said. "I eat

carefully. I exercise. I am fit. I am also genetically disposed toward a certain plumpness which, I thought, pleased you."

"This is not the place . . ."

"I'm well aware of that," Elena said. "But where is a good place and when will we next be there? You said I am like my aunt. I am. She taught me to face situations when they arise, to accept confrontation rather than allow incidents to become infected."

"I didn't —," Iosef said, holding out his hands.

"You did," she said. "And you are smart enough to know that you did. I would not love you if I thought you were a self-deluded generic man."

"You are being too sensitive," he tried.

"That is what generic men say when they wish to avoid responsibility. The woman is being too sensitive. Perhaps the man is being too insensitive. Do you wish to marry me?"

"Yes," he said. "Definitely. Without question. As soon as possible."

"Good," Elena said.

A door opened behind her. She could hear the tapping of shoes behind her.

"Let's talk to Paulinin," Iosef said as a slight older woman in a dark suit walked past them quickly, a pile of files cradled in her arms like a baby.

"Iosef, I am what I am destined to be."

"And that is what I want," he said. "I —"

"Later," she said as he advanced and stood in front of her. She touched his right hand with her left and his cheek with her right hand and then turned to continue down the corridor.

A few dozen steps farther and they were before a heavy metal door. The door was unnumbered and there was no plate on it indicating what lay behind. Elena knocked.

Paulinin did not look pleased when he answered the door to his laboratory. Elena and Iosef were no happier to be here.

"The dead man on the subway," Elena said.

"Your case?" asked Paulinin, adjusting his glasses with the back of his hand.

The scientist was of average height, a bit on the thin side, with wild white hair that was beginning to show definite signs of thinning. He wore a less-than-clean lab coat that had once been white but was now tinged with hues whose source neither of the detectives wished to consider.

"Our case," said Elena. "May we? . . ."

"Come in," Paulinin said, throwing open the heavy metal door and turning his back on his guests.

They stepped in, and Paulinin pushed the

door shut behind them. A fluorescent bulb dying slowly tinkled deep inside the vast room which had once been used for file storage. It had been a haven for Paulinin for at least two decades.

The man was, at best, eccentric. More likely he was a bit mad.

Paulinin was twenty paces ahead of them, maneuvering around familiar objects that formed the maze of his sanctuary — laboratory tables covered with metallic and glass contrivances, most of which were his own peculiar invention and which no one else would know how to use, stacks of books and scientific journals on the floor and on lower tables and two desks, one of which was missing several drawers. Along the walls were shelves up to the top of the ten-foot ceiling. On the shelves were cardboard and wooden boxes, each with a large number in black on its sides. There were also jars ranging in size from a gallon to five gallons or more. Something floated in each of the jars. A brain, a kidney, a small animal, and, somewhere, the left leg of Porfiry Petrovich Rostnikov; and, according to Petrovka lore, the brain of Josef Stalin.

Elena and Iosef wended their way toward Paulinin, who now stood behind a table on which lay the naked body of a man who appeared to be about fifty. The corpse was neither fat nor thin, tall nor short. He was not particularly handsome; neither was he ugly. Stripped of his suit, the dead colonel was simply a corpse with seven deep, long, clotted knife wounds on his neck, arms, and stomach.

Paulinin's arms were out and resting next to the body. When he leaned forward, the strong overhead light cast a shadow in the sockets of his eyes. The visitors to Paulinin's lair had a wide variety of options with which to respond, ranging from amusement to discomfort and fear.

Iosef thought Paulinin would have been a particularly sad and isolated creature were he not sustained by his own paranoia, delusions, and self-confidence.

"This should be Emil Karpo's case," Paulinin said.

The closest thing the scientist had to a friend was the silent pale detective. At least once a week they lunched together. Karpo was a good listener. Paulinin was a talker.

"We take the cases we are assigned," Elena said.

"I didn't suggest otherwise," Paulinin said with irritation. "I made an observation. It is bad enough that those bunglers up there" — he looked up toward the ceiling — "treat the dead with ignorance and no respect," he went on. "Do you know what Bolgakov did?"

Neither Elena nor Iosef knew who Bolgakov was.

"Woman, dead inside the Kremlin gift shop," Paulinin said. "Greek. Just fell. Boom. Like that. No one saw. She was in a corner, supposedly alone. And Bolgakov, that oaf who could not see an elephant without an electron microscope, looks at the body, declares she had a heart attack. Case closed. The great Bolgakov has spoken. I get the body after they have pawed it with no sense of respect or dignity. I read the report. Broken nose. Bolgakov says she fell on her nose when she had her attack. Cheek bones are intact. Bone in the nose is thin. The nose had been broken before, twice. One rib had been broken before. Simple X rays showed that. Given her weight, even if she didn't fall flat, the nose should have been flattened, pulp. You understand?"

"Perfectly," said Iosef patiently.

"Heart attack," Paulinin went on. "Pills in her purse for angina. Bolgakov, the language expert, can read the pill bottle in Greek but just enough to make out the medication. I get the bottle. Can I read Greek?"

"I do not know," said Elena.

"I cannot," Paulinin said with a smile. "But I do not pretend to. I find a Greek. There's one at the newsstand on Kolpolski Square. I give him the bottle. The pills belong to the woman's husband. She was carrying them for him. I go back to the body, look at the heart, the arteries. Bolgakov had not bothered to open her. There was nothing wrong with her heart till it stopped. She died of a stroke brought on by a blow to her head. Something hit her in the face. She fell back and struck her head. Hematoma under the hair. Any idiot could see it if he looked, but not the great Bolgakov, chief medical examiner for the Homicide Division."

"So what did happen?" asked Iosef, knowing that they would not get to the dead man before them till Paulinin's story was over.

"I asked to see the husband of the dead woman. He was leaving with the body that very day. They had waited two days to get the dead woman to me. I talked to Karpo. He stopped the man at the airport and brought him here. You know what I found?"

"What?" asked Elena, resisting the urge to look at her watch.

"Signs of broken capillaries in the knuckles of his right hand. That is what I found. They had fought. He had punched her. She had fallen and the fools upstairs had missed it."

"He confessed?" asked Elena.

"Of course," said Paulinin. "I laid out the

evidence. One, two, three, four, five. Built a tower of steel truth. He was a wife beater. Greece has as many as we do in Russia, but possibly Russian women have thicker skulls."

He looked directly at Elena, who met his eyes.

"Interesting," she said. "The man on the table."

"You want some coffee? Tea?"

"No, thank you," said Elena.

Both she and Iosef had made the mistake in the past of accepting Paulinin's offer of coffee or tea. They had suffered for their attempt to get on his good side, not knowing at the time that he had no good side. The coffee had come in small glass jars with hints of white powder and something that did not look like coffee grounds floating in the tan liquid. They had drunk the vile brew, trying to avoid the floating dots.

"Business, then," said Paulinin. "My friend here," he said, touching the hairy chest of the corpse, "and I have had a long talk. He told me all about his attacker."

With this Paulinin looked down at the face of the dead man, whose eyes were closed.

"And he told you?" Iosef prompted.

"She is five foot and six inches tall, or within an inch. Approximately one hundred and twenty pounds. About thirty years of age.

Right-handed but with a sprained wrist. Strong. Determined. If you find her, I can definitely identify her from the description given by our friend."

He went silent and looked at each of the detectives with a knowing, secret smile.

Iosef briefly considered not asking Paulinin how he knew all of this, but that would be cruel. The man had nothing but his skill and vanity and the need for a small appreciative audience.

"Two of the surviving victims of this woman said she had used her right hand," he said, holding up his right hand as if clasping a knife. "The others didn't remember. Our friend here was stabbed by someone with the knife in the left hand."

"A different attacker?" asked Elena.

"No," said Paulinin. "Same knife in all the attacks. Same general pattern, but this time the strokes came across from the left and were not as deep. Mind you, they were deep, but not as deep as those she had delivered in the past with her right hand. Hence, there is something wrong with her right hand, probably a strain. She strikes hard, very hard. She could well cause herself injury. The spacing and location of the blows suggest an attacker without plan or pattern. She simply lashes out, probably screams when she attacks. Her height is evident from the angle of the wounds, and her weight is more than suggested by the depth of her thrusts."

"And you can identify her?" asked Elena.

"Bolgakov didn't bother to examine my friend here closely. Look at his fingers."

Both detectives leaned forward to examine the white fingers.

"Under the nails of his right hand," said Paulinin. "He held up his hands to ward her off after the first two or three blows, but it was too late. He touched her face or arm. There were tiny, very tiny pieces of surface skin under his nails. Definitely a woman."

"DNA," said Iosef.

"Absolutely," said Paulinin. "Find her. Look for a woman with a weak right wrist, possibly bandaged. You know her height, her general description. Questions?"

"We have spoken to those who have survived this woman's attacks. They have given us a description," said Elena, removing the artist's sketch from her pocket. "They say this is a reasonable representation."

Paulinin adjusted his glasses and leaned forward to examine the sketch.

"She is not that thin in the face," he said. "Given her weight she could not be. Your surviving victims got only a glimpse before they were struck. They had childhood images of witches to pull from deep inside their surprise and fear."

"We will adjust the sketch," Iosef said.

"It will help, but you are seeking a woman, not a witch. She probably looks like a mouse. No, not a mouse, a timid rabbit, unnoticed, shy, and then she strikes. And then she is gone."

"You know this to be a fact?" asked Elena.

Paulinin stepped back, clearly offended.

"My friend here told me," he said. "By his wounds, his former life, his whispers without words that only those of us who listen closely can hear. I gave you facts. Any more questions?"

"None," said Elena.

"Then go," he said. "My friend and I still have much to talk about."

"What goes on in here is nothing compared to what goes on in the streets," said the paunchy man with the clean-cut goatee and short-trimmed dark hair.

They were in the club and bar called Loni's on Kropotkin Street. Loni's took up two floors of a former ten-story apartment building. It was vast and dark and smelled of alcohol, sweat, and the ammonia being used by the cleaning crew. Six women were working slowly, sweeping, mopping, scrubbing graffiti from the walls, taking down torn posters of leather-clad, electric-guitar-holding young men with open mouths and angry faces, and putting up fresh posters very much like the ones they removed. The women moved silently, pushing buckets of water ahead of them.

The paunchy man in a black T-shirt was Karoli Stinichkov. He was the day manager. His duties involved seeing to it that Loni's was ready for the nightly crowd — clean, well stocked — and that the money from the preceding night, which ended at almost four in the morning, was correctly accounted for.

Karoli had a partner who worked evenings and nights. The men met late every afternoon for an hour, and every morning for an hour, to hand over the keys and give a report to the other.

This worked well because neither man liked the other. They were brothers-in-law. The sisters they were married to didn't like either of the men.

"You've got crowds of homosexuals hanging around in front of the Bolshoi, drug dealers right in Derzhinski Square where State Security can look out the windows of Lubyanka and see them. You've got . . ."

"Misha Lovski," Emil Karpo interrupted.

"Misha Lovski?" the man asked.

"Naked Cossack," said Zelach.

"Oh, him," said Karoli. "His name is Lovski? Between you and me and nobody else, he's a bastard son of a bitch. But what can we do? They like him. They go crazy for him. Between you and me and nobody else I don't understand half of what he says, but then I don't really have to listen to him or any of them much. My partner's here at night."

"When was he last here?" asked Karpo.

"My partner?"

"Lovski."

The gaunt detective made Karoli nervous. He had a great deal to hide, though almost none of it was related to the prick who called himself and his group of addle-brains Naked Cossack. Karoli shrugged and reached for the Diet Sprite with ice that was bubbling on the bar.

"You mean performing? That was last week. Wednesday, I think. They're due back on Saturday. Saturday is a big night."

"He come in here when he's not performing?"

"I'm told," Karoli said, looking at the ice in his drink. "He likes to be patted on the back, praised. The skinheads buy him drinks and things."

"Things?" asked Karpo. "Drugs?"

"Things," Karoli answered. "We don't sell anything but soft drinks and alcohol and a few

87

things to eat. Chips. They love chips. You know how many bags of chips we sell every week?"

"I do not," said Karpo.

"Eight, nine hundred, maybe more," said Karoli proudly. "We get all kinds from a plant outside the city. They have a deal with some potato farmers in the north."

"Misha Lovski," Karpo repeated. "He was in here two nights ago."

"Wait, Yervonovich is still here. He doesn't sleep. Bartender. Knows everybody. Wait."

Karoli motioned to one of the nearby cleaning women, who came over, a rag in her hand.

"Go in the back. Get Abbi," he ordered.

The woman looked at the two policemen and moved slowly around the long bar and through a door.

"Between you and me and nobody else," Karoli said. "A lot of the skinheads like Naked Cossack because of the girl, the redheaded girl who backs him and pretends to play."

"Anarchista," Zelach said.

"That is right," Karoli confirmed. "Crazy business. At another club, the Cossack and the girl pretended to have sex during a song he was singing about wanting to be an American Indian and scalp slaves. Sick stuff. And he is not the worst. Filth. But it is a good living. I like the old stuff. Rock 'n' roll. Elvis. Bill

Haley. Johnny Rotten."

A man staggered out through the door behind the bar. He wore no shirt and there was a dark stain on his tan slacks. The man was hairless and looked ancient and hung over.

"Abbi," Karoli said. "Cops. They have questions. Answer them. We don't want trouble."

"When was Misha Lovski last in here?" asked Karpo.

"Naked Cossack," Zelach explained.

"Cossack," Abbi repeated, followed by a cough. "Last here. Yesterday. The day before. The Iron Maidens were on. I remember."

"That was the day before yesterday," Karoli explained.

"What?" asked Abbi, straining to hear. "I'm going deaf from the damned music. I wear earplugs. Thick ones, but it drives through my head like a sharp nail. What did you say?"

"Who was he hanging around with?" Karpo asked loudly.

Abbi scratched his head and searched his pockets. He came up with a crumpled cigarette, looked at it, and threw it on the floor.

"We just cleaned back there," a large woman said.

"Pick it up, Abbi," said Karoli.

Abbi nodded, sighed, and leaned over to pick up the cigarette. When he stood on uncertain legs, Karpo repeated the question.

"Everybody," Abbi said. "Everybody wanted to touch him or the girl. They didn't mind. They never do. There were two skinheads who took it on themselves to protect him and the girl, stayed with them. Big guys. Kids."

"With whom did he leave?" asked Karpo.

"Leave? I don't know. I think it was the skins. The other two guys from the band, Naked Cossack's band. They weren't here. I think the girl was here, the crazy one with red hair. Maybe not. The skins. I saw the Cossack with some skins."

"Names?"

"The skinheads? Real names? I don't know real names. Bottle Kaps and . . . let me think, Heinrich. That's it. Bottle Kaps and Heinrich. Tattoos on their arms. Nazi stuff. SS, swastikas. Stupid talk."

"Where can we find Bottle Kaps and Heinrich?" asked Karpo.

"Find them? Here, tonight. Almost every night," Abbi said. "Tonight especially. Death Times Four is on. Their lead . . . what's his name? . . ."

"Snub Nose Bullet," Zelach supplied.

"Yeah, Snub Nose Bullet," Abbi confirmed

with a smirk, plunging his hands into his pockets. "Loud, very loud. Screeching. Drums. Steel. I need some sleep."

"Go in back," said Karoli. "Get some sleep."

Abbi nodded and went back through the door behind the bar.

"Yes," said Karoli. "He's a drunk but an amazing bartender. He's like an artist. Drunk one second and then when the customers hit the bar he becomes an acrobat. I think he used to be an accountant. Me, I used to sell office supplies."

"We'll be back tonight," said Karpo. "Tell no one. Not even your partner."

"Then don't tell him you told me you were coming back," he said. "I've got enough grief with him. When I have enough saved, I'm going to buy him out or sell out and start my own place. The hell with my wife. The hell with her sister. A man can only take so much. You know what I mean?"

The detectives turned, crossed the room, opened the door, and went out into a light falling snow.

Porfiry Petrovich read the note, neatly printed in ink on a piece of paper that showed the creases of a double fold.

The note read:

Take the green rubles in a simple bag on the Two leaving M. for V. on Thursday. Contact will be made en route. Contact will give you the words *Nicholas's Secret*. Give contact the suitcase after contact gives you a package. Do not open the package. Deliver it to Ivan. Collect fee remainder from Ivan.

The note was unsigned. Rostnikov laid it flat before him and looked up at the Yak, who gave a slight tilt of his head to indicate that he waited for his chief inspector's response.

"*Two* is the number-two train leaving from *M.*, Moscow, on Thursday. Green rubles are not rubles. They are another green currency, probably dollars, half a million American dollars."

Rostnikov paused. Today was Thursday.

"Go on," said the Yak.

"There is nowhere to go until you give me more information."

Porfiry Petrovich wanted to take off his leg and scratch the stump. The itching was demanding, almost unbearable. He sat motionless.

"The message was intercepted," said the Yak. "The sender, who was being watched, was taken into custody. What you have is a copy of a one-sided telephone conversation.

The call was from the sender's apartment in Odessa to a phone booth in Moscow. The Odessa phone line was tapped. The receiver at the phone booth said nothing. By the time a car arrived at the booth, the receiver was long gone. In the course of interrogating the sender — a very old man who unfortunately died under the strain of vigorous questioning — it was determined that the old man had simply been hired in a bar by a woman he could not identify. He was given a handful of rubles to make the call and repeat exactly what is on the sheet before you. Security forces considered it a dead end, possibly drugs, smuggled currency. They lost interest. There wasn't enough information for them to board the train and search all the luggage for a bag of money. And even if they found such a bag, it would prove nothing."

"And I am to board the Trans-Siberian Express tonight, find the person with the bag of money, and? . . ." asked Rostnikov.

"I am not interested in the money or the man," said Yaklovev, suddenly standing. "Though you are to bring both to me. What is more important, I want the package. Look at the next item in the folder before you."

Rostnikov opened the folder and pulled out the xeroxed sheet of two pages copied from what must have been an old book.

"Read," said the Yak.

The two pages dealt with court intrigue during the decline of the reign of Czar Nicholas I. There was speculation on the relationship of Russia to Japan, the growing hostility between the two countries over offshore islands in the Sea of Japan. Highlighted in yellow marker were the words: "believed to have been a secret treaty signed by the czar and the emperor of Japan. The document supposedly disappeared or was stolen en route from Vladivostok to St. Petersburg."

Rostnikov looked up.

"Speculation?" asked the Yak.

"The person with the suitcase full of money is buying the document?" Rostnikov tried.

The Yak said nothing.

"Such a document would have little political or economic significance even if it did exist," Rostnikov said. "Agreements made by a Czar a hundred years ago would not be honored today and it would do little good to attack the royal family. It is ancient history."

"Go on."

"And there is little reason to see a connection between this intercepted message and the supposed document."

"And so you believe the pursuit of this package is not worthy of action?"

Behind the Yak, through the window,

Rostnikov could see the snow beginning to fall. It heartened him. Winter was his season, the season of most Muscovites. A clean white blanket of snow. Crisp chill air. He considered pointing out the falling snow to the director and thought better of it. Instead, he said, "I believe it is worth pursuing."

His reasons for making the statement needed no further comment. There was something the Yak was not telling him. There was probably a great deal the Yak was not telling him.

"Take one of your people with you."

"Sasha Tkach," Rostnikov answered without hesitation. "He has no immediate assignment."

That was true, but the chief inspector had other reasons for wanting the less-than-stable detective to accompany him.

The Yak turned his back and walked to the window, hands folded behind his back. He was looking at the falling snow.

"It will not be easy to locate the courier," said the Yak. "But I have great confidence in you, Porfiry Petrovich."

"I shall do my best to merit such confidence," said Rostnikov.

"Pankov will hand you tickets for you and Tkach on your way out. The number-two train leaves a few minutes before midnight.

You are in separate first-class compartments. If the courier is a professional, and it seems that he or she is, then they are likely to be in first class, if for no reason other than to protect the suitcase full of money. You have twelve hours to prepare. Take the entire folder. You have one-way tickets. As soon as you find the package, the courier, and the money, you are to fly back to Moscow from the nearest airport. Pankov will take care of all travel arrangements and provide you with necessary expense money. You will return whatever you do not use directly to him."

Rostnikov rose, steadying his leg with both hands as he did so. He picked up the file folder and his notebook and turned toward the door.

"No one sees the contents of the package," the Yak said, his back still turned. "It is to be delivered to me unopened."

"Unopened," said Rostnikov. He closed the door gently behind him and stood before the desk of the moist-foreheaded Pankov.

Without a word Pankov handed Rostnikov a thick envelope, and the chief inspector departed. Three minutes later he was in his office, door closed, behind his desk. He dropped the folder and envelope with the tickets and cash on his desk and quickly removed his artificial leg as he sat. He began scratching the stump as he settled back. Ecstasy. Pure delight. Better than Sarah's Chicken Tabak. Better than walking in the snow. Better than winning the senior weight-lifting title in Ismailovo Park. The itch slowly spread and Rostnikov worked on it as he reached for the phone on his desk with one hand and pushed a number on the keyboard.

"Come to my office," he said and hung up.

The itching slowly departed and Porfiry Petrovich reconsidered the delights of life. Scratching an itch was very good, but Chicken Tabak, sex, snow, and the rush from lifting massive weights had now moved high above it on his list of pleasures.

He put his legs down, the front of the desk hiding the artificial leg he had not replaced on the chance that the itch would return.

Rostnikov had believed very little of what Yaklovev had told him, but that didn't matter. The assignment was clear and probably not as difficult as it appeared to be on the surface.

A knock.

"Come in."

Sasha Tkach entered. Rostnikov motioned him across the small space and nodded at the chair on the other side of the desk. Sasha sat.

"How would you like to take a trip?"

"Where?"

"Siberia, the Trans-Siberian Express."

"To China?"

"Vladivostok."

Sasha brushed the lock of hair from his face. He did not look pleased by the prospect of the journey.

"When?" asked Sasha.

"Tonight," said Rostnikov.

"Maya is coming back tomorrow," he said.

"I am pleased to hear that," said Rostnikov. "You can call her. Tell her to move in with the children, get resettled, have the apartment to herself. Does Lydia know Maya is coming back?"

"Yes," said Sasha. "I should be here."

"Perhaps not," said Rostnikov. "Perhaps Maya would welcome a few days or so without the awkwardness of reunion. And you would have time away from Lydia."

"That would be good," Sasha admitted.

"Can you keep her away from Maya and the children?"

"No," said Sasha. "She paid for their return tickets. She wants to see her grandchildren. Maya knows. She understands."

"Good. Tonight. Number-two train. I'll pick you up in a cab around ten. Have you ever been to Siberia?"

"No," said Sasha.

"It can be cold, beautiful," said Rostnikov.

It can also be quite deadly, he thought.

"Do I have a choice?" asked Sasha.

"Refusal is always an option, but refusal has consequences," said Rostnikov. "That is not a threat, Sasha. It is an essential moral essence of life."

"I have some work to finish," said Sasha, standing.

"Call Maya from here; your office," said Rostnikov. "It is police business. I'm sure Director Yaklovev will not mind." He was equally certain that the Yak was listening to the conversation. "Pack enough for seven days," he added.

If things went well and they found the courier and the package, they might be back sooner, possibly much sooner, but they had to be prepared to travel all the way to Vladivostok if necessary.

Sasha nodded and left the office.

Rostnikov thought the younger detective was in serious need of a change of scenery. It would probably be snowing in Siberia. He could spend hours looking out at mountains, losing himself in a meditation he would not recognize as meditation.

Rostnikov sat back and turned his chair toward the window so he could watch the snow and plan how he was to find his quarry, on a train full of people, when he had no idea who he might be looking for.

A bag of half a million American dollars, or deutsche marks or French francs or British pounds, would be reasonably large even if the bills were in large denominations. Starting with the first-class passengers, he would have Sasha make his way through the train, examining every piece of luggage. A passenger who carried a sizeable bag with him or her at all times would be a certain target. Distracting the carrier might be difficult but Rostnikov enjoyed a game of distraction.

Because of his leg, Rostnikov's task would be the diversion of individual passengers. The agile and innocent-appearing Sasha Tkach would do the search of each compartment.

It was a reasonable plan, but there had to be contingencies. He would work them out. Later he would work them out.

But now he began to think seriously about lunch.

Chapter Five

There were plainclothes police officers at every one of the twenty-two stops of the Kaluzhsko-Rizhskaya line, the orange line, of the Moscow metro. Some carried newspapers, pretending to read. Others carried briefcases and wore watches, which they checked periodically as if they were late for an important meeting. A few were more creative.

Most of the officers, regular users of the metro system themselves, were aware that the more successful businessmen, government officials, and Mafiosi of the city seldom used the underground. Although there was a clear class distinction, there were still many well-dressed men in the age group of the men who had been attacked.

One young officer named Mariankyov assigned to the Cheryomushki station dressed up like a gypsy, or what he thought a gypsy looked like. He was the most conspicuous of all the police officers. Gypsy men alone on the platform at a metro station or at a bus stop were open warnings that a pickpocket was present. The truth was that the gypsy pickpockets had long since learned to dress more conservatively.

People avoided Mariankyov, except for one old man in an overcoat who bumped into him as he rushed to catch a departing train. Moments later Mariankyov discovered that his pocket had been picked.

By noon, five women had been picked up based upon their resemblance to the drawing each officer carried in his memory and his pocket. The women were brought to Elena Timofeyeva and Iosef Rostnikov, who headquartered in a small office at the Tretyakovskaya station at the center of the line.

One of the women was the wife of a Portuguese leather buyer. The woman had been in Moscow for only one day and carried no knife. She was released.

Another woman was an actress with the Moscow Theater Company. Iosef knew her slightly from his theater days. She carried no knife and found the arrest interesting. She was released.

The third woman did have a small folding knife in her purse, along with a can of Mace. She was terrified of muggers and not particularly at ease with the police. She had once been accosted by a drunk on her way to work as a hotel maid. She was released.

The fourth woman was Chinese. She was released.

The fifth woman was not a woman at all but a transvestite prostitute coming home from an unsuccessful morning, which did not surprise either of the detectives since the man was incredibly homely. He carried a razor in his pocket. It was an ancient straight razor. He said the sight of it usually deterred people who did not understand or appreciate alternative life-styles and careers. He was released.

None of those arrested had a sprained wrist.

While all this was going on, more than fifty thousand people traveled to work, home, sightseeing, and nowhere in particular on the metro system. The system opened each morning at six and closed at one the following morning. That gave the cleaning crews a little over five hours to clean the platforms, walls, pillars, and tracks, and repair any broken windows or chipped paint. The cleaning crews worked quickly and generally efficiently, depending on who headed each particular crew.

There was a lack of funds for metro repairs and cleaning, though the stations were more cosmetically acceptable than the interior of most of the city's hotels. The metro system was a symbol of Russian accomplishment, a source of pride along with the space program and the Trans-Siberian Railroad system. The mayor of Moscow was a man who built his career on the image of the city, and he saw to it that the metro stations were clean and well-maintained. Efficient, sometimes magnificent, each station — all built during the Stalin era — was in a different style.

Guidebooks told tourists that they should not miss a tour of the metro stations, and few of them did.

One of the most opulent examples of the old Soviet system was the Komsomolskaya station, dedicated to the Komsomol, the Young Communist League, whose members provided labor during construction of the metro.

Many metro stations had undergone name changes after the fall of the Soviet Union. If the Komsomolskaya had undergone such a change, few Moscovites who rode it were aware of this rejection of Communism. It was still and would probably remain the Komsomol station to all who rode it.

One of the regular riders was Toomas Vana. Toomas, born in Tallinn in Estonia, had come to Moscow to work in the office of the state gas company when he was fourteen. His father had been an unpopular and very corrupt commissar in Estonia, who thought the way for his son to achieve political position at a high level in the Soviet Union was to move the boy to Moscow. Toomas had, indeed, moved up, but not politically. He earned his university degree and developed a passion for gas. He wanted, not political power, but to be the world's foremost authority on natural gas and its uses. At the age of forty-six he was certainly among the elite of the world in that knowledge.

And Toomas had a very valuable skill which added to his stature. Tallinn, Estonia, is sixty miles across the Gulf of Finland from Helsinki. The Estonians of the region spoke a language almost identical to that of Finland, and until the age of fourteen when he was sent off to Moscow he had regularly listened to and watched Finnish television, a link to the Western world available to few in the Soviet Union.

Toomas traveled frequently to Finland to consult on that country's attempts to expand its use of natural gas.

This morning Toomas did not have the correct change. He stopped at the change machine and then proceeded to the automatic gate and dropped in his coins.

The platform was crowded. It always was around lunchtime. Toomas stood against a pillar, briefcase in one hand, a report on the cost of pipeline repairs in the other. Moscow was heated and cooled by natural gas. The gas company was still a great government bureaucracy to be reckoned with, the largest natural-gas company in the world.

Had he not stood on this same platform at this same pillar thousands of times before he would certainly have looked up at the decorated arched ceiling with its massive, ornate, and multilamped chandeliers running the length of the platform longer than a soccer field and nearly as wide. He would have noted the arches above the pillars echoing the elegant medieval theme of the station. He might have looked straight up, as he had many years earlier, at the huge, multicolored mosaic of a warrior with shield and lance upon a prancing white horse and admired the elaborate design of curlicues and flowers that framed it.

But this was today and his mind was on rusting gas pipes.

He barely noticed the woman walking slowly in his direction. People were moving. She would pass him and move to the edge of the platform to look for an incoming train. Toomas never bothered to move for the train until he heard it coming with a roar down the tunnel. Then he would make a slow turn, always to the right, and place himself exactly where the train door would slide open. He knew the spot. He didn't have to think about it. Now he heard the first distant rumble of the approaching train.

The woman stood in front of him. She was probably going to ask him a question about the train schedule, or perhaps she was going to ask him for some coins, which he would not give her. To encourage one is to encourage all, he thought. He read the report.

And then the report exploded in his hands, split in two, and he felt a sudden pain, saw a flash of bright light. The world turned into a sparkling light show. Fireworks. Strobe lights. A bomb, he thought. Terrorists. Chechins. A bomb. They had bombed underpasses and now a metro station. It made sense.

He knew he had slumped back against the flat pillar. Toomas did not panic. Someone or something was punching him in the stomach. An aftershock from a bomb? Wait. Was there a gas main under this station? A gas explosion? It had happened before, many times before, but there was no gas main under the platform or nearby.

His head ached. The fireworks stopped. The punching ceased, leaving nausea. Toomas felt himself passing out. At least he thought he was passing out. In fact, he was dying.

Inna Dalipovna stepped back and turned away from the falling man in the dark suit. She tucked the knife into her deep coat pocket. She would wash it when she got home. She would sharpen it with oil on the rectangular stone when she got home. She would use the knife to make dinner for her father tonight. She would use it to slice the sausage into the thin, almost transparent slices he liked to heap upon his bread.

The attack had been quick. Some people thought it was probably a husband and wife quarreling. Some people pretended to see nothing. Most on the crowded platform did not notice. When it was over, however, a woman screamed. Inna, now at the end of the platform, nearing the escalator steps, heard the scream above the noise of the crowd and the approaching train.

The screaming woman, who stood hand in hand with her six-year-old granddaughter, looked down at the man who lay before her, his right eye socket a small pool of blood, his neck pulsing red, and spots of darkness quickly forming and spreading on his white shirt and dark suit.

"Don't be afraid, Grandma," the child said. "It's just a dead man."

Inna did not look back. Her wrist felt numb. She had used her right hand, had taped it thickly and tightly with white adhesive. She had planned to thrust without turning her hand, but when she had seen the man standing there, had known it would be him, she had forgotten everything, had gone into some kind of automatic state, had let it take over. And now she felt both pain and satisfaction. Only when she reached the street and stepped into the falling snow did she examine herself for bloodstains. She could see none. No one had looked at her strangely so she assumed that her face and neck were untouched, but she paused at a window to be sure.

The woman looking back at her was the one she saw each morning in the mirror. It was not her own face but the face of her mother.

No policeman had appeared during or immediately after Inna's attack on Toomas Vana. There had been no policeman on the platform for a very good reason. None had been assigned to this station.

The Komsomolskaya station was on the red line, the Kirovsko-Frunzenskaya line, not on the line where Inna had attacked before.

Five minutes later when Elena and Iosef were informed of the murder they realized that there were now more than ninety stations where their killer might strike. To patrol the stations in two shifts would require about two hundred officers. The chances of their getting two hundred officers assigned to the case were nonexistent.

They would have to find another way to the woman or wait for her to make a mistake.

Sasha had tried to pack. It was useless. The scuffed but serviceable dark-leather suitcase that had once been his father's lay open on the bed. His mother, who had been in the apartment uninvited when he arrived, had criticized him as he placed the first item, a pair of trousers, at the bottom of the case.

"You will squash it," Lydia had shouted.

She was a wiry wraith who denied her near deafness, loved Sasha and her grandchildren to the point where she would die for them, and drove her son nearly to madness each time they spoke.

"It will be fine," he said.

"You will pile things on it. It will wrinkle. You will not have a pair of decent pants. Where can you get pants cleaned and pressed on a train?"

He flattened the pants with the palms of his hands and reached for the first of the three shirts he had placed on the bed.

"That is not the way to fold them," Lydia said, arms folded.

"It will be fine," Sasha said, the first sign of impending defeat in his tone.

"You fold along the seam, sleeves back," she said. "The way you are doing it . . ."

"Would you like to pack for me?" he asked, closing his eyes.

"Yes, why don't I pack for you?" his mother said, stepping to his side.

Sasha stepped out of the way and watched her fold, invade his drawers, select items from the bathroom and closet, and keep up a running commentary on each item.

"This is worn at the cuffs. See? Frayed. You need a new jacket. I will get you a new jacket."

He did not argue.

"What size are you now? You've lost weight. You do not know," she said with a what-am-I-going-to-do-with-you sigh. "I used to know. Don't worry. I will figure it out. Shirts, you need shirts. Who ironed this shirt? Maya?"

"You did," he said, leaning against the wall, defeated.

"I will iron it again. When you have worn a shirt all day on the train, do not try to clean it. Do not wear it again. Put it in a plastic bag."

"There will be no room in the suitcase for clothes in a bag. You are stuffing it full of things I don't need."

"Change your socks every morning," she said.

"You are packing enough for a month," he

said. "It will weigh as much as I do."

"In the other room, on the table. I brought you a book to read so you don't get bored."

"I will be working," he said before he could stop himself.

"It is about learning to relax," she said. "I read it. It has done wonderful things for me."

She scurried around, looking for more to do, taking one thing out and replacing it with another.

"I look forward to reading the book," he said.

"We have forgotten something," Lydia said. "I know! A small plastic bag to keep your toothpaste in so it doesn't squish out and ruin your clothes."

"I will get one," he said.

"Go see if you have one," his mother ordered.

He escaped from the bedroom and took his time bringing the plastic bag back. He had called Maya, told her what had happened. She had asked if he could find some way to keep his mother away from the apartment for the first few days while he was gone. He said he would try.

"I do not dislike her, Sasha," she said.

Sasha was not sure he felt the same way about his mother.

"She wants to see the children," he said. "How can I? . . ."

"Tell her I will call her soon, that, that I have had a breakdown . . . no, she will come with doctors. I do not know what you can tell her."

"I can tell her anything," Sasha had said. "The problem is that she will not listen."

"I know," Maya said.

They had spoken a few minutes longer, holding back, putting away till they had face-to-face time together the important things that had to be dealt with, the important things other than the omnipresence of Sasha's mother.

And now Sasha stood watching his mother stuff the suitcase beyond its reasonable capacity.

"And this is last," she said, holding up a pair of binoculars. "They were your father's. You can look out the train window with them."

"Thank you," said Sasha, having no intention of using the binoculars. Were she returning to her own apartment that night he would have considered removing half of what she had packed and hiding it. But that would probably not work. His mother was certain to search the two rooms to be sure he had not done just that.

This was madness. He was thirty-five years old.

"Mother," he said as she struggled to zip the bag closed. "For the first few days, when Maya and the children come back . . ."

"Tomorrow," Lydia said, standing back to examine her handiwork.

"Yes." He had promised Maya he would try and so he would.

"I won't be here," his mother said, turning to Sasha. "I have to go to Istra for a while."

"Istra?"

"You do not know where Istra is?" she asked, looking at her son as if he might be feverish.

"I know exactly where it is," he said. "About forty kilometers from here off the Volokolamsk Highway."

"On the bank of the Istra River," she said.

"That is right."

"Why are you going there?" he asked, his curiosity replacing for the moment his pleasure at having achieved instant success.

"To spend some time with Matvei," she said, walking past him into the room that served as living room, dining area, and kitchen.

Sasha followed her quickly.

"Matvei? Who is Matvei?"

"Matvei Labroadovnik, the famous painter,"

she said, looking around the room for something to straighten or at least change.

"The famous . . . I've never heard of . . . why are you going to spend time with this Matvei La . . ."

"Labroadovnik," she supplied. "He is very famous. We are considering marriage."

Sasha felt slightly dizzy. He reached back for the arm of the couch, found it, and sat heavily.

"He is living in a dacha in Istra while he helps with the restoration of the Cathedral of the Resurrection," she said, finding a chair that had to be moved a few inches to satisfy her sense of decor.

Sasha's mother had retired from her government job four years earlier. She was now nearly sixty years old, and as far as Sasha knew she had had nothing to do with men since his father had died when he was a boy.

"How did you meet him? How old is he?" asked Sasha, bewildered.

"You want some tea? Pepsi-Cola?" she asked.

"Water," he said.

She nodded, moved into the kitchen area, and got him a glass of water from the noisy tap.

"Matvei is fifty-six years old. His mother lives in the building where I have my apartment. We have met frequently. We have much in common."

"Like what?" asked Sasha.

"Art," she said.

"You have never shown the slightest interest in art," he said.

"You haven't noticed," she said, sitting across from him, continuing to scan the room for imperfection.

"Art?"

"And movies."

"You don't like to go to movies. You can't hear them."

"You are wrong," she said. "I love movies."

Sasha had an insight, or thought he did.

"And he is famous?"

"Very."

"And he is well paid?"

"He has a great deal of money. He is in great demand."

Sasha sought desperately for a reason why this man might be interested in his mother. If it wasn't for her money, then what? Lydia was no beauty. Lydia was no aesthete. Lydia was a meddler and a tyrant.

"He is healthy?"

"Like a swine," she said with a small smile. "Tall, robust. When we get back, you can meet him. I'll see that he dresses up."

There was a mystery here for which Sasha

did not have the time, energy, or proper source of information. He recognized the possible blessings of seeing far less of his mother, but he was a detective and the evidence sat before him.

"Does he know I am a policeman?" he asked.

"Yes, of course," she said. She stood up suddenly and said, "I will go shopping, get food, some new clothes for the children for when Maya gets back . . . Sasha," she said, picking up her oversized black purse. "You must promise me something."

"What?" he asked.

"On the train, you will stay away from women."

"I will be working with Porfiry Petrovich," he said.

"That has not stopped you before."

She walked over to her seated son and touched his cheek. "You are too much like your father," she said.

"My father? My father? . . ."

"Had a weakness." She sighed. "For the ladies. He was handsome, weak, but he had a bad heart."

"You've never told me this before," he said.

"You knew he had a bad heart. It killed him."

"No," he said, "about the women."

"I must have," she said. "How could you not know after all this time? I had best go do some shopping now. You should eat before you go."

"Yes," he said, not wanting to hear any more surprises from his mother. "I should eat."

"Is there anything you would like special for dinner?"

His mother never asked such questions. She simply made what she wished and expected anyone at the table to enjoy it, though she was a terrible cook.

"No," he said. "Whatever you choose."

She nodded as if he had made a very wise decision, and marched out the door.

When the door closed, it struck him. He had carried on an entire conversation with his nearly deaf mother without having her fail to understand him.

His mother had changed in what appeared to be an instant. Had it been gradual? Had he been too preoccupied to notice? He took out his notebook and pen and wrote the name Matvei Labroadovnik in it. He would make some calls, ask some questions.

The building on Brjanskaya Street was about half a hundred paces from the entrance to the Kievski Market, across the Moscow

River from the heart of the city. There was no name on the building, just an address, and the building itself was no more than a few years old; it was a relatively simple, clean, yellow-brick six-story structure.

It was not the kind of building in which one might expect to find one of the wealthiest men in all of Russia. The truly wealthy new capitalists and those who aspired to be and lived on the edge of success were in the prestigious buildings in the center of the city.

Nikoli Lovski could have his office wherever he wished. He owned six radio stations, two newspapers, a paper company with a supporting forest in Siberia, and a piece of several banks and stock in a large number of foreign companies, not to mention considerable land, mostly in the growing suburbs of the city.

The only real clue to Nikoli Lovski's wealth was the quartet of armed men in the lobby of the building. Two of the men, wearing well-trimmed dark suits and ties, carried automatic weapons in their hands and stood at ease on opposite sides of the smoothly tiled lobby. Another man armed with an equally formidable weapon stood behind a bullet-proof-glass plate, ceiling-high, behind which sat a very pretty dark woman with a pie-shaped speaker's screen directly in front of her.

Few would have noticed the fourth man, who stood inside an open elevator in a gray uniform. He seemed to be the elevator operator. The very slight bulge under his jacket and the fact that a modern elevator would need no operator were enough to demonstrate to Emil Karpo that he was probably the most formidable member of the quartet.

There were no other people in the lobby. Karpo and Zelach moved to the reception window, the sound of their shoes echoing.

"We are here to see Mr. Lovski," said Karpo.

"Names?" the pretty dark woman asked.

"Inspectors Karpo and Zelach. I called earlier."

The woman nodded and said, "May I see your identification?"

Both men pulled out their identification cards and held them up to the window. The armed man behind the glass glanced at the cards and nodded to the woman, who shook her head.

"Are you armed?" the woman asked.

"Yes," said Emil Karpo.

She looked at Zelach.

"Yes," he said.

"You will have to leave your weapons with me," she said.

A metal drawer slid open in front of Karpo.

"No," said Karpo. "We cannot."

In fact, Karpo could if he so chose, but he was not prepared to give in to the power of a capitalist trying to make him feel inferior. It was not Karpo's feelings that were at issue. He had no feeling about the demand, just an understanding that to comply would put himself and Zelach into the position of accepting their capitulation.

"Then Mr. Lovski will be unable to see you," she said.

"Please tell Mr. Lovski that under section fourteen of the Moscow City Criminal Investigation Law of 1992 we can insist that he accompany us to Petrovka for questioning. If he refuses, we have the duty to arrest and fine him for violation of the law."

"Fine him?" the woman said with the hint of a smile. She knew that money meant nothing to her employer.

"And hold him a minimum of twenty-four hours in which we can interrogate him in addition to a fine," said Karpo. "Call him."

"Are you sure you wish to antagonize Mr. Lovski?" she asked.

Lovski was a new capitalist. Karpo was an old-line Marxist-Leninist. He had been forced by the reality of corruption in the Communist Party of the Soviet Union and the crumbling of any true hope for a principled revival of the party to put aside the beliefs on which he had based his life. People like Lovski were the new Russia of the privileged few and wealthy who had replaced the privileged few and politically powerful. Lovski, a Jew whose media regularly attacked Vladimir Putin and his regime, had suffered several indignities, courtroom confrontations, and even nights in jail. Each time he had emerged, determined but a little closer to the edge over which Putin did not yet have the power to push him.

The woman nodded, pushed a button that cut off sound through the screen, and picked up the phone. She hit a single number and began speaking. Karpo and Zelach could not hear her. The conversation was brief, the button to the screen was pushed, and the woman said, "The elevator will take you up."

"Thank you," Zelach said.

Karpo said nothing. He moved toward the elevator with Zelach at his side.

"Section fourteen of the Criminal Investigation Law?" Zelach whispered.

"Yes," said Karpo as they neared the elevator.

"Is there really? . . ."

"Not since 1932," said Karpo.

They stepped into the elevator. Since there was no law, Karpo was willing to pick and choose what would serve his assignments till a law existed. When there was a coherent body of law, which there might never be in this new Russia, he would obey it to the letter. Karpo believed in the law, wanted clear rules and guidelines, but he would exist without them and think only of bringing in the guilty and putting the evidence of their guilt before Chief Inspector Rostnikov. What happened after that was something he chose not to consider.

The elevator moved up slowly. The armed man who pushed the buttons folded his hands in front of him and stood back where he could watch the two policemen. The elevator came to a stop so smoothly that when the doors opened Zelach had the impression they had not moved.

The entryway before them was covered in white carpet. There was a single dark wooden door in the wall with no name on or near it.

Karpo and Zelach moved forward to the door, the armed elevator operator behind them. The door popped open. Inside was a large room with a well-polished wooden floor. At a very modern white desk sat an old man in a suit and tie. The old man had thick white hair and small, remarkably blue eyes.

He looked up at the three men and said, "You have ten minutes, no more. Mr. Lovski has an important engagement."

Karpo nodded. He did not think that they would require more than ten minutes, but if they did, he would take whatever time he felt was needed.

The old man's eyes met Karpo's. Karpo was accustomed to people looking away from his ghostly appearance. This old man did not. The old man nodded at the elevator operator, and a door behind the old man's desk opened.

Karpo and Zelach moved forward with the elevator operator at their backs. They walked through the door and it closed behind them.

The office was as remarkably modest as the building itself. Through the large double window one could see the Hero Tower several hundred yards away and the Moscow River beyond it.

There were four comfortable, soft black-leather chairs and a matching couch against the wall. A conference table with six chairs stood in the corner next to a low wooden table with a marble top, on which rested a large samovar and a line of cups, saucers, spoons, and a bowl of sugar cubes.

Behind the wooden desk before them sat Nikoli Lovski. Both detectives recognized the man from both newspaper and television pictures and they knew his voice when he suggested that they be seated.

He was a man of average height, a bit stocky

124

and no more than fifty years old. His hair was thinning and dark and his face was full, with deep-set eyes. He wore a white shirt and an orange tie. His jacket was draped over the back of his desk chair.

Karpo and Zelach sat. The elevator operator stood behind them near the door.

"Tea?" asked Lovski. "Or I can get you coffee? I am particularly partial to strong tea with water brewed, as it was meant to be, in a samovar. The one over there belonged to my mother's father and his father before that. It was the only possession the family had that was worth anything in rubles or memories."

"I'll have . . ." Zelach began.

"Nothing," said Karpo.

"I will," said Lovski, reaching under his desk to press a button.

The office door opened and the old man entered. Lovski held up one finger and pointed to himself. The old man moved to pour him a cup of tea.

"Your son is missing," Karpo said.

"I have two sons," Lovski said.

"Misha," said Karpo, knowing that the man behind the desk knew which son was missing. "We have reason to believe he has been kidnapped. Have you been contacted with a ransom demand?"

"No," said Lovski, accepting the cup of tea

from the old man, who quickly left the room.

Karpo was reasonably sure the man was telling the truth. "You may be contacted very soon," he said.

Lovski nodded and drank some tea. "And I will pay any reasonable amount, providing it can be demonstrated that it is not a scheme of Misha's to get money from me. He is not beyond that."

"How can that be demonstrated?" asked Karpo.

"Simple," said Lovski, licking his lips. "I shall demand that they deliver to me the small finger of his left hand. I will check it against his fingerprints, of which I have a set. Misha would not cut off his own finger. He needs it to play that piece of steel garbage he calls a guitar."

"Do you have any idea who might want to hurt your son?" asked Karpo.

Lovski smiled and said, "Anyone in his right mind. Have you seen him, heard the filth he spews? He has even written a song about me, calls me the wealthy Jew in the steel tower, the Manipulator of Metropolis. He says I should be flattened by a female robot, my penis ripped from my body. I understand it is one of his more popular songs."

"It is," said Zelach.

"You've heard it?" asked Lovski with some interest.

"Yes," said Zelach.

"And?"

"It is what you say, though there is a pulse to the music that . . ."

"It is possible that he has not been taken for ransom," said Karpo.

"You mean someone who hates him has already killed him or is torturing him somewhere?" asked Lovski, taking another sip of tea.

"There are many possibilities," said Karpo.

Lovski nodded. "There is another possibility," he said. "I am a member of the Russian Jewish Congress."

"I am aware of this," said Karpo.

"My newspapers, television stations have been critical of Putin and his regime. This you also know."

It was Karpo's turn to nod. "So, you believe he may have been taken by someone who wants to put pressure on you to stop your attacks on Vladimir Putin?" Karpo asked.

Lovski smiled. "Nothing so simple," he said. "A few months ago Putin attended a rededication ceremony at Marina Roscha, the Chabad Lubavich Hasidic synagogue."

"I remember," said Karpo.

"What do you know of the synagogue?" asked Lovski.

"It was one of only two allowed in Moscow

during the Soviet era," said Karpo. "It was untouched until the fall of Communism. Since then it has been attacked three times. In 1993 it was almost destroyed by fire. It was bombed in 1996 and 1998. And it has been restored and rebuilt."

"Yes," Lovski said with an approving nod. "And Mr. Putin was there to proclaim that the new Russia would not tolerate anti-Semitism. My newspapers covered it, put Putin on the front page and on the television screen. Putin was not just making peace with a handful of Jews. He was making a peace gesture toward me."

Karpo nodded.

"You think it is my inflated ego making this assumption?"

"No," said Karpo. "Your ego, as you call it, is clearly large, but your interpretation bears serious consideration."

"Meaning?" Lovski prompted.

"Your son may have been taken by an individual or group, anti-Semitic in nature, anti-Putin in philosophy, who wants to put pressure on you to keep you from supporting Putin."

"Yes."

"But they have not yet contacted you?"

"No, but when they do it may not be for money. It may be to tell me that Misha is safe as long as I keep up my attacks on the regime."

"It is a possibility," said Karpo.

"It is more than that," said Lovski. "Inspector, I confess that I have been contacted. My receptionist took a message this morning. The caller said to tell me that Misha is alive for now."

"Was the caller a man or woman?"

"The receptionist said it was a man, or, to be more accurate, a young man."

"Anything else?" asked Karpo.

"I do not want my son to die," he said. "I don't want to see him or hear from him, and I would prefer it if he were somewhere far away. South America would be fine. I understand there is a second and third generation of fascists there who might like his kind of hatred, but I do not want him dead. He is young. People change. I did. Perhaps in ten years, twenty years, he will change, perhaps for the better. I'll be an old man and far beyond wanting a reconciliation, but he will have to live with whatever that means to him. Officers, give me your number. If I am contacted I will call you, but only if I feel certain that whoever called means to kill Misha no matter what I do. I will try to keep that from happening by promising them and delivering a bonus for his safe return, if that is what they want. I will not, however, change my policy toward Putin. For now, he is relatively safe from attack by me. I have no illusions. Our president has donned a yarmulke for political reasons. He bears no great love for Russia's Jews. There is a price I will not pay to free my son, but the price I am willing to pay is quite high to insure that he is safe."

"Safe except for a finger," said Karpo.

"He will have to be a singer without a guitar perhaps," said Lovski with a shrug. "I know little of such music."

"There is a guitarist with Dead Zombies with two fingers missing," Zelach said.

"That is comforting," said Lovski. "Now, if you have no more questions . . ."

Karpo rose. Zelach did the same. Lovski picked up the phone and was talking to someone before the detectives reached the door, which was opened for them by the elevator operator.

Five minutes later they were on the street.

"Thoughts?" asked Karpo.

Zelach shrugged.

"He hates his son," said Karpo.

"No," said Zelach. "He loves his son. He loves him very much."

Karpo nodded. Karpo trusted his own sense of reason, but he had learned to trust Zelach's feelings if not his intellect.

Chapter Six

"Do you think the sun will eventually burn out?" asked Rostnikov.

He was sitting in the Paris Café a few hundred yards from his apartment on Krasikov Street. The Paris Café bore no resemblance to anything Parisian, nor was it a café. It was a small shop that was sometimes open and sometimes not, depending on the whims and health of the old couple who ran it. There were six plastic tables with four chairs at each. The decor was simple. A painting of a dark jungle that looked decidedly un-Russian, with its huge palm trees and high waterfall in the distance, was the only decoration. The menu choices were almost as limited. In fact, there was no menu. The old woman or old man simply told you what was available at that moment in time besides coffee, tea, *kvas*, and vodka. Today, Rostnikov and the three people at the table with him had a choice of flat almond cakes of unknown vintage or puffy, small chocolate muffins of great durability.

Rostnikov had ordered two of each.

Like most Moscow cafés, this one smelled of pungent, acrid Russian tobacco. The man and woman across from him were contributing to the smell. The four of them were the Paris Café's only customers at the moment.

"The sun?" asked the man, looking at Rostnikov without understanding.

The man was large, perhaps forty, clean-shaven and rather resembling an ox. He wore a flannel shirt and solid-blue tie over his navy-blue coat. The woman at his side was a bit younger than the man. Her face was plain though her skin was smooth, unblemished. She was thin, nervous, dark, and wore a look showing that she was prepared for battle.

The man had been introduced by the woman as Dmitri. No last name had been given. The woman was Miriana. She had given no last name. Rostnikov needed none. Miriana was the daughter of Galina Panishkoya who sat heavily to Porfiry Petrovich's right, her hands in her lap, looking at her daughter who did not meet her eyes.

Both Miriana and Dmitri were smoking cheap Russian cigarettes.

"Time is perhaps infinite, but our solar system, our galaxy, and certainly our lives are not," said Rostnikov.

"I want my children," Miriana said, looking

defiantly at Rostnikov.

"You abandoned them, Mirya," Galina said flatly. "You left them with me and . . ."

"Things have changed," said Miriana, cutting off her mother, not looking at her. "Dmitri and I are getting married. The girls are mine."

"But Mirya . . ." the older woman tried.

"No," her daughter cut her off. "They are mine. The law is on my side."

Galina looked at Rostnikov, who pursed his lips. He considered touching the grandmother's shoulder to reassure her, but reassurance would come from action not gesture.

"Then you shall have the children," Rostnikov said. "They are packed, ready. We anticipated this. My wife and I are looking forward to having the apartment to ourselves. Your mother can join you."

"My mother . . ." Miriana began.

"Or perhaps she can get a small room," said Rostnikov. "I know someone who might help."

Galina sobbed.

"Perhaps . . ." Dmitri began but stopped when Miriana raised her hand.

"You are bluffing," the younger woman said.

Rostnikov shrugged.

"You do not want the children to go with

me," Miriana continued.

"I do not want the sun to burn out," said Rostnikov, "but I believe it is as inevitable as the fact that all of us who sit at this table will die and eventually be forgotten."

"Dmitri and I have a great deal of traveling to do in our business," Miriana said, stubbing out her cigarette and holding out her hand for Dmitri to give her another. He did so and lit it.

"I see," said Rostnikov.

"I might consider leaving my children with you if I can be compensated for being away from them."

"You have been away for two years and seem to have survived," said Rostnikov.

"But a mother's heart has been full of concern," she said, with no sign of concern in her voice that Rostnikov could discern.

"Understandable," said Rostnikov. "What would you consider a fair compensation for our continuing to keep these children and your mother?"

"Two hundred rubles a month," she said.

"Two hundred," Rostnikov repeated as the old man placed a plate of cake and muffins on the table and retreated. "That is acceptable. Cake?"

Dmitri reached for a muffin.

"You can begin payment immediately, tonight," said the woman.

"Begin payment?" Rostnikov said, carefully slicing the small cake with a knife the old man had placed next to it. "Yes, the payments can begin tonight. That would be nice. Very generous."

Rostnikov tried the cake. It was slightly stale but he could still detect the flavor of almonds. He dunked the hard slice in his coffee.

"Well?" asked Miriana. "The first payment."

"Yes," said Rostnikov, putting the cake down on a small plate before him and wiping his hands on the napkin next to it. He put out his hand.

"What are you doing?" the woman asked.

"Waiting for my first payment," said Rostnikov. "Time is passing. I've encountered no one in my experience who is getting younger."

Miriana looked at her mother, who had been looking down and now was staring at Rostnikov.

"You expect me to pay you?" she said.

"For keeping your mother and children, yes. The cake is not at all bad. You should try a small piece. I'll cut it for you."

He reached forward with the knife to cut the cake. Miriana stood. Her green cloth coat was draped over the back of her chair. The chair looked as if it were going to fall backward. Dmitri, half-finished muffin in his left hand, reached over with his right to steady the chair.

"We'll pick up the children," the standing woman spat.

"As you wish," said Rostnikov, taking the second slice of cake and offering it to Galina, who shook her head.

"I don't think . . ." Dmitri began.

"No," said Miriana, "you do not. He is bluffing. He doesn't want us to take the children. We will call your bluff. Let's get them."

"Let me finish my cake and please have a slice. It really is reasonably good."

"No more stalling," Miriana said, still standing.

"Maryushka," Galina said. "Please."

"The law," Rostnikov said, breaking off a small piece of cake and popping it into his mouth. "You mentioned the law. I know a bit about the law. I am a policeman."

"That doesn't frighten us," said Miriana.

Dmitri's eyes revealed that he might not fully share his companion's courage.

"After having given it a moment's thought, I think we will simply keep the girls," said Rostnikov. "And you and your friend can go away and not be heard from again."

Miriana leaned over the table, her face a foot from Rostnikov, who met her eyes.

"I am going to take this to the courts," she said. "We will see what they say. I did not abandon my children. I had an accident. I was in a hospital in Lithuania, near death for more than a year. I thought I was going to die. I didn't want the girls or my mother to know. Thanks to God I made a miraculous recovery."

"That is what you plan to tell a judge?" asked Rostnikov.

"Yes," she said. "I have now recovered and want to reunite my family."

"Or collect several hundred rubles a month," Rostnikov added.

"If that would be better for my children," she said, sitting.

Rostnikov wiped his hands and wrapped the remainder of the cake in his paper napkin. Dmitri had already finished the second muffin.

"Miriana Panishkoya," said Rostnikov. "Father of children unknown."

"His name was Anatoli Ivanov," she said. "He died in an oil-tanker explosion."

"He died in prison," said Rostnikov.

Miriana looked at her mother.

"Your mother did not tell me," Rostnikov said. "Nor did she tell me that you have been arrested eight times that I am certain of, in several cities including Moscow, Tiraspol, Minsk, and Yalta. Five of those arrests were for attempts to rob men you had picked up as a prostitute, twice for selling drugs, and once for petty theft of clothing from an Italian-owned shop. You have not spent the last two years recuperating from accident or illness. Shortly after you abandoned your children, you were sent to a women's prison in Lithuania."

Miriana sat glaring at Rostnikov, who calmly placed the covered piece of cake in his jacket pocket. Her right hand shot out suddenly, fingernails aimed at his face. Rostnikov caught her hand with his own.

Dmitri moved, grabbing Rostnikov's arm. Still holding Miriana's wrist, Rostnikov reached over with his right hand, palm open, into the face of the man across the table. A sudden powerful push and Dmitri tumbled back, his chair falling with a clatter to the floor.

"Sit," said Rostnikov, calmly releasing the woman's wrist.

This time he did touch Galina's shoulder to reassure her that everything was under control. Galina was not at all sure. Dmitri had clambered from the floor and was moving quickly toward Rostnikov, who reached under the table to plant his false leg on the floor before rising to meet the ox who moved toward him.

"No," Rostnikov commanded firmly.

Dmitri did not obey. He pushed the table aside and went for the older man. Rostnikov took a step forward and rammed the charging man in the chest with his head. Dmitri halted. Rostnikov reached out and grabbed the man around his waist, lifting him from the ground. Dmitri punched frantically at the head of the smaller man, who had begun squeezing. The blows fell on the side of Rostnikov's head. He squeezed harder. Dmitri groaned and stopped punching. Rostnikov turned and placed the man on the chair in which the policeman had been sitting.

"Ribs," Dmitri groaned. "Broken."

The old man who owned the Paris Café appeared, looked at the table, chair, and groaning man and asked, "Will there be anything else?"

"No, Ivan," said Rostnikov.

"I'm going to be sick," Dmitri said.

"The muffins," Rostnikov said. "Ivan?"

"This way," said the old man, helping Dmitri out of the chair and leading him toward the rest room. "Do not throw up on the floor."

Rostnikov faced the stunned Miriana, who

stood, mouth slightly open, watching Dmitri being led away.

"This is not right," she said, and then to her mother: "You know this is not right. You do not do this to a daughter. You don't know how hard it has been for me. I am entitled to something."

"Perhaps," Galina began, looking at Rostnikov. "We could get a small apartment. You, me, and the girls, Maryushka. I could get you a job at the bakery. We could . . ."

Miriana laughed. She wept and she laughed.

"You, me, and two little girls in a room? Me working in a bakery? Have you no ears, Mother? Have you no eyes? Can't you see what is real?"

Rostnikov considered speaking but decided to let the scene play out.

"You are my daughter," Galina said.

"No," Miriana said. "I am a woman you gave birth to thirty-six years ago. And then we became strangers. My father must have been very smart. I must have gotten everything from him. I see nothing of me in you."

"I see nothing of you in my grandchildren," Galina said softly.

"Mother, I live in pain," Miriana said. "Can you understand that? In pain?"

"We all live in pain," Galina said, stepping

toward her daughter. "We are blessed if we have someone to share the pain and the small good things."

The younger woman fell into her mother's arms. Galina wrapped her big hands around her daughter and let her cry. Rostnikov watched silently. And then Miriana stepped back.

"I need money," she said, wiping her red eyes with the sleeve of her dress.

"I have a little," Galina said. "In the apartment."

Rostnikov took out his wallet. There was not much in it except for two bills, one of which he handed to the weeping woman.

"That is all," he said. "There will be no more."

"You don't understand," Miriana said, taking the bills. "I have nothing. What little looks I have are almost gone. I . . ."

Rostnikov stood silently. Ivan and Dmitri emerged from the small rest room.

"He did not throw up," the old man announced. "Not yet."

"Thank you, Ivan," said Rostnikov, handing the old man his last remaining bill. "I am sorry about . . ."

"Something to tell Kolya and Anasta when we get home tonight. Nothing is broken."

Dmitri reached out to put his arm around

Miriana. She shrugged it off and headed for the door. He was a step behind her, moving slowly, in obvious pain.

At the door, Miriana turned, looked at her mother, and said, "I'm sorry, Mother."

With that, the man and woman left the café. Galina took a few steps toward the door. Rostnikov put out a hand, not touching her but making clear that he thought it best if she stopped.

"My only child," Galina said, turning to him.

"I know," said Rostnikov. "Come. Let's bring the cake home to the girls and Sarah. You really should try a piece."

"I work in a bakery," Galina reminded him. "I am surrounded by cake."

"Take advantage of the pleasures of cake and children together and don't worry about the sun. We have millions of years."

"I wasn't worried about the sun," Galina said.

Inna Dalipovna sliced the sausage while her father drank his soup and read a report. Though the knife was sharp the sausage was very difficult to cut, especially using only her left hand. Her right wrist would bear almost no pressure. She had taped it tightly, which helped, but not enough.

"What is wrong with you?" Viktor said, looking over the top of his glasses at her.

"I think I sprained my wrist," she said.

He put down the report and exhaled at the annoyance of having to deal with the problem. "How?" he asked.

"I fell on the street." She went on painfully slicing.

"Tomorrow go to the clinic," he said. "If it is broken, they can fix it. If not, they can tape it better."

"Yes," she said, biting her lower lip to keep from wincing with the pain of holding down the sausage.

"I have broken more bones than you have fingers," he said. "Take a few pain pills. Go to the clinic in the morning."

"Yes," she said, feeling the tears in the corners of her eyes as she finished the final slice. She put the plate next to his bowl. He went back to his report, tearing a thick slice of bread and dipping it into what remained of his soup.

Inna sat and ate carefully, letting her right hand rest in her lap.

"No television tonight," he said. "I have to work. I need silence."

Inna nodded. She wanted to know what was being said about the man on the subway platform, but she could wait. She could read a little. She might even take one of the pills she was supposed to take three times a day. It might help the pain though it wasn't for pain. It was to keep her sedate and calm. She did not want to be sedate and calm.

"The bread," he said. "You didn't slice it. How can we make sandwiches if . . . oh, yes. Your wrist. I'll slice it. Hand me the knife."

"I'll get the bread knife," she said, starting to rise.

"That one will do," he said, holding out his hand.

She could not give it to him. He could not have it. It was her instrument, something like a religious icon, something he could not touch.

"Well, give me the knife," he said with irritation she well recognized. His daughter was a lunatic. Inna was slow. Inna was a chain around his neck. Inna was a servant.

She swept her hand toward the knife and sent it spinning off the table toward the refrigerator.

"Inna," her father said in exasperation.

"I am sorry," she said, rising quickly. "I will clean it."

She reached for the knife and took two steps to put it in the sink. Then she opened the drawer and pulled out the brown-handled serrated bread knife. She kept it sharp. She kept them all sharp but none as sharp as the one she had placed in the sink. It would need special work in the morning when her father had left. It might have nicks from its flight across the room, a smudge on the handle. She didn't see anything immediately.

"Here," she said, handing him the bread knife.

"Why don't you go to bed early?" he asked. "After you clean up and do the dishes."

Inna knew it was more than a suggestion.

"Yes," she said.

"Take a pain pill and your regular pills and go to sleep. I will work in here."

"Yes."

"Eat something," Viktor said, picking up a handful of red sausage slices with a fork and depositing them on her plate.

He watched her pick up a piece of sausage with her fingers and put it to her mouth, taking a small bite.

"Use your fork," he said.

She nodded and picked up the fork. He went back to his report.

"I am reading a book," she said.

"Good."

"It is about the metro system," she said.

"Good," he repeated, giving her a small false smile followed by a look that made it clear he wanted to hear no more about the metro and sore wrists.

It was always like this. Sometimes her father talked about business, the government, about a plan he had made to save or earn money for his company. She was expected to nod and be attentive. She was not expected to understand.

There were many good things about her father. He had never struck her. He had never punished her. He had provided her with food and a home and enough clothing. He had never shouted at Inna or called her names. He had simply made it clear that she was a burden to be tolerated and not listened to, if he could avoid doing so.

And that was, as she remembered, how he had treated her mother. Inna was just the continuation of her mother. She wondered how he might react if she told him what she had done and planned to continue doing. Would he scream, hit her, pull her hair? It might well be worth telling him if she thought he might really do something other than make a phone call, have her taken away, and go back to reading his reports.

Inna waited till she was sure her father was finished with his dinner and then, using only her left hand, she slowly cleared the table while he drank coffee and made notes.

"What is the book?" asked Nina, standing next to the bed where Porfiry Petrovich was packing his suitcase.

Nina was eight years old and for the first two months she and her twelve-year-old sister, Laura, had lived with the Rostnikovs she had said nothing. Now, still very serious and thin, she was explosive with questions about everything.

"It is a book about policemen," Rostnikov said.

The girl shook her head knowingly, her hands clasped behind her back, her body twisting slowly from side to side.

"Russian policemen?" she asked. "Like you?"

"American policemen," he said. "In a place called Isola."

He finished filling his bag, looked down, and removed the Ed McBain paperback novel *Jigsaw* and placed it in his pocket. It was badly dog-eared. He had read it three times over the past decade and looked forward to returning to it. He closed the suitcase.

"You are ready?" Nina asked.

"I am ready," he said, straightening up and looking at her.

"My grandmother says you are going to Siberia," she said. "What did you do wrong?"

"Many things," he said. "Many things. But I am going to find a criminal. I will be back in a few days. I'm going on the Trans-Siberian Express."

"What is that?"

"The greatest train in the world," he said, sitting on the edge of the bed. "Almost six thousand miles long, the longest continuous railroad in the world. They began building it from Moscow and from Vladivostok in Siberia on the Sea of Japan in 1891."

"Two places?"

"They met at a bridge in Khabarovsk in 1916. I'll show you on the map. It is one of the world's greatest accomplishments, one of Russia's greatest triumphs. Thousands of miles of track had to be built and rebuilt. It cost more than a trillion rubles."

"How much is that?"

"If you take rubles and piled them on top of each other, a trillion would reach almost to the space station."

"The space station is as high as a star," the girl said in awe.

"Not that high, but high enough. The train goes over hundreds of bridges and through almost a hundred tunnels, traveling at one hundred and twelve miles an hour between stops."

"You've been on it many times," she said.

"Never before," answered Rostnikov, trying to think if he had forgotten something.

"Can I go with you?"

"Perhaps another time," he said. "Perhaps when you are grown you can go with your husband."

"I am not married," she said seriously.

"Perhaps you will be," he said, satisfied that he could think of nothing further to pack. "Let us go in with the others."

"I am not going to get married," the girl said. "I am going to be a foot doctor."

"A noble ambition," he said, taking her hand. "You can be my foot doctor."

"I'll only charge you half," she said. "Because you have only one foot."

"Most generous and fair. Maybe your sister will become an engineer and she can work on my other foot."

"She wants to be a plumber," Nina said as they moved through the bedroom door into the living room–dining room area. "Like you."

"An equally noble ambition," said Rostnikov.

Sarah, Galina, and Laura were seated at the table. The adults had said nothing to the children about the meeting with their mother.

Sarah Rostnikov was talking about a concert they would be going to while he was gone. They had an extra ticket. Sarah's cousin, Leon the doctor, was appearing with his quartet. Leon played piano, had a particular passion for Mozart, and made lots of money in his practice catering to those who could afford his services and held the widespread and almost mystical belief that Jewish doctors were far better than those who were not. Rostnikov was not a fan of classical music though he went dutifully to such concerts and found that he could lose himself in a dreamy, open-eyed meditation almost approaching the near-nirvana he felt when he lost himself in the pragmatic magic of a plumbing problem.

Sarah looked up at him and smiled. He nodded to show that he was packed. Sarah was still a beauty. Her natural and shiny red hair had grown out following her surgery and she had regained some but far from all of her former plumpness. Her pale smooth skin was a bit more pale than he thought looked healthy, but she'd survived. Except for the frequent headaches, Sarah had recovered enough to go back to work at the Dom music shop on a half-time basis.

Not for the first or thousandth time, Rostnikov thanked whatever gods might be (or common genetic chance) that their son had turned out to look like his mother. Porfiry

Petrovich was not ugly, but he knew that he possessed the flat, homely face common to millions of Russians descended from dozens of generations of peasants. He was comfortable with his face, the face of his own father, and his body, the compact solid body that had earned him the nickname of "the Washtub."

"The cake is good," said Laura, who bore a resemblance to her mother even more striking than Iosef's to Sarah.

"Your grandmother is the giver of all cakes and cookies," he said. "Look at me. I have grown fat with the sweets she brings home from the bakery."

"You are not fat," Nina said, touching his stomach. "You are round and strong and have a plastic leg."

"Thank you," said Rostnikov.

There were five chairs at the table. Three matched. The other two did not. One of the solid metal chairs with the slightly padded seat was always left open for Porfiry Petrovich, who had learned from experience that the last few inches before he hit a chair with a slight thud could do great damage to a wooden chair. He had destroyed two of them and taken falls that would have embarrassed him had anyone but Sarah been present when they happened.

There was a mug in front of his place, his Dostoyevsky mug, white, with a drawing of Fyodor on the side. Dostoyevsky had been the favorite author of Porfiry Petrovich's father. Porfiry Petrovich was, in fact, the name of the lawyer in *Crime and Punishment* to whom Raskolnikov eventually confesses. It was a name that played at least a small part in Rostnikov's becoming a policeman when he got out of the army. He had been a child soldier. He had lost the use of his leg to a German tank outside of Rostov.

Sarah poured hot coffee into his mug and Rostnikov nodded thanks.

"Are you going to do the weights?" Laura asked.

It was one of the high points of the girls' day. Rostnikov would solemnly open the cabinet under the television and CD/cassette player, pull out his bench and heavy rings of weights, turn on something by Dinah Washington, Sarah Vaughan, or Ella Fitzgerald, and in his black gym shorts and one of his sweat shirts with the sleeves cut off, he would do curls, presses, and crunches with appropriate grunts and sprays of sweat. His favorite shirt was a black one with the words "The Truth Is Out There" in white letters across the front.

The girls would watch, sitting on the floor,

enthralled by the spectacle of the powerful one-legged man turning red, the veins of his muscles expanding in purple bands.

"Yes," Rostnikov said. "Very soon."

Tonight he would wear his Chicago Bulls red sweat shirt, his second favorite. He would do his regular routine, shower, dress, call the cab, and then pick up Sasha and head for the train station.

"Which way is Siberia?" asked Nina.

"Toward the rising sun," said Rostnikov.

"I had a dream about the sun," Laura said.

They all looked at the girl.

"In the dream," she said, "the sun faded away slowly, so slowly you couldn't be sure it was disappearing."

"Were you frightened?" Rostnikov asked with great interest.

"No," she said. "It was in no hurry and neither was I, and something or someone said 'Don't worry.' I think it was you."

"It was," said Rostnikov. "I have been thinking about the sun."

Galina looked at him, remembering the conversation in the Paris Café with her daughter and Rostnikov's curious comments about the sun.

"What have you been thinking?" Laura asked.

"That it is a miracle," he said. "That if

mankind has anything to worship, it is the sun. The ancient religions were right. We owe all to the sun. But the sun does not need our worship. It does not think. It simply is. Just enough of it means life. Too much exposure is dangerous."

"I do not understand," said Nina.

Rostnikov looked at Sarah, who smiled.

"Nor do I," said Porfiry Petrovich. "Nor do I."

"Are you going to do the weights now?" asked Laura.

"As soon as I finish my coffee," he said.

The weights were round like the sun and the full moon. There was a wholeness to the circle. The circle Director Yaklovev had given him was not whole. It was not bright, a flawed icon. There was much he had not been told about his mission and much he had been told that rang of Russian fairy tale more than the reality of three hundred pounds of weights on a steel bar.

"Are you going to be in the weight-lifting contest in the park? Grandmother says you are."

"I am," Rostnikov said, removing the bench, bar, and weights from the cabinet under the television in the living room.

"Will you win?" Nina asked.

"Perhaps," he said. "But there are other

strong men in Moscow, many, and they do things to help them win."

"Like what?" Laura asked as he slid the weights onto the bar.

"Take pills, herbs they think will make them stronger, legal pills," he said, making sure the weights were balanced.

"Is that fair?" asked Nina.

"It is legal," he said, getting next to the weight and lifting it so that he could set it atop the bracket at the end of the bench.

"What else do they do? To win?" asked Laura.

"When the judge claps his hand, the competitor must lift," he said, lying on his back. "If one is watching the judge, one can begin an instant before the hands come together and have a fraction of a second more for the lift."

He was reaching for the bar now, looking at the weights on either side.

"Do you do these things?" asked Laura.

"No," said Rostnikov.

"You do not want to win?" the girl pressed.

"Yes, I want to win," he said, "but I want to win knowing that I have followed the rules, my rules. If I do not, there is no pleasure in winning, simply a trophy which I do not feel I deserve. You understand?"

"Yes," said the girl. "I think."

"Good," said Rostnikov, gripping the bar. "Now, when you are ready, clap your hands."

Misha Lovski, the truly Naked Cossack, tapped his forehead on the steel bars to the driving beat of his own voice and guitar being played at concert volume.

He could feel the vibrations when he put his hands to the walls or wrapped them around the bars. The music had been playing for hours. He didn't know how many hours. It might even have been days. He had tried to sleep but the bright lights and pounding music made it impossible.

He sang along with himself now.

Keep the clubs beating faster.
Keep the fists driving harder.
Drive them back against the wall.
Nail the fuckers one and all.
If you don't kill them, they'll kill you.
Do it to them before they do it to you.
You know who they are. Line up along
   the street.
Pull it out and beat your meat.
Slam the running slant-eyed freaks.
Smash the screaming Jewish beaks.
Ram the rotten queers and geeks.
Shout like Cossacks as they fall.
Then have a pint of blood alcohol.

His voice was almost gone. All that came out was a hoarse croak. He had cried and laughed, huddled in the corner with his mattress. He had crapped and pissed in the plastic bucket, using torn-up sheets of old newspaper that had been left for him. With his fingers he had eaten what they had given him, though he had no idea what the brown mush in the bowl was, something like meat mixed with kasha. And they had given him just enough water, also in a pot.

Like a trained monkey he had learned that when the lights went out and the music stopped, the door to the room beyond his cage would open, revealing nothing, and he would be expected to put out his bowls, which would be replaced by others.

He had tried to talk to the person whose footsteps he heard. He had tried each time.

"What do you want?" he had demanded the first time. "Money? Call my father. He'll pay. Just get it done."

No answer. Just a door closing. The next time it was, "Get me something to wear, you bastard, you *gol-uboy*, queer fucking bastard."

No answer. Just a door closing. Then, after hours of light and blaring music, "Leave the lights on. Keep the music coming. It gives me something to do, something to sing and beat."

157

No answer. Just a door closing. The last time it had been but his hoarse croak, "Turn it off. No more light. No more music. If I don't get some sleep, you will kill me."

No answer, so he added, "The hell with you. Drive me mad. Drive me crazy. I will go *okhvet,* nuts, but I will emerge a mad genius, more popular than ever, and I will find you and beat your head in with my guitar, drag you on stage and beat you till your putrid blood and brains run and smell. See, you inspire me. I have just written the words to a new song. I will call it 'Surviving the Cage.' "

This time, just before the door closed, he heard a sound in the darkness, perhaps a laugh. It wasn't much but he held onto it, tried to place it. But before he could, the lights were on and he heard his own voice screaming over the speaker, "Kill your mother. Kill your father. You never asked them to be born."

He reached through the bars for the cracked metal bowl of brown mush and the cup of warm water. As he ate, he rocked his head. He knew it was only a matter of time before he was completely mad. The problem was that he did not know how much time had passed.

He stopped rocking. An idea had come. A project. Something to keep him busy. Yes.

He smiled and looked beyond the bars at the far wall behind which he was certain they were watching him.

He touched the fuzz of his growing beard, leaving a stigma of brown mush, and smiled cunningly toward the wall.

The Naked Cossack had a plan.

Chapter Seven

Zelach had dined with his mother in their small apartment which she kept impeccably neat and clean, smelling and looking like something from a different era, a different place. The place it looked like was an apartment in Voronezh south of Moscow, near the Ukrainian border. Zelach's mother had been born there, a gypsy who did not look like one and who escaped to marry a slow-witted but decent Moscovite policeman who thought her quite beautiful. Akardy Zelach had been born six months after they had married. She had never, to this very day, told him of his gypsy blood. There was no reason to do so. The boy had looked like his father the moment he was brought painfully into the world.

Zelach's mother loved her son and worried about him. He had talents but no great intellect. He was a follower, and when she died she wondered whom he might follow.

They ate boiled potatoes, thick fish soup,

and bread with water.

"I must work tonight," he said as he ate.

"I know," she said.

He had not told her before this moment, but her comment did not surprise him. She almost always knew when he had to work, when his mind was on something other than the meal or the television screen. She usually knew what he was thinking. This did not disturb him. It was reassuring.

The words to one of the Naked Cossack's songs kept running through his head:

Spit on your friends. Shit on your friends.
  They'll do the same to you.
Just clasp their hands and walk in step
  when you agree on what to do.
On what to do, on what to do, and who to
  do it to.

"Akardy," his mother said.

"Yes."

"You are bouncing your head while you eat."

"A song I can't . . . it just . . ."

"Listen to the song," she said, tearing off a piece of bread. "It may tell you something."

Emil Karpo ate alone in his room, which was about the same size as Misha Lovski's

161

cell. The room held very little furniture — a cot near the single window whose shade was almost always pulled down, a chest of drawers, a free-standing simple wooden closet, a desk in front of a floor-to-ceiling bookshelf filled with files of cases he had worked on, open and closed cases, and cases that he had never been assigned but were still open.

What free time Karpo had, he gave to those files and their challenge.

He ate one cucumber, one tomato, one onion, a thick slice of unbuttered bread, and a piece of plain boiled chicken he had prepared on his hot plate on the dresser.

There were two lights in his room, one a bulb in the ceiling, the other a small table lamp.

The only color in the room was a painting above the dresser, a painting of and by Mathilde Verson, a gift from her. The woman in the foreground looking up the hill to a barn was definitely Mathilde, though her face was turned. Mathilde, the woman of the city, the part-time prostitute whom he had paid once every two weeks for her services until she had stopped taking the money and they had become something more than client and provider. That lasted three years, four months, and six days. She was shot in the crossfire between two Mafias, gangs disputing territory or trying to make a point which may not have been clear to either gang.

The phone next to the computer rang. He picked it up and said, "Yes."

"Emil," came Rostnikov's voice. "I am going on a train ride."

Karpo said nothing.

"Sasha is going with me. To Siberia."

"Yes."

"While I am gone, you are in charge."

"I understand."

"I left the file on the subway attacks on your desk."

"I shall read it in the morning unless you feel I should get it immediately."

"No, just be acquainted with the case, should you be needed. In an emergency, you can reach me on the Trans-Siberian Express, the number two. I'll be in compartment twelve, car three-two-seven-eight."

Karpo did not bother to write the number. He would remember it.

"Yes," he said.

"Emil, as I recall, you can see the sun over the hill in your painting of Mathilde. Is that correct?"

Karpo did not have to turn to the painting.

"That is correct."

"Then I have a very important question. Is the sun rising or setting? Have you ever asked yourself that question?"

"No," Karpo said, now turning to the painting.

"Look at it with fresh eyes and tell me what you think when I return."

"I will do so."

"You are working on the Lovski case tonight?"

"Yes. Zelach and I are going to a club called Loni's where Lovski was apparently last seen."

"Find him," said Rostnikov. "And don't forget the sun."

He hung up and Karpo turned his wooden chair so that he could face the painting above his dresser.

Pavel Cherkasov dined, as he had planned, at the Uzbekistani restaurant on Neglinnaya Street. There was a good crowd, but Pavel had assured himself a table near the wall with a few bills passed to the maître d'. With a bottle of Aleatiko wine to guide him, Pavel, as planned, had started with *maniar,* moved on to *shashlik,* followed by an order of *Tkhum-dulma.* He ordered a second bottle of wine and turned to the patrons at the next table, a well-dressed couple in their fifties.

"A glass of wine?" he offered.

The man smiled and Pavel motioned to the

waiter, who came over quickly. He knew Pavel from previous visits, knew the man would leave a big tip if he were served quickly and if the waiter smiled or laughed at his jokes.

"The other night I came in here," Pavel said in a whisper to the couple at the next table after the waiter had moved to get two clean glasses. "I said to the waiter, 'I'm so hungry I could eat a rat.' And the waiter replied, 'Then you've come to the right place.' "

The woman gave a slight tic of her left cheek that might have signaled offense or a touch of amusement. It encouraged Pavel, who poured wine from his bottle into the glasses the waiter had brought.

"Listen, listen," he said, raising his eyebrows. "An American and a Russian go to hell and the devil says, 'You have a choice of American hell or Russian hell. The difference between them is that in American hell you get one bucket of shit to eat every day. In Russian hell, you get two buckets.' The American takes American hell. The Russian, to the American's surprise, takes Russian hell."

The woman and the man to whom Pavel was speaking were definitely not amused, but Pavel chose not to notice.

"A year later," Pavel said, "the American

and the Russian meet. 'How is your hell?' asks the Russian. 'Just as promised,' the American answers. 'One bucket of shit to eat every day. And Russian hell?' 'Just as I expected. The shit deliveries seldom arrive, and when they do come they are late and there are never enough buckets to go around.' "

Pavel laughed. The couple did not.

"We are late for an appointment," the man said, motioning to the waiter for the check.

"One more," Pavel said, laughing. "When I was here yesterday, I told the waiter there was a dead cockroach in my soup and he said, 'I'll call my manager, but you should know there will be an extra charge for the funeral.' "

The couple rose without the check and headed for the door. Pavel kept laughing. On the train, he would find a captive audience in the bar. He had dozens of train and travel jokes and even more about drinking. He checked his watch. He had brought his suitcase with him. It was tucked under the table, which was not at all odd in Moscow. One never knew when luggage or a coat might disappear from a checkroom.

It was nearing time to go, but he still had at least ten minutes for a cup or two of syrupy thick coffee. Pavel was not drunk. He was, however, at his limit and could use the coffee to return to the ground. Pavel was a professional.

He ordered his coffee, told the waiter another joke, and looked around the room with satisfaction. In a few days, he would have enough money for that gourmet trip to America. His English was good enough for him to get on the stage during open-microphone sessions at a comedy club in New York. He had tried it before. The crowd had been small and the audience minimally polite, but he had new material now. He was not one to give up.

He glanced around the room as he drank. There was the hum and clatter of conversation and plates, the shuffling of moving waiters and customers departing. He had an idea for a little joke in English. He would play on his slight Russian accent. He would begin his set in New York by saying, "Ladies and gentlemen, I am a Russian, but my English is perfect so let's conversate." He removed one of the lined cards from his pocket and with his pen made a note of the remark.

At a table on the other side of the restaurant another diner, back to the room, watched Pavel in the large ornate mirror on the wall. The watching diner had come in a minute after Pavel, given the maître d' even more money than Pavel had, and pointed to this table.

The watcher heard nothing of Pavel's jokes but watched him eat, pay his bill, rise, pull his suitcase from beneath the table, and head steadily toward the exit. The watcher had motioned to a waiter a second after Pavel had called for his check. To insure a quick departure, the watcher had overtipped the grateful waiter.

The goal was to stay close to Pavel Cherkasov in the city, on the train, to wait till the exchange was made, then to seize the prize and, possibly, the money. This, the watcher well knew, would require the death of the joke-telling courier and probably the person to whom the money was to be delivered. There might even be more who got in the way.

The watcher was prepared. The stakes of the job were high but the assignment was routine. It would be executed with precision and maybe, thought the watcher, with a touch of irony, which was far more interesting than coarse jokes.

Perhaps the one-legged policeman would appreciate the irony when the time came. The watcher respected the Washtub and sincerely hoped that he would.

"*Yah golahdyeen,* I'm hungry," Iosef said.
Elena Timofeyeva and Iosef Rostnikov had

not had dinner. They had rushed onto the metro platform, having paused only to call Paulinin, who was still in his laboratory.

"Do not let anyone touch him," Paulinin had said. "Do not let any of the butchers upstairs get near him. No one should get near him till I talk to him."

Iosef had hung up the phone and turned to Elena. "He's coming. He wants to talk to the dead man."

"Paulinin is mad," Elena observed as they moved out of their temporary underground office and ran for the train just pulling in.

When they pushed their way onto the train, Iosef had turned to Elena and declared his hunger. She too was hungry, but she was on a diet. Elena was sure that she would be on a diet her entire life. Not for the first time she wondered what would happen if she were ever to have children. She remembered the photographs of her mother before she was pregnant with Elena and after. The *before* mother was plump and pretty. The *after* mother was a far different, heavier person: still pretty, but definitely tired.

They were packed tightly and talking was difficult so they said nothing till they got to the Komsomol station. There the body of Toomas Vana was being guarded by three young uniformed police officers, who told gawkers to keep moving.

Elena and Iosef stepped near the body, avoiding the pool of blood that had formed under him, spreading out in an amoebic deep-red pattern.

"Has anyone touched him?" Elena asked the nearest uniformed policeman.

"Not since we have been here," the young man said, glancing over his shoulder at the mutilated corpse. "I was on the street with my partner in our car. A woman told us someone had been killed. Then he" — he pointed to the third policeman — "showed up." The third policeman was one of the uniformed detail that had been assigned to work the platforms.

"Good," said Elena. "Witnesses?"

"Them," the young policeman said, nodding toward a child who held the hand of a woman and seemed to be consoling her. Elena moved toward the two, who stood a dozen feet away. People moved past, glancing at the dead man.

"You saw what happened?" Elena asked gently.

The woman nodded, her hands trembling.

"And you?" Elena asked the little girl.

"Yes," she said.

"Your name is? . . ."

"Alexandra," the child said. "The man is dead."

"I know," said Elena.

"My grandmother is frightened."

"I see. What is your grandmother's name?"

"Sylvia. Her name is Sylvia."

"The person who did that to the man. What did he look like?"

"It was a lady," Alexandra said. "She hit him and hit him and he was bleeding and bleeding and she ran away up the stairs. That way."

The girl pointed toward the escalators at the end of the platform.

"What did she look like?" asked Elena.

Sylvia gulped and shook her head.

"Like a lady," Alexandra said. "Like Mrs. Duenya, my teacher. A little like Mrs. Duenya. She had a knife. The lady. She made a noise. She hurt her hand. This one. This is the right hand."

"Yes, it is," said Elena, looking back at Iosef, who was standing over the body. "Is that the hand she had the knife in?"

The girl nodded. "It was hurting both of them, the man and the lady, only the man is dead and the lady went away."

"Did you see anything else?"

"Two big boys took the man's bag when he dropped it. They ran away. That way."

This time she pointed to the opposite end of the platform from the one toward which she had said the woman had run.

"They stole it," the girl said.

"It appears as if they did," said Elena. "Did the lady say anything?"

Elena looked at the grandmother, who was still trembling. The little girl held the older woman's hand and patted it gently.

"My grandma does not watch television," Alexandra confided almost in a whisper. "She has not seen people bleeding and killed and things. I tried to explain to her."

"Yes," said Elena. "Anything else you can tell us about the lady?"

The grandmother shook her head.

Alexandra said, "Yes. He was her father."

"Her father?"

"She called the man *At'e'ts*, 'Father,' " said the child. "Two times while she was hitting him, like this." The child raised her fist as if she held a knife and jabbed out, saying, " 'Father, Father.' Like that. Just like that."

They could hear the sound, feel the vibration and the noise, coming from Loni's when they were about a hundred yards away. A guitar screeched.

"Jimi Hendrix," Zelach said as they walked toward the door. A very big pair of men wearing leather vests and no shirts on their shaved chests stood guard.

"The player is Jimi Hendrix?" asked Karpo.

"No, the sound. Whoever is playing is imitating Hendrix."

"I see," said Karpo, who did not see at all.

At the door the sound was a screaming, sharp-nailed scratch down the spine. The two men in leather vests stood in front of them. Karpo and Zelach took out their wallets and showed their identification.

"I'll check with the manager," one of the two men said.

"You may check with the manager after we are inside," said Karpo. "We do not require permission."

The two big guards looked at each other and then at Karpo and Zelach.

"You do here," one of them said. "Mr. Trotskov has friends."

Which meant that Mr. Trotskov was paying off a Mafia and very likely local police. At least that was what the big man at the door implied.

"You will step back and let us pass," Karpo said calmly.

"Just wait till . . ." the big man started, and Karpo stepped forward so his face was inches from the guard.

"We will not wait," he said. "You will open the door and we will pass."

Karpo's pale face stood out in the light

above the door. His black clothing made that face look like a floating death mask. Something in that mask, the eyes, made the big man say, "Fine, go in." He nodded to the other man, who opened the door. "Primo," the first guard said, "go tell Mr. Trotskov that the police are here."

There would be no need to point out to the owner who Karpo and Zelach were. They stood out in the blaring smoke-filled crowd of young people. With Karpo in front, the detectives made their way through a sea of young men with bad teeth and tattoos as colorful as those of a Siberian convict. Swastikas, skeletons, guns, knives, churches, women, angels, and devils adorned the chests, arms, and even cheeks of both young men and women who, drinks or cigarettes in hand, swayed to the music and parted with scowls as the policemen moved through them to the bar.

Behind the crowded bar, the man they had spoken to earlier, the one called Abbi, stood serving. He was clean-faced and looked sober, with a fresh blue T-shirt and hands moving professionally to keep up with the orders.

Abbi spotted the detectives and moved toward them behind the bar. "You were here this morning, right?"

It was almost impossible to hear him over

the screaming of Death Times Four on the small stage.

"That is right," said Karpo. "We are looking for Bottle Kaps and Heinrich."

"I don't know anyone with those names," Abbi said, looking at the nearby customers who were listening to the conversation.

"You knew them this morning," Karpo said. "If they are here, point them out. If you will not, we will close this place."

"They," Abbi said, nodding at the crowd, "would tear you apart."

"That is not your concern," said Karpo.

"What is happening here?" asked a man of about forty who came up behind the bar. He was short with a neatly trimmed mustache. He wore a gray pullover shirt with short sleeves. Inscribed on the left side of the shirt were the words *Top Sail* in English.

"We are looking for two people who call themselves Bottle Kaps and Heinrich," said Karpo.

"Why?" shouted the man. "I'm Yevgeny Trotskov, the manager."

"They were seen leaving here two nights ago with Misha Lovski," Karpo said.

"Naked Cossack," Zelach supplied.

"Naked Cossack? I don't think he was here two nights ago," Trotskov said, shaking his head.

The music suddenly stopped. The crowd shouted. The lead singer, Snub Nose Bullet, gave the crowd the finger and bit his lower lip. He was thin and bare-chested and had the chiseled face and nose of a Romanian. The crowd loved it. They shouted obscenities back at him and laughed and applauded and banged their bottles and glasses against tables and the bar.

"He was here," said Karpo. "Point out Bottle Kaps and Heinrich."

"They said they'd close us down," said Abbi.

Trotskov smiled knowingly. "We can discuss this in my office," he said, reaching out for Karpo's arm. Karpo did not move. He met Trotskov's eyes, and the bearded owner of Loni's knew that this man was not interested in a bribe.

"They will kill you," Trotskov said, his eyes scanning the crowd.

"I told them," Abbi said.

"Zelach," said Karpo. "Go to the door. Fire four shots into the ceiling. If anyone attacks you, shoot them."

"You're —" Trotskov started, but he could see that the Vampire before him was not bluffing.

"If one of us is hurt or anyone has to be shot," said Karpo, "Loni's will cease to exist."

The madman is prepared to die, Trotskov thought. He looked at the other policeman, the unkempt one with the glasses who did not seem to be as interested in dying as his partner.

"Listen," Trotskov said, turning to Zelach.

"To the door," said Karpo. "Fire."

Zelach blinked and turned to head for the door, prepared though not pleased at the prospect of dying in this place or, for that matter, in any place.

"Wait," said Trotskov. "Wait. They're over there. Table near the stage."

There were four people at the table. None of them were looking their way.

"Bottle Kaps has a red heart with a knife through it tattooed on his left arm. Heinrich is the big one with the swastika on his chest. Don't tell them I pointed them out. Please."

Karpo started for the table, a temporarily relieved Zelach at his side. Zelach had long ago learned that the man with whom he was working seemed to be without fear. He did not appear to value his life. Zelach, however, valued his very much, though he often thought himself nearly worthless. Luck had put him where he was in the Office of Special Investigation. At times like this he thought it had been bad rather than good luck.

Karpo moved to the table with Zelach at his

side and looked directly at the one with the red heart with a knife through it tattooed on his arm.

"You are known as Bottle Kaps," Karpo said.

All four young men at the table looked up. All four were skinheads. All four were drinking beer and smiling.

Bottle Kaps looked away from Karpo, ignoring him, and continued saying to Heinrich at his side, "So, I tell the little ant that if he does not return it I will crush his head with my boots."

People at nearby tables had stopped talking to watch how the confrontation was going to play out.

Karpo said, "We have some questions to ask you."

The four at the table ignored the gaunt policeman and kept talking.

Zelach looked around, moving his hand up his side in case he had to reach for his gun. They could, thought Zelach, simply go outside, wait till Bottle Kaps and Heinrich came out later. He did not really care if they had to wait half the night, given the alternative that Karpo was now pursuing.

Karpo took the table in two hands and flung it on its side against the two to whom he was talking. Glasses and bottles and ashtrays and keys flew. Heinrich fell to the floor. Bottle Kaps slid back on his chair. The other two at the table stood facing the detectives.

"I have questions," Karpo said calmly. "It would be easier to sit quietly and talk than to come with us, but the choice is yours. Make it now."

Bottle Kaps let out a grunt and pushed the fallen table out of his way. Zelach was sure he was going to charge at Karpo. Heinrich held out a hand to stop him.

"No riot," he said. "You talk. We listen."

Heinrich started to pick up the table. He needed help from Bottle Kaps and both of the others who had been seated at the table.

There was a moment now when Zelach felt certain that someone would jump on his back, stab him in the neck, beat him with a chair. He wanted to turn and face the crowd behind him but he held firm, doing his best to pretend he felt as confident and unafraid as Karpo looked.

Death Times Four had missed the confrontation. They had gone through a door in the wall behind the stage. When they came out, looking angry as hell, they were greeted not by cheers but by a silence.

"Out of the grave," Snub Nose Bullet screamed at them. "The sun is down. It's night. The night is ours."

Then his eyes met those of Karpo.

Snub Nose Bullet, whose real name was Casimir Rolvanoshki, had seen many people dressed like vampires, but he had the impression that he might be seeing a real one for the first time. That was what the silence was all about.

Hell, this one might be here to destroy them all for mocking the living dead. Snub Nose Bullet was ready. Vindication. He hit a chord and launched into a song he had written and rehearsed only that afternoon.

He wanted to give Karpo the finger, give death the finger, but the best Casimir behind his own mask could do was to give a less-than-powerful sneer before he started singing.

"We will sit here," Karpo said above the music, moving the chairs of the two young men who had been sitting with Bottle Kaps and Heinrich.

Karpo had to have a plan. Zelach was certain of that now. He would not be constantly challenging these people if he were not confident, did not know exactly how they would react. Karpo knew more about the law than anyone in the Office of Special Investigation, perhaps even more than Inspector Rostnikov himself, and knowing the law at this point in Russian history was no small accomplishment. On a day-to-day basis, Zelach had no idea what the law might be on any crime. He trusted Karpo. He trusted the others. He had no choice.

Death Times Four howled and shouted. Snub Nose Bullet leaned toward Karpo and sang-shouted, "Swine in brown and swine in blue. They will step all over you."

The four skinheads at the table remained standing, looking at Karpo, waiting for him to make a move.

"Shrapnel Spew," Zelach muttered.

He had spoken softly but somehow the singer on the low stage leaning toward Karpo heard him and hesitated. The mess of a policeman with glasses, the sweating blob, was right. The line was from the Estonian group Shrapnel Spew. Casimir had not made it up this afternoon — not the song nor the words. He had simply remembered them, and there he stood doing something he had never done before. He was singing and playing someone else's music. The song was obscure, but somehow this policeman had recognized it. Casimir was sure there was no one else in the room who had any idea of the disaster.

Casimir stopped singing, kept playing, and pointed a finger at Zelach. Everyone watched, not knowing what was happening. Death Times Four was giving this slouch of a policeman the sign that he was good. Snub Nose

Bullet did not give his blessings easily, and to a cop?

"Sit down," said Heinrich.

Karpo and Zelach sat and so did Heinrich and Bottle Kaps. The other two reluctantly moved away.

Karpo paused but an instant before asking his first question. The hesitation came from a completely unexpected source. Emil Karpo, perhaps for the only time in his life since he was a child, had lost control. No one watching him could have known. He looked the same as he always did, but he knew his actions had been unnecessarily provocative.

Was it this place? These people? The deep realization that this is what had become of the nation for which he lived, the cause in which he had believed? He was in the belly of a dying beast, the heart of chaos. This place was a cancer. These people were spreading it. And they were only a symptom. His head beat with the first pangs of migraine. The smoke, the noise, the realization, the lights. Pain. He wanted to get this over quickly and get to the darkness of his room. And because he wanted it over quickly, he chose not to give in, to move slowly, to challenge the pain.

"Two nights ago you were seen leaving here with Misha Lovski, the Naked Cossack," he said.

Neither of the young men answered.

"Where did you go?" he asked.

The two young men looked at each other. The look between them said that they both recognized the madness in the eyes of this pale spectre.

"We left him in the street and went home," said Heinrich.

"Right outside in the street," Bottle Kaps confirmed, shaking his head.

"No, you did not," said Karpo.

Zelach sat silent, listening.

"What is this about?" asked Bottle Kaps.

"Misha, the Naked Cossack, is missing," said Karpo.

"Missing?" asked Heinrich. "Gone?"

"We want to find him," said Karpo. "We want you to tell us where he is."

"Us? We do not know. Go find some of those rappers. They probably killed him. They hate him, hate us all. We would not hurt the Naked Cossack. He is a symbol of our battle."

"Battle with whom?" asked Karpo. "About what?"

"You, everyone, the weak bastards who are turning Russia over to the Jews," said Bottle Kaps.

"And the niggers, the *chernozhopyi*," said Heinrich. "And the Chinese. The *rappery*. And . . ."

"I did not say we thought he was kidnapped, killed, or even hurt," said Karpo. "I said only that he is missing."

"We don't know where he is," Heinrich said.

"No," said his partner.

"You will come with us," said Karpo, starting to rise.

"Why?" Heinrich protested.

"Because you are lying," Karpo said. "If Misha Lovski is dead, you too will die."

"This is crazy," said Heinrich. "You think he is dead and you just want someone to blame because his father is rich and —"

The band was wailing a few feet from Karpo's throbbing head. He wanted to slowly rise, take the guitar from the shouting robot, and methodically rip out each string.

"How do you know his father is rich?" asked Karpo.

"He told us," said Heinrich.

"He told no one," said Karpo. "He is ashamed of his father. Someone else told you."

Bottle Kaps gritted his teeth and looked at Karpo with a last pretense of anger.

"We do not know where he is. We do not know who took him."

"What," asked Karpo, "makes you think someone took him? One assumption we made was that he went away on his own, but your answers confirm that he has been taken. You will come with us."

The band continued. Karpo could take no more and for that reason he remained seated, looking calmly at the two young men across from him.

"We are not going with you," said Heinrich. "We did nothing."

"Then," said Karpo, "we shall have to shoot you. I shoot well. I'll probably not kill you. We need one of you to talk. Akardy Zelach on the other hand is nearsighted, a poor shot. A bullet from his weapon could strike anywhere on your body. I'll shoot you."

Karpo looked at Heinrich.

"Detective Zelach will shoot you," Karpo went on, looking at Bottle Kaps.

"Then what will happen to you?" asked Heinrich. "Look around."

"From your place on the floor, if you are still conscious and alive, you can watch and bear witness. Now we leave or you die."

The feeling of sharp glass entered Karpo's brain. The light burned deep as if he were looking into the sun.

But both of the younger men believed this pale madman. They had encountered brutal policemen in the past, policemen who enjoyed beating, policemen who might get so worked up that they would shoot to kill, but nothing like this one. He was, once again, not bluffing.

"Let's go," Heinrich said.

Death Times Four had changed songs. Akardy Zelach neither liked nor recognized what they were now playing.

Chapter Eight

Igor Yaklovev, director of the Office of Special Investigation, former KGB colleague of Vladimir Putin, a man who plotted his destiny carefully and with great ambition, sat in his favorite chair in his boxer shorts and a T-shirt, watching television.

On the table in front of him sat his nightly glass of brandy atop a plain white porcelain coaster.

The Yak lived alone. He had once had a wife. She had proved to be a constant nuisance. She was gone. He did not miss her.

He checked his watch. In less than an hour, Porfiry Petrovich Rostnikov would be on the Trans-Siberian Express. That trip was the most important item on the director's list. It was not that finding the son of Nikoli Lovski was not important. Handled correctly, it could be the key to a formidable base of support when Igor Yaklovev decided it was only minimally risky to call in his markers and make his next move up.

The Yak was not interested in sex. The Yak was not interested in money; nor was he interested in posterity or popularity. Life was brief. To make it interesting, he had decided early to play a game, not terribly different from a board game like Risk or Monopoly. He would slowly, patiently, acquire power, as much power as possible. His goal was to become the most powerful man in Russia without the public having any idea of his existence. Once he had achieved his goal, the game would be over. He would exercise his power, dictate policy to politicians, soldiers, the media, enjoy the fruits of having won.

Igor Yaklovev did not think a great deal about why he had taken this path in life. He was sure that it had something to do with his ineffectual father, who struggled, took orders, worked in a government automobile factory, and died young without a complaint. His mother had accepted whatever fate the government chose to give her or not give her.

Igor had chosen the Communist Party to escape the same fate as his parents. He had never been convinced of the ideology, but it was open to manipulation. He had seen that as a very young man. And he had come far, savoring briefly the fall of each opponent in his path, opponents who were usually too preening or stupid to realize that they were engaged in a game. The Yak had never looked back at the bodies of those who had fallen.

He did, however, at this moment, look at the body on the television news show. In front of a videotape of the draped white form on the metro platform, a serious white-haired man at the news desk in the television studio said that the dead man was the latest victim of the Phantom of the Underground.

Russian media elevated major violent criminals to a new level by giving them names. The Yak did not think that "Phantom of the Underground" was particularly inventive, but that did not matter. What did matter was that this case belonged to his department and that the office was getting publicity. Publicity was fine as long as the Yak's name was not mentioned and the criminals being sought were caught or killed quickly.

He turned up the volume with his remote control as a route map of the Moscow metro appeared on the screen. Each station where an attack had occurred was on the purple line, except for the most recent. Each station where an attack had been was marked with a large red circle.

The face of Toomas Vana appeared on the screen. He looked vaguely familiar, a serious, middle-aged man in a suit, a business type, nothing out of the ordinary except that he was an important engineer working for the gas company.

The videotape of the subway platform returned to the screen as the newscaster prattled on about the police not issuing a statement and the public in panic.

A grizzled, nearly toothless man in a workman's shirt and jacket, wearing a cap, looked to his left offscreen. A handheld microphone was under his chin.

"I'm afraid, yes. I admit it. This crazy person could be anyone. She could jump off a train I am going to get on and do what she did to him."

He glanced over his shoulder at the sheet-covered body being looked at by a wild-haired man in an out-of-date police-department coat.

The frightened man had nothing to fear, the Yak thought. He does not fit the profile. The killer had better taste in men.

"They should have policemen all over every metro station," the grizzled man sputtered, now warmed up, living his few minutes of minimal fame. "They should have soldiers. They should be searching women for knives."

While that, the Yak knew, would not be possible given the volume and flow of traffic on the metro system, the man's comments did give Yaklovev an idea. Perhaps the latest attack was not by the same woman, by the Phantom of the Underground. Perhaps this latest one was a copycat, and Toomas Vana was a particular target. Or perhaps she was simply a second madwoman taking advantage of a door that the Phantom had opened. Such things had happened before.

Rudolf Bortkovich, the Kursk schoolteacher, had confessed to forty-two murders of young men and women when he was caught, but he steadfastly denied four others that clearly fit his mode of operation. He was convicted of all the murders, but the police and the KGB had known that those four had been committed by a copycat. When Bortkovich was caught, the killings ended. His copycat had lost his cover and was now walking the streets.

The man leaning over the body, which was now only partly covered by the sheet, turned his head. Paulinin. Iosef and Elena were not in the picture, but the Yak knew they were nearby. Paulinin was a nearly private treasure but he could become an anvil if he talked to the media. The Yak was reasonably sure that would not be allowed to happen.

The next news item came on. A heavy snow was falling in Moscow. A weather map appeared. Igor Yaklovev pushed the red button on his remote and the image on the screen disappeared with a snap.

There would be reports on his desk in the morning on both the disappearance of Misha Lovski and the metro murders. He would have to wait for Porfiry Petrovich's progress report. It might be days before it came. No matter. Igor Yaklovev was a very patient man.

He finished his brandy, carried his glass into the kitchen, washed, rinsed, and dried it, and placed it carefully back in the cabinet over the sink.

It was still relatively early. The Yak required and wanted no more than five or six hours of sleep. Sleep was a necessary inconvenience.

He moved to his bedroom, picked up a small pile of folders from his desk in the corner, and moved to his bed. He propped up the pillows, put on his reading glasses, placed the first file, which bore a large red stamp of SECRET, on his lap and opened it to the cover page which read: *Preliminary Psychiatric Evaluation of Senior Detective Inspector Emil Karpo.*

Porfiry Petrovich sat next to his wife on the bed. Galina and the girls were asleep in the living room. When he left, he would move as quietly as his telltale leg would allow him and hope that he woke none of them.

The small television set was on, on the low dresser, but there was no sound. Sarah, had, since her illness, found it difficult to fall asleep. She often watched television quietly while her husband slept. Neither the light from the screen nor the sound kept him from falling into a deep sleep within a minute or two of his deciding that the day had ended.

Sarah wore the nightgown, the blue one, Porfiry Petrovich had bought her for her last birthday. Porfiry was fully dressed, leg attached, sitting on the end of the bed as they spoke.

"Your appointment is at two," he said.

"I know," Sarah answered, smiling at him. "I am feeling fine. Don't feel guilty."

While Sarah would never bar her husband from one of her medical appointments, she sometimes preferred that he not be there, particularly if she was not feeling well and thought that the news might not be good. She preferred to be the one telling him.

"I will call you from wherever we are," he said. "You are sure you feel well?"

"Very well," she said, touching his cheek with her warm palm.

He did not believe her but he smiled back and said, "Good."

"Iosef and Elena will be here tomorrow night if they do not have to work," Sarah said.

"I know."

"And Galina and the girls are here."

"I know."

"Porfiry Petrovich, I will be fine."

"I know," he said, taking her hand and glancing at the metro map on the screen.

Something about it struck him. Sarah could feel the change in his hand. He did not get up to turn up the volume. The red circles on the screen fascinated him.

"What?" she asked.

"A minute," he said, rising awkwardly and moving to the telephone, his eyes still on the television screen.

He dialed and waited. It rang nine times before he hung up. He tried another number. The answer came in three rings.

"Have I awakened you, Anna Timofeyeva?" he asked. "It is Rostnikov."

"You have not awakened me," his former boss in the procurator general's office said. "I go to bed late. I get up late."

"Is Elena home?" he asked.

"She just arrived. I will get her."

"How are you feeling?" he asked.

"Considering that I have survived three heart attacks and have begun having long conversations with Bakunin, I am surprisingly well."

Bakunin was Anna Timofeyeva's cat.

"I will come to visit when I get back. I have an assignment."

"That would be nice. How is Sarah?"

"She is right here. I will let you speak to her after I talk to Elena."

There was a pause and Elena Timofeyeva's voice came on. "Chief Inspector," she said to the man who was scheduled to soon be her father-in-law. "You want a report on the metro attacks."

"No," he said. "Unless you have caught the woman."

"No, but we think she is attacking men who remind her of her father. A little girl who witnessed tonight's attack heard her address the man as 'Father' before she stabbed him. Paulinin is working on a report. It will be ready in the morning."

"Do you know why she has moved to another line for her attacks?"

"No," she said.

"I think I may know," he said.

"Why?" asked Elena.

"She ran out of *K*'s on the purple line," he said. "She has moved to another station beginning with the letter *K* on another line. It might be a good idea to concentrate on metro stations whose names begin with the letter *K*."

"But why would she? . . . Yes, she is mad."

"She has a reason, but you may well not find it till you find her."

"I'll call Iosef right away," Elena said.

"Don't hang up," Rostnikov said. "Your aunt wants to talk to Sarah."

Rostnikov handed the phone to his wife and pointed to his watch. It was time to go.

"Anna," Sarah said, accepting her husband's kiss.

He picked up his suitcase and moved to the door with a wave. Behind him he could hear Sarah talking about wedding plans. Something in Sarah's voice suggested that there might be a problem, but he did not have time to find out what it was.

He closed the bedroom door behind him and walked as slowly and quietly across the room as he could.

The snow was soft and deep and still falling and falling. Plows were grinding down the major streets, sometimes in military tandem, leaving narrow white ridges between them. Taxis and buses moved slowly behind the plows.

In the light from the late-night street lamps, people lifted their legs high walking through the drifts on sidewalks which would not be swept and shoveled till morning.

Through their windows those who had not gone to bed, and some who should have but could not bring themselves to, watched the thick snow that covered hard asphalt and cracked concrete, that decorated drab buildings and added a holiday touch to the niches and roofs.

Parked cars wore white snow caps that came to a peak, and trees became festive with whipped-cream leaves.

It was an annual event, a silent, private celebration to welcome the first real snow.

For some, the snow meant protection, real or imagined, from street drunks, rattling cars, shouting couples. Crime dropped in the winter, though not as much as those who considered the snow their protection might think.

For some, the snow was simply clean, simple. A single hue that glistened with the lights of night and billowed with the gray-cloud glow of day. Life was complex on dry streets or in the rain. Danger could come from anywhere. It was no different in any large city of the world. But in Moscow, people, many people, said a silent prayer asking for respite from the storm, the isolation of the white hills.

The ice rinks in the parks would be cleared for hockey and skating. Hills would be evened down for sledding. Cross-country skiers would move quickly past trees and venture onto streets and, it would be agreed, people were in a far better mood than they were in the summer heat.

The people of Moscow did not mind bundling up, covering their heads, wearing boots, wrapping scarves around their faces, seeing their breath before their eyes.

There was magic in the winter. There was hope.

And there were also delays like those of the buses and cabs moving carefully to avoid a skid and crash.

Inna Dalipovna was late because she walked home from the metro station. She did not want to get to another station and move to a platform where she might be recognized. She was afraid her father would get to the apartment before her and be disappointed because his dinner was not ready. She needn't have worried. Viktor Dalipovna was later than his daughter. A meeting had gone on too long, but he couldn't avoid it. And then he could find no cab at the cab stop and there were huge crowds on the metro. While Inna felt protected by the snow, Viktor was annoyed.

Misha Lovski had no idea it was snowing.

Porfiry Petrovich had seen the snow coming and had, in the name of his director, ordered a car from the motor pool and a police driver. For a short time, it looked as if he would not be able to find a car or driver. The cars were all out dealing with traffic accidents and dangerous street corners. He had finally reached a man in the motor pool who owed him a favor. The man agreed to drive Rostnikov himself.

Once in the car, the going had been slow. He picked up Sasha Tkach half an hour late and it began to seem genuinely possible that they might miss the train. The driver was skilled and willing to take risks. There was no choice. Even when they were less than a mile from the station and Sasha might well make better time walking, there was no possibility of Rostnikov being able to walk through snow.

Rostnikov and Sasha sat silently, Porfiry Petrovich in front with the driver, Sasha in back. They all watched the snow. The driver checked his dashboard clock from time to time. He was determined to meet the challenge.

Ten minutes before the train was due to depart, the unmarked police car pulled into the broad drop-off area in Komsomolskaya Square in front of the train station. He maneuvered through cars, hotel vans, tourist coaches, green cabs and yellow cabs to get the policemen to the doors of the station.

Lights filtered through the snow. The dark top of the station with two windows over the arch looked like the hood of an ancient hangman.

Five minutes later, Sasha Tkach and Porfiry Petrovich Rostnikov waited in line to board the Trans-Siberian Express. There were five people ahead of them, a couple and their small child, a boy. The father was wrestling two suitcases up the steps of the train. Behind him, trying to protect her son from the frustrated flailing of her husband, the woman held the boy's hand and led him cautiously up the steps. Directly in front of Sasha and Porfiry Petrovich were two old men talking in English. Finally, Rostnikov climbed the metal steps with a minimum of awkwardness and the help of his left arm. The right was occupied with his suitcase.

If they had to go all the way to Vladivostok, it would be seven days, six nights, more than four thousand miles. It could be a long trip.

Part II

Tracks

Chapter One

Life on earth is short at best
The cities are a game of chess
Copper domes and statuettes
Victories with marble breasts
Leave the burden with the rest
Watch the sleepers phosphoresce
Trans-Siberian Express

There were eighteen carriages in the train, plus a dining car. The narrow corridors of the carriages were crowded. Sweat, grunts, hurrying, pushing. Languages. English, French, German, Chinese. Faces to match the languages. Some laughter. The shrill voice of a woman in Russian asking, "Petrov, are you behind me?" Petrov answered above the crowd and the awakening sounds of the train engine.

In 1857, N. N. Murav'ew-Amurski, governor of eastern Siberia, commissioned a military engineer named

Romanov to explore the possibility of a railroad to connect Siberian cities to each other and the western metropolises, including St. Petersburg and Moscow. Romanov came up with a plan. The Russian government gave it no support till the czar became interested in the possibility of such an enterprise in 1885. Entrepreneurs from Germany, France, Japan, and England came forward with offers of help, but Czar Alexander III feared strengthening foreign influence in eastern Russia and decided to use government money for the project. In 1886, Czar Alexander approved a report from the governor of Irkutsk in Siberia.

The czar wrote: "I have read so many reports from the Siberian governors that now I can admit with sadness that the government did almost nothing to meet the needs of this rich, neglected region. It is time to correct that error."

In 1887, three expeditions were launched, each headed by an engineer appointed by the czar. One expedition was to find a path to Zabaikalskaya, another to explore the construction possibilities through middle Siberia, and the third to examine the feasibility for a connection to the South-Ussuriyskaya railroads. Following the expeditions, the czar appointed a Siberian Railroad Construction Committee, which declared that the "Siberian railroad construction is a great national event which should be built by Russian people using Russian material."

Rostnikov searched for his compartment. Most passengers were already stowing their bags in the compartments designed for four people. Western tourist agencies booked their clients together, four Frenchmen in a compartment, four Americans in another. But a compartment of Russians could be next to one with four Chinese or Americans, and a woman traveling alone might find herself in a compartment with three men. And another car might be filled with Russians, except for one with four Greeks. Sometimes tourists going nowhere but on a train ride asked to be placed in a compartment with Russians.

When Rostnikov found his compartment, he was greeted by a reasonably polite conductor, who said, "Your ticket."

Rostnikov handed the ticket to the man, who took it and gave him another.

"You have been switched to the next compartment, thirty-one."

Rostnikov did not bother to ask the reason

since the compartment was nearby and he knew there could be a dozen good reasons for the move or a dozen bad ones. The conductor probably did not even know.

So, whether by design or chance, Rostnikov found himself wedging into a compartment where three men sat speaking English. There was a small white table next to the window of the compartment. A bottle of vodka sat on it with glasses. The men had the tentative air of people who were getting acquainted.

"Excuse me," Rostnikov said in English, lifting his suitcase toward the high luggage rack. The three men, two who appeared to be in their seventies and one who might be fifty, nodded at him. The slightly rotund youngest man said, "Welcome. Need some help with that?"

Rostnikov recognized the old men as the two who had boarded the train in front of himself and Sasha.

"I am able to manage," Rostnikov answered. "Thank you."

"A glass of vodka to toast our journey and new friends?" said one of the men.

Rostnikov finished stowing the suitcase and accepted the offered glass.

"*Zah vahsheh zdahrov yeh ee blahgahpah-looch'yeh*, health and happiness," said the man who had handed Rostnikov his glass.

Rostnikov repeated the toast and touched his glass to those held out by the three men. And then he drank.

After receiving the report of the committee, Alexander III wrote a directive to his son, Czarevitch Nikolya Alexandrovitch, stating: "I order the start of construction of a continuous railroad across all of Siberia. I want to connect Siberian regions rich in natural resources with the rest of the Russian railroad system. This is my will. I want you to use the funds of the Russian treasury to complete this historic enterprise."

On May 19, 1891, at ten in the morning, the first religious ceremony to bless the new project was held at the foundation of what was to become the Vladivostok station. Czarevitch Nikolya Alexandrovitch, the future czar, was present and laid the first stone and a silver plate designed in St. Petersburg and personally approved by the emperor, Alexander III, himself. Construction had officially begun on the railroad that would twenty-five years later transport the future czar and his family to their death.

Rostnikov learned the names of the men

who introduced themselves. One, a tall, lean American who looked a bit like a very old Gary Cooper, shook Rostnikov's hand and said his name was Robert Allberry.

"And this is Jim Susman," Allberry said, nodding at a short man with a freckled bald head with a thatch of gray-white hair.

"And this," Allberry said, nodding at the youngest man, "is David Drovny. I say that right?"

"David Drovny," the youngest man said, offering his hand.

Drovny had the chest and build of an opera singer. He was heavy, on the verge of fat. The roundness of his face was given some line by his close-trimmed dark beard and mustache.

Most of the Trans-Siberian Railroad was built in nearly impossible weather over minimally populated or nonpopulated forest land. The roadbed had to go across strong Siberian rivers, around or over dozens of lakes, through swamps and permafrost. The most difficult section was around Baikal and Lake Baikal. Rocks had to be blasted to build tunnels and supporting structures and bridges.

The Railroad Construction Committee estimated the cost of road building at 350 million gold rubles. To keep costs down, the committee established conditions for the Ussuriysk and western Siberia sections. The proposed width of the roadbed was narrowed. Ballast layer was made thinner. Lighter rails were used. Major construction was to be used only on the biggest bridges. Smaller bridges were built of wood. The Circum-Baikal loop to the south of Lake Baikal alone needed two hundred bridges and thirty-three tunnels.

Rostnikov stepped into the corridor. Traffic had thinned. A conductor was walking through, calling out that the train would be taking off. Other Russian trains might be late, but not the Trans-Siberian Express.

Rostnikov went in search of Sasha Tkach. He passed the large white metal samovar in the corridor which provided hot water at all times for drinks and instant foods for those who did not want to spend the time or money going to the dining car.

He found that Sasha was in the same car, an end compartment. He had been placed with three French businessmen.

It appeared that Pankov had done his work. Rostnikov spoke English and was with two Americans and an English-speaking Russian. Sasha's French was nearly perfect. Rostnikov did not pause as he passed the door. He did not pause till he was on the narrow platform between two cars. Sasha joined him.

"Our adventure begins," said Rostnikov.

The most difficult problem in building the Trans-Siberian Express was not the distance, cost, or dangers. It was labor. The problem was dealt with by hiring workers in different sections and transporting them to Siberia, each group working separately, all destined to join. In western Siberia there were as many as fifteen thousand workers from western Russia, European Russia. The Zaaylal-skaya section employed forty-five hundred workers from all areas. And in middle Siberia, the most dangerous of the three legs of the railroad, most of the workers were convicts and soldiers. Throughout the construction sites were peasants, youths seeking adventure, men who thought they could make a steady living which they could send or bring home to their families.

No one knows how many workers died from floods, plague, sustained temperatures of fifty degrees below zero in the winter and over one hundred degrees in the summer, cholera, landslides, anthrax, bandits who came in packs and stripped smaller work teams of their money and clothes before killing them, and tigers made winter-hungry.

Some estimate as many as ten thousand people died building the railroad. Others say this figure is far too low.

The train lurched a few feet forward. Rostnikov and Sasha Tkach steadied themselves on the metal doors. The train lurched three more times and began to move, very slowly, so slowly that they were aware of their movement at first only by the passing images on the platform, the people waving good-bye, tourist-agency representatives sighing with relief, uniformed police, the arches of the station itself.

Then, with a thrust, the train began to pick up speed.

"No one will sleep for hours," Rostnikov said. "Excitement. Almost everyone will rise early to look through their windows. The first movement out will be at lunchtime. Most will want to go to the dining car. It may be the only time they go. That is when we begin our search."

Sasha nodded.

"You looked at your timetable?"

"I did," said Sasha. "There are so many stops. More than one hundred and thirty, stops every few hours. We can't check at every one. We would get no sleep."

"Most of the stops are only for a few minutes so people can stretch their legs, buy some trinkets, chocolates. We will take turns watching to see if someone gets off with a suspect suitcase or someone of interest gets on. It is most likely that the transaction will take place at one of the larger stops. We have three days till we get to Novosibirsk," said Rostnikov as the train rattled forward, the lights of Moscow glowing a faint yellow through the falling snow outside the window.

It was not much of a plan, but Rostnikov did not intend to simply wait.

"We begin our search now," he said. "We walk through the train, noting any luggage or people who might be suspicious. Most important, look for a person who does not leave his or her compartment or does so only with a suitcase."

The chances of success seemed very slim to Sasha Tkach, but the responsibility was not his and the chief inspector did not appear to be concerned. But then Porfiry Petrovich was not a man who showed excitement.

Rostnikov pointed to his left, the direction he wanted Sasha to take, and he turned to the right, toward the car from which they had come.

"Porfiry Petrovich," Sasha said. "My mother is planning to get married."

Rostnikov hesitated. "Perhaps the sun will burn out sooner than we think," he said. "Tell me more in the morning."

The sun? What did the sun have to do with it? Sasha wondered. On more than one occasion in the past, Sasha had given serious consideration to the possibility that the chief inspector had moments of great eccentricity.

Almost all the work done on the railroad was by hand. Axes, saws, shovels, miners' hacks, wheelbarrows. Despite the primitive tools and weather, 600 kilometers of railway were built every day. Not only were thousands of miles of track laid, but one-hundred-million cubic feet of earth was moved. In just one 230-kilometer span, the Circum-Baikal Railway, fifty protection barriers against landslide had to be constructed, thirty-nine tunnels blasted and reinforced, 14 kilometers of support walls built with concrete. Just the cost of the tunnels with support walls was more than ten million rubles.

In October 26, 1897, temporary traffic began from Vladivostok to Khabarovsk. In 1898, the western-Siberian section from Chelybansk to Novosibrsk was put into operation. The middle-Siberian section from Ob'River to Irkutsk was completed in 1899. In 1905 regular traffic began. Only one track had been laid. There had not been enough money to lay a track running in each direction.

Pavel Cherkasov was more than slightly bothered by the coincidental appearance of the barrel of a man who shared the compartment with him and the two old Americans. Pavel recognized Chief Inspector Rostnikov of the office of Special Investigation. There was no doubt. He recognized the face, and his impression was confirmed by the man's distinct limp.

He had never met Rostnikov, and he was quite sure Rostnikov had never seen him or a photograph of him. Pavel had a computer. It was not with him. Far too large and he did not like carrying laptops. Pavel was a professional. He kept track of supposed friends and potential enemies. There were web sites with photographs of the Washtub. People had e-mailed him photographs via scanner of the policeman and many others whom it would behoove him to recognize. Pavel, in turn, had occasionally put out some information on people and places to avoid or be wary of. And Pavel had an excellent memory.

The possibility of the detective's being on the train by chance was slim to nonexistent, though it was certainly a possibility. However, the chance of the policeman being in the same compartment defied the odds. It was most likely that Rostnikov had some information on the transaction. It might be very little but it might be enough to present some danger.

No matter. He would find out how much help Rostnikov had with him. He would guard the blue duffel bag containing the money, put it, if necessary, in a safer place than the compartment carrier. He had a number of thoughts about that. It would all be done tomorrow, after breakfast.

He lifted the duffel bag to his lap, zipped it open, and removed a pair of blue pajamas and a white robe. He did this casually, laying the items on the seat next to him, wanting them to see but pay no attention. Even if Rostnikov was watching him, it was most unlikely that he would consider the boldness of Pavel's carrying more than half a million British pounds under his nightclothes and underwear.

"Gentlemen," he said in English to the other three people in his compartment as he zipped the duffel closed and deposited it casually on the rack over his head. "I asked a young friend of mine who his father was. He answered, 'Comrade Putin.' I asked who his mother was. He answered, 'Russia.' I asked him what he would like to be when he grows up. He answered, 'An orphan.' "

The two old Americans laughed and Pavel immediately said, "Two Jewish women meet on Kalinin Street. One is holding the hands of her two little boys. 'Well,' says the one woman, 'how old are your children?' And the other woman answers, 'The doctor is six. The lawyer is four.' "

Again his compartment mates laughed.

Pavel had many more. He put any thoughts of Porfiry Petrovich Rostnikov in a little mental box to be opened when he did not have a willing audience.

In 1904 the Japanese attacked and defeated the Russian fleet in the Sea of Japan at Port Arthur, near Vladivostok. Troops had to be sent to the front to protect the coast of Siberia. The Trans-Siberian Railroad could handle only thirteen trains a day. The czar ordered the elimination of civilian services on the line. Transferring troops was also hampered because a portion of the Circum-Baikal section of the line had to be used. Part of that line, the connection of the west and east coasts of Baikal Lake, was not completed. Trains were ferried on a 3,470-ton icebreaker called *Baikal*, which could carry up to 25 loaded cars at a time. When winter came and the lake froze Siberian-solid, tracks were laid across it and 220 cars a day rattled across. There are no reports of the ice giving way.

After the war with Japan, the czar ordered an increase in the capacity of the Trans-Siberian Railroad. To increase the speed of the trains, the earth bed was widened, light rails were replaced by heavier ones, rails were laid on metal plates instead of wood, wooden bridges were torn down and replaced by others of concrete and metal. A second track was begun in 1909 and completed in 1913. New branches were also built.

By 1912, 3.2 million passengers traveled on the Trans-Siberian Express, but during World War I the Russian railway system, suffering from shortages, began to break down. It was further devastated by the Russian civil war. Cars and locomotives were destroyed, bridges were burned, and passenger stations bombed.

When the czar was overthrown and the White Army defeated, rebuilding began. During the winter of 1924–1925, the badly damaged Amur Bridge was rebuilt. In March of 1925, traffic on the railroad was opened again. It has not once been interrupted in more than seventy-five years.

Porfiry Petrovich bypassed his compartment, where the three men were drinking and laughing. He considered joining them to work on his English, but he knew there would be time for that and that his English was certainly passable.

He found the dining car. It was almost empty. People were settling into their compartments. The dining-car seats were comfortable. Through the windows he could see the last lights of the outskirts of Moscow growing more apart and more dim and small.

He took the Ed McBain novel out of his pocket and began to read. He would have liked to remove his leg but that would have to wait till he returned to his compartment, where he would immediately tell the others how he had lost it. The two old men with whom he shared his compartment had mentioned that they were veterans of World War II. They might want to discuss their own experiences, but then again they might not. Rostnikov's explanation of his own participation in the war was always short and precise.

It invited no conversation but discouraged no comment.

"I was a child," he said. "A very young boy soldier. I made a mistake and my leg was run over by a German tank. The ground was muddy. The leg would not die. Not long ago it was necessary to remove it."

Story done. He did not want to go into details. Most who had served in an army did not press him.

He planted both his good and his artificial leg on the floor and opened his book. The train jostled, but he was not prone to motion sickness.

There were a few others in the car, a couple in their late thirties or early forties talking softly in Russian, pointing out the window. A woman of about fifty, slight, thick glasses, alone, sat with her elbow bent on the train seat and her head resting upon her hand. She looked sadly and deeply into the night.

Rostnikov was absorbed in the text of the ragged paperback. The Deaf Man was killing people again, confounding Carella and the others. Rostnikov did not wonder if he would be caught. He knew. He had read the novel three times before.

Even absorbed in the book he was aware that someone had sat across from him. He did not take his eyes from the page but he could see the figure of a woman, sense her presence and perhaps the faint smell of perfume. When he finished the chapter, Rostnikov looked up.

The woman was about forty, lean, wearing a tan skirt and blouse. She was quite beautiful. She was looking directly at him. She smiled. Rostnikov smiled back.

Over the woman's shoulder Porfiry Petrovich saw Sasha Tkach enter the car. Rostnikov blinked his eyes once without looking at Sasha. The blink was enough. Sasha understood. He backed out of the car.

"Are you traveling alone?" the woman asked in Russian in a surprisingly deep voice.

"Yes," he answered. "And you?"

"The same," she said. "I think I know you."

"I think that not likely," he said. "I know I should remember you if we had met."

"Thank you," she said, widening her smile and holding out her hand. "I am Svetlana Britchevna."

Rostnikov leaned over somewhat awkwardly. Her skin was tender but her grip was firm.

"I am Ivan Pavlov," he said.

"Forgive me," she said. "I'm a bit forward, I know, but I anticipate a boring trip and the more interesting people with whom I can converse the more quickly the time will pass."

"The scenery during the day is supposed to be magnificent," he said.

"I know," she answered, straightening her skirt. "I've seen it many times. I travel the line frequently, three or four times a year. I'm an engineer. Electrical. Safety checks on various plants throughout Siberia. There are no stops on the line of any great interest to me till we get to Novosibirsk."

"Nothing of interest is likely to happen before then?" asked Rostnikov.

"I speak from experience," she said pleasantly. "And you?"

"I have never traveled on this train before."

"No," she said with a smile. "I mean, what do you do?"

"I am a plumbing contractor," Rostnikov said. "Not terribly interesting to others."

"But you find it so," she said.

"Yes."

"As I find computer programs. You know about plumbing, then?"

He nodded.

"My husband and I have a problem," she said, leaning forward as if she were about to share an intimate secret. "We have cast-iron drain pipes in our basement. They are rotting. We're planning a new fixture. Do we have to, should we, use galvanized iron again?"

"No," Rostnikov said, putting his book in

his pocket. "A no-hub fitting can get you into the stack with minimum difficulty. With special adapter fittings, copper or plastic supply lines can take over where the galvanized leaves off. It can usually be accomplished with the right tools, some no-hub clamps, spacers, a few sanitary crosses, possibly a tee and a riser clamp, using the right tools."

"I think we had better get a plumber," she said.

"It is really not difficult," Rostnikov said. "You live in Moscow?"

"Yes," she said.

"I would be happy to come to your home and examine your problem."

"I couldn't . . ." she began.

"No," he said. "Plumbing is my pleasure."

"But it might not be simple."

"That would be even better," he said.

"We will talk again," she said, rising and offering her hand. He took it.

"That would be pleasant," he said.

The woman turned and left the car. Rostnikov turned his eyes to the window, finding the last village lights before the plunge into darkness. In the reflection from the window a few seconds later he saw Sasha Tkach, who sat where the woman had been.

"Who was that?" Sasha asked.

"A very beautiful woman."

"That I could see. What did she want?"

"To find out if I am a plumber," said Rostnikov.

"If you are a plumber?"

"Yes. I believe she knows who I am."

"Why would she approach you?" asked Sasha.

"A very good question. She wants me to know that she knows."

"Then she doesn't believe you are a plumber?"

"No," he said. "She was playing a game. Like chess. She begins the game with a small move of a pawn. She asks me about a plumbing problem she does not have. I think she was pleasantly surprised that I was able to answer her question."

"What does she want?" asked Sasha. "Is she the one with the suitcase?"

"Perhaps. I don't think so. The question is, Why does she want me to know that she knows who I am?"

Sasha shrugged. It was the sort of problem Rostnikov relished.

"She has something to gain by my knowing of her presence."

"FSB?" asked Sasha.

"Very likely," Rostnikov answered.

FSB, the Federal Security Service, *Federal'naya Sluzhba Bezopasnosti*, the heir to most of the empire of the former KGB. The FSB was even headquartered in Lubyanka, in Derzhinski Square, the former headquarters of the KGB.

The FSB, established in April of 1995, is overseen by the procurator general of Russia and has over seventy-five thousand agents. The FSB's primary mission is civil counterespionage, internal Russian security, organized crime, and state secrets. Terrorism, international borders, drugs, and various other classified areas are the province of the Russian Security Ministry, MBR, *Ministertvo Bezopasnosti Rushkii*. The MBR has more than one hundred thousand agents. That leaves the SVR, the Foreign Intelligence Service, whose numbers are unreported.

"And she did tell me something which may be important," Rostnikov said.

"What?"

"That the transaction will almost certainly not take place before we reach Novosibirsk."

"She told you that?"

"I believe so. It will be an interesting trip. Do you want to try to sleep?"

"Too noisy in my compartment," said Sasha.

"Mine too," said Rostnikov. "Let us talk about your mother and her impending marriage."

Chapter Two

Rich man leave your wealthiness
Wanderer, your solemn dress
Seafarer, the sea's caress
Beowulf, your angriness
Time to take a second guess
Time to make a pact with death
Trans-Siberian Express

"It is a bad idea," Elena Timofeyeva said.

She had almost used the word *stupid* instead of *bad* but had caught herself in time. She was standing in the doorway of the apartment she shared with her Aunt Anna. Her right boot was resisting her efforts to make it take leave of her foot.

She looked up at Iosef Rostnikov, who had both of his boots off and had entered the apartment.

"You want help with that?" he asked.

"No," she said, and with an awkward effort and a mighty pull the boot came off, taking the long woollen sock with it. She almost fell.

Perhaps her diet plan needed reconsideration.

Anna Timofeyeva sat in her comfortable chair near the only window in the room. She had been looking into the snow-covered courtyard in the first light of dawn. The children bound for school had not yet made tracks across the field of white that came up to the level of the seats of the benches circling the center of the covered concrete square.

Her cat, Baku, had been sitting on her lap. When her niece and Iosef had opened the door, the cat had lazily leaped to the floor and gone over to sniff at them.

Anna had never been bitter over her tragedy, the heart attacks which forced her to retire as procurator of Moscow before she was fifty-five. Anna had worked her way up from assembly-line worker to Communist Party leader for her factory, to regional assistant procurator, to her final position in Moscow. She had regularly put in fifteen-hour days, frequently worked days at a time fueled by duty, coffee, thick soups, and sandwiches of fatty meat.

The Soviet Union had prided itself on the equality of women. Movies, newspapers, posters showed women as leaders, workers, soldiers, the equal of men. The truth, as she had learned early in life, was the exact opposite. Women were considered inferior, and often those put in token positions of authority were chosen because of their party loyalty and a nonthreatening lack of intellect. Anna Timofeyeva had been a notable exception. She had taken pride in her achievement, but she had taken enormous satisfaction in her work.

And then, so suddenly, it was all over. The brown uniform that she had worn for sixteen years was traded for bulky skirts and sweaters; the large office for a small one-bedroom apartment.

Anna had never married, had never shown or had any interest in men as anything but people for whom she worked or who worked for her. She showed no greater interest in women as friends, companions, confidants, or lovers. She had tried sex with two men and one not particularly pretty but quite slim woman many years earlier. None of the three encounters had given her any satisfaction.

And so Anna sat in her apartment, read, and welcomed the company of her niece, which she would soon be losing when Elena and Iosef married. From time to time Porfiry Petrovich would visit, either to ask for her advice or simply to sit with her and drink some tea. All too often she was visited by Lydia Tkach, Sasha's mother, who had an apartment down the hallway and around the corner.

It was Porfiry Petrovich whose idea it had been for Lydia to move into the apartment complex. Anna could still pull some strings. Lydia could have afforded much better, but she was content to move half a corridor from Anna and to knock at the door uninvited so that she could relate her woes in a very loud voice to the captive former procurator.

Recently, however, there had been great respite from Lydia. Lydia was seeing a man, a painter named Matvei Labroadovnik. She had told Anna all about him. Anna would have bestowed a medal, one of the dozen or so she had in her drawer in the bedroom, to the man if he were to end Lydia's daily visits. But, at the same time, she felt uneasy the single time the man had come with Lydia to be shown off. Intuition, which came from years of talking to liars on multiple sides of the law, had taught her when someone was wearing a mask. The man had been wearing a mask of satisfied contemplation. Behind the mask, Anna was certain, was a racing mind. But that was Lydia's problem. For the moment, he was Anna's ally.

"Tell Aunt Anna what you want to do," Elena said to Iosef, moving to the seat opposite her aunt.

Elena and Iosef had been up all night, meeting with the dozen uniformed officers assigned to their case, trying to come up with an idea they could present to the Yak, talking to Paulinin, who, they discovered, was even stranger than usual after the hour of midnight.

Paulinin had kept his right hand reassuringly on the head of the naked corpse of Toomas Vana during their entire conversation in the laboratory. From time to time Paulinin had looked down at the mutilated face of the dead man and smiled reassuringly.

The corpse was as white as the snow falling two stories above and outside Petrovka. The multiple wounds formed an odd pattern.

"We have had a very interesting conversation," Paulinin said. "He has told me about his life and the woman who killed him."

Elena wanted to ask what the dead man had said, but she still was not sure of the proper protocol with the odd scientist in the dingy laboratory jacket. Was he waiting for her to ask a question or would he be offended by being interrupted in his musings? Iosef had been the one to speak.

"What has he told you about the woman?"

Paulinin, hand still on the dead man's head, twitched his nose to push his glasses back an infinitesimal notch, and said, "The woman loved him. She loved the others she attacked too. But she was reluctant to tell him, to tell them. She always strikes her first blows someplace vulnerable, the neck, eye, scrotum, nothing consistent, shy about admitting her purpose. She jabs. Here. There."

Paulinin pointed at various wounds before continuing.

"And then, she strikes hardest at the heart, always at the heart, always the hardest blow. This time it caused her enormous pain. She used her right hand again. She has trouble maintaining her attack. The blade goes this way and that. The thrusts are growing weak. She tried her left hand. Remember?"

"Yes," said Elena.

"But," Paulinin went on, "it was not natural, it did not give her satisfaction. You want to know how I know?"

"Yes," said Iosef.

"Because she went back to the right hand in spite of the pain. The right hand. The heart."

"She wants to break his heart," Elena said before she could stop herself.

Paulinin pondered her comment and nodded his head in agreement.

"Yes, something like that. She loves him. You said the little girl on the platform heard the attacker call the man *Father*."

"Yes," said Iosef.

"She loves her father," said Paulinin. "I loved my father."

"But you didn't kill him," Elena said.

"Of course not," Paulinin said in exasperation. "And I don't believe she has killed her father. She is sending him a message he cannot hear. Maybe she will kill him. Meanwhile, her wrist has a very severe sprain, possibly it is broken. She is probably feeling great pain. But that will not stop her from attacking again. The same kind of man, well-dressed, possibly carrying a briefcase, tall, between the ages of forty-five or so and fifty-five or sixty, from what my friend" — and here he gently patted the dead man's head — "has told me."

"Why does she attack on metro stations beginning with the letter *K*?" Iosef asked.

"How should I know?" Paulinin returned with irritation. "I am not a psychiatrist. Maybe her father's name begins with a *K*, or maybe something happened to her on a metro platform that began with a *K*, something when she was a little girl. Now she cannot remember which *K* station it is. Maybe her name begins with a *K*. Maybe a million things. When you find her, ask her and tell me."

They had left Petrovka and walked miles in the nearly empty streets through the snow, talking, and Iosef had come up with his plan. Now he stood in Anna Timofeyeva's apartment. He reached down to pick up the cat,

231

which did not complain, and said, "I will wear a suit and tie, put a little gray in my hair, carry a briefcase, and travel from station to station spending time on each K platform."

"He will make himself a target for a madwoman," Elena said, looking at her aunt.

Anna Timofeyeva was a solid, heavyset woman with a wide nose and a distinctly Russian face. Her best feature was her large brown eyes, which she fixed on whomever she spoke to, giving her full attention, or, in some cases, the semblance of full attention.

"The likelihood of this woman finding you," she said, looking up at Iosef, "is not great. There is no shortage of potential victims for this . . ." She almost said "poor woman" but stopped herself and simply said "woman."

"You see," said Elena.

"And who knows if and when she will strike again?" Anna went on.

"Her favorite time seems to be between nine in the morning and three-thirty in the afternoon," Iosef said.

Anna pondered the answer and said, "She is not free to attack early and she must be somewhere in the late afternoon. Perhaps she has a night job. Most likely she has no job at all but she has something to do, somewhere to be."

"The likelihood that she will find you," Elena said, "is very small."

"But," her aunt said, "what other plan do you have? More police on the platforms? We know you cannot get them. Your plan cannot hurt."

"Cannot hurt," Elena exclaimed, rising from her chair. "It can get him killed."

"The woman is not big," Iosef said. "I'll be alert. And there are not really that many men in suits and ties, carrying briefcases, on the metro. They are above the ground in cabs and private cars."

Elena considered trying to reach Iosef's father, but Rostnikov was on a train to Siberia. Iosef was his only son. He would surely dissuade him. She could go to the Yak, but she was certain he would see nothing wrong with the plan. He would not be the one making a target of himself on the metro platform, and the Yak had no great fondness for Iosef. Elena considered that it might even be possible to simply order Iosef not to do it. She was the senior inspector on the case. But to issue him an order in this situation might be a blow to their relationship.

She looked up at Iosef cradling the cat in his arms. He was no fool and he had several advantages in the situation. He had been an actor. He would not overact his role as a businessman. He was an ex-soldier, a combat veteran of the Afghanistan disaster. He had a keenly developed sense of danger.

Elena had little choice.

"All right," she said, stepping in front of him and reaching out to pet Baku. "But I will be there every moment."

Iosef smiled.

Inna's mother's name had been Katyana. Inna's mother had been perfect. Katyana, Inna thought as she sat at the table, her wrist wrapped tightly and resting under a bag of ice, had betrayed her daughter by dying.

Inna adjusted the bag on top of her wrist. The wrist no longer hurt in the same way. It was now either numbly frozen or burning.

Inna's life was no life. She took her pills and existed to please her father. There was nothing else. She was trapped, too frightened and too dependent to walk away. Where would she go? She had no other relatives. What would she do? She had no skills.

Viktor Dalipovna was her life. She had to take care of him. What if something should happen to him? Things happen, you know. He could have a heart attack, be killed in a robbery, get hit by a car or truck. One of the women he sometimes spent the night with might kill him in his sleep for the money in his wallet, his watch, his ring. He did not take good enough care of himself in many ways. His diet was bad. Inna fed him healthy meals. She never argued or disagreed with him. She snuck vitamins into his food, cut every speck of fat from his meat, even watered his vodka but ever so slightly.

Inna looked around the room. She would have to get up soon, retape her wrist, work through the pain, get her father's dinner ready. Had she taken the medicine? She couldn't remember. Had she meant to? Probably not. She was not supposed to take too much. But she had been taking none of it.

She put the question to her mother, whose ghost sat across from her on the other side of the table. The dead Katyana was the same age as when she had died, a mature, plump, pretty woman.

"Did I take the medicine?" Inna asked.

"Yes," her mother said. "Don't you feel it?"

"No."

"Then perhaps you did not take it," Katyana said. "We can count the pills. We can keep count so you will know. Prepare a sheet of paper, write the date. Make a check mark when you take the pill."

"Yes," said Inna, but she knew she would not do it. It was curious. Each day, she woke up certain that she could keep track of everything, pills, shopping, cleaning. She needed no list. But then she discovered that she could not remember if she had taken a pill or eaten lunch. In the grocery, she could not remember if the night before she had onions or potatoes or whether the night before she had served his favorite salad, *sahlad eez reedyeesah,* sliced radishes with salt and sour cream. That particular dish did not matter. He would not care if he had it every day.

"It is just the idea of not being able to remember," she explained to her dead mother.

"I know," Katyana answered. "How is your wrist?"

"It . . . I don't know."

"Take off the ice," her mother advised. "You have had it on too long."

Inna removed the top bag of already melting ice and slowly lifted her hand. "It hurts," she said.

"You might have to go to the clinic," her mother said.

"They would know what I have been doing," she answered.

"How? A woman hurts her wrist. How would they know?"

"I am not good at lying."

"Then you will suffer."

"Yes," she said, biting her lower lip to hold off the pain as she moved her hand.

"A little suffering is not a bad thing," her mother said. "But when the suffering is more than a little you should do something."

"I will be fine," Inna said.

"I worry about you," her mother said.

"Why?"

"Because you are crazy. You are crazy and you don't take your medicine. You know that both of these things are true."

"Yes."

"And?"

"I cannot stop. I will grow even crazier if I stop. I love my father. He must know. I must drive it into his heart. He must know. He must reach over and smile sadly and say something, anything, like 'You are my daughter.'"

"He is not that kind of man," Katyana said.

"I know," said Inna, resting her throbbing arm in her lap. "I must go shopping."

"Make a list," her mother said.

"I don't need one," Inna said.

"This is not a good day for you to show your love," Katyana said gently. "Do not go in search of your father on the trains."

"I search for both of us, for you," Inna said.

"I know, but not today."

"Tomorrow?" Inna asked, almost pleading.

"Tomorrow, if you must," her mother said with a smile.

"I will be nothing if I do not go," Inna tried to explain. "I will disappear. My body will be here but I will have no thoughts, no meaning. You understand?"

"Perfectly," her mother said.

"I don't, but I know it is so."

And then her mother was gone. It was always like this. She would be there and it would be quite natural. She would not be there and that would be natural too. Inna knew her mother was dead but she did not have to address this reality. In fact, she chose to address no reality at all other than keeping herself reasonably clean, taking care of her father, and keeping the knife very, very sharp.

Chapter Three

The world is long, there is no consolation
For those who join at the end of the line

Porfiry Petrovich sat at a table in the dining car with the three other men from his compartment, the Americans dressed casually and the slightly dapper, somewhat portly man with the neatly trimmed beard, wearing a suit and tie, who had identified himself as David Drovny — a dealer in men's clothes on his way to Vladivostok to approve a shipment of material from Japan.

Meanwhile, Sasha was making his rounds of the eighteen cars in search of the suitcase. Meals were the best time for such a search because people would be in the dining car. Even if they were not, he would make up an excuse, be at his charming boyish best, apologize, ask for help with something, and without giving himself away examine the luggage, perhaps even swaying slightly and reaching out to touch a particularly interesting suitcase, to balance himself, and feel for its contents.

"Never made it this far during the war," one of the Americans, the tall one named Allberry, said. "Liaison with Russian intelligence near Rostov."

"OSS?" asked the other American, Susman.

The tall American nodded and said, "I helped get some information from our people to the Russians," said Allberry. "We'd broken the Nazi codes. It helped a little. Always wanted to come back."

"And here we are, Bob," said the smaller, bald American with a sigh. "I never made it past Rome. Landed in Casino. Thought about making this trip from the day the war ended. Then the Cold War. Ellen died last year. Figured, what the hell."

"What the hell," Allberry agreed, patting the other American's shoulder.

Rostnikov listened to the men at his table talk and looked out the window past a forest of birch trees that came almost to the train tracks. Snowdrifts stretched up the trees, and nooks in the fleeting branches were tinged with the soft whiteness. From time to time he could see an isolated dacha or two, sometimes four or five in a group, retreats for the upper-middle class, their roofs decorated with tufts of snow.

On the table before the four men was a plate of hard-boiled eggs, another of fried eggs with small slices of ham, an urn of black coffee, slices of black bread, and small cups of yoghurt.

"The breakfast," Drovny said in English, buttering a thick slice of bread, "is standard fare. Nothing you would not get in a second-class hotel in Irkutsk. But the lunch and dinner . . ."

"Good, huh?" asked one of the Americans.

Drovny smiled and said, "Rice with minced mutton."

Plov eez bahrahnyeeni, thought Rostnikov.

"Boiled beef tongue, roast pork with plums, goulash, beef Stroganoff," Drovny went on. "Not the equal of some of the restaurants I could take you to in Moscow, and nothing like Paris, but palatable."

"I'm a steak-and-potatoes man," Allberry said. "Doing it so long, it's in my blood. But I'm willing to try. I remember back in those months with a Russian intelligence general we had a dish with beef, veal, and chicken in gelatin served with a mustard sauce. Sounds terrible, right? But it was damned good."

"*Kholodets*," Drovny said. "That is what it is called. Served with *charlotka*, a creamy vanilla and raspberry-puree dessert. Delicious."

The American laughed. "I'm afraid we

241

weren't near any of that."

"Yes," said Drovny, reaching over to pat the man's arm in congratulation for his willingness to experiment with the standard cuisine of the country he was visiting. "And you?"

He was looking at Rostnikov.

Rostnikov had already told the men that he was a plumbing contractor; but he was, like Drovny, a Russian. "I am willing to try any food," he said.

"A large man with a large appetite," said Drovny with a big grin, as if he had made a joke.

Rostnikov looked around the car. All the tables were full. He did not see the woman he had spoken to the night before, the one who had given him the name Svetlana Britchevna.

"This egg," said Drovny. "It reminds me of something."

"What's that?" asked one of the Americans.

"It reminds me of a funny story," Drovny said. "Two flies go into an insect restaurant. The first fly orders shit with garlic. The second one orders shit but adds, 'Hold the garlic. I don't want my breath to smell bad.' "

The two Americans laughed. Rostnikov smiled as the joker asked, "Which is more useful, Russian newspapers or Russian television? The newspaper," he answered himself. "You can wrap fish in it."

Five cars down, Sasha Tkach was slowly making his way through the train. His plan was simple. He would check the empty compartments, the ones in which the occupants were dining, out in the corridors, or visiting with other passengers. He kept a list of the cars and compartments and checked them off. He would return periodically to see if unchecked compartments were empty.

If a compartment were, at the moment, unoccupied, he would slide open the door when he was confident no one in the corridor was watching, then quickly look at the luggage and reach out to feel particular pieces. In five cars, he had found nothing promising.

Some people passing had looked at him as he moved slowly or loitered. He gave them his best smile and a good morning. The smile still worked, though he did not feel it.

Sasha had no great hope of finding that for which he searched, but he persisted. There would be a stop in twenty minutes. He would have to suspend his search and get out onto the platform. This was proving on the first day to be an exhausting assignment.

Sasha continued, recalling his brief conversation with Porfiry Petrovich the night before.

243

"The man's name?" Rostnikov had asked. "The one your mother says she might marry?"

"Matvei Labroadovnik," Sasha had said. "He is working on the restoration of the Cathedral of the Resurrection in Istra."

"Matvei Labroadovnik," Rostnikov repeated, searching his memory for the name.

"She says he is famous," Sasha had gone on.

"And you believe? . . ."

"That he knows my mother has money. That he is not a famous painter. Either that or he is ninety years old, half blind, and slightly mad."

"You don't think a man could be interested in your mother?"

"Do you?"

"She has her good points, Sasha."

"Such as?"

"She is generous."

"But she charges a great deal for her generosity. Attention, great respect, and the right to dictate how I live."

"She loves you and your children," Rostnikov tried.

"She smothers us with love, on her terms," said Sasha. "She is a smothering . . . I do not know."

"Would you not be happy if she indeed

had found someone?"

"I would be relieved, overjoyed. I would throw a party. There would be dancing. But I don't believe it."

Rostnikov had his doubts too but he went on, "We will check on this painter when we get back to Moscow."

"And if they decide to marry before we get back? He may want to marry her quickly before he has to meet me, deal with me."

"Are you concerned about losing your mother's money?"

"A little, perhaps," Sasha admitted.

"You are concerned about losing your mother," Rostnikov tried.

"As strange as it is, that may be the case," said Sasha with a deep sigh. "I have grown accustomed to her nagging. Maya would be happy to see her gone. Maya does not care about the money. The children would probably be happy too."

"We are not talking about Lydia dying," said Rostnikov. "Only about her getting married."

Sasha laughed. The few other people in the car had looked at him. "You know why I am laughing?" he asked.

"I think so," said Rostnikov.

"I sound like I am jealous," Sasha said, putting his hand to his chest. "That is what the woman has done to me. I will be thirty-six years old on my next birthday and I still feel like a child when I am with her."

Rostnikov said nothing. This was an important moment of realization for Sasha Tkach.

"I think," he said, no longer laughing, "I think I understand something. It sounds crazy. The problems I have had with women during my marriage."

Rostnikov was well aware of Sasha's weakness. It had almost cost him his marriage and at least twice had jeopardized his career.

"It is my mother I want to hurt," he said. "It is my mother I want to show that I am interested in other women."

"It is a theory," Rostnikov admitted.

"It seems right," said Sasha with excitement. "You should have been a psychiatrist."

"If simply listening qualifies one, then perhaps you are right, but I would give you a caution, Sasha. What seems clear and true and right when it is night and one is tired and on a train rocking into darkness may not seem quite so right in the sunlight."

And Rostnikov had been right. Now, going through the train in search of a suitcase he probably would not recognize, Sasha thought his whole theory about his mother had been little more than nonsense.

Sasha moved forward, sometimes sensing

when someone was in a compartment or catching a glimpse of movement or form on a seat. He had such a sense as he passed the next compartment and was about to open the door of the empty one just past it when a woman's voice called.

"You missed me."

Sasha turned back. Standing in the doorway of the compartment he had just passed was the quite-beautiful woman who had been talking to Porfiry Petrovich in the lounge car the night before.

She was wearing a tan skirt and a matching sweater with the sleeves rolled up. Her hair was down and she was smiling.

"I wasn't looking for your compartment," Sasha said, finding it difficult to draw upon his charm.

"Come in," she said and walked back into the compartment and out of Sasha's sight.

Sasha paused, considered, and moved slowly back to the woman's compartment, trying to come up with a tale, hoping a creative lie would present itself.

She was sitting near the window, looking up at him, the morning light cast on the left side of her face, a slight shadow on the right. Her lips were full, red, her smile playful.

"Sit, please," she said, pointing to the seat opposite her.

"I was on my way to —" he began, but she was shaking her head and he stopped.

"I don't know how much time we have until the people I am sharing this compartment with return," she said. "So please examine the luggage. Satisfy yourself."

"I don't know —" he tried.

"You are wasting time," she said.

Sasha brushed the dangling lock of hair from his forehead and quickly examined the luggage.

"Satisfied?" she asked.

He sat back and nodded to show that he was, at least with his search.

"We passed in the lounge car last night," she said. "I had just spoken to the plumber and you were about to do so. My name is Svetlana Britchevna."

She held out her hand. Sasha took it. Firm grip. A feeling he recognized stirred and he willed it to go away. She held the shake and the feeling battled Sasha's will. She released his hand and sat back.

"I did exchange a few words with a one-legged man in the lounge car," he said. "I did not catch his name."

She cocked her head to the side and made an almost imperceptible negative nod.

"And what is your name?" she asked.

"Roman Spesvnik," he said.

"And what do you do, Roman Spesvnik?" she asked.

She was toying with him. He knew that. He knew she expected lies. Oh God, did she also sense his weakness for aggressive women?

"I work in the government information office in Moscow," he said. "Utilities division. Gas, electrical power."

He knew a little about the job. His mother had held such a position until her retirement.

"Roman," she said, looking out the window, showing a near-perfect profile, "this will be a long trip with beautiful scenery. But one can spend only so many hours a day looking out the window even at the most beautiful of mountains and forests and the most quaint of villages."

Sasha said nothing.

"It is good to have company on a long trip, don't you think?" she asked.

There was provocation in her words. Sasha knew them. He recognized them. There was a magic thread with an invisible hook reaching out to him.

"Yes," he said.

"You are traveling alone?" she asked.

"I . . . yes."

"Good, then perhaps we can provide each

other with company. Are you married, Roman?"

"Yes."

"So am I," she said. "But my husband is far away and, to tell the truth, not very good company recently."

And then it got even worse.

"I understand that there is a single compartment open in the next car," she said. "I've already inquired about moving into it. The conductor can arrange it."

She was older than Sasha. That he could tell, but there was a confident sophistication which was overwhelming.

"Shall I do that, do you think?" she asked.

"It is not up to me," he said.

"Oh, yes, it is," she replied.

This could not be happening. It must not happen. Not again. She had caught him unprepared. There was nothing gradual in her approach. She was giving him no time to think.

Sasha took a deep breath and said, "Then I recommend that you save your money and remain in this compartment where you have people to talk to."

"Roman," she said. "Don't make a mistake. I'm not suggesting anything that need be shared with anyone else, not even with the plumber you barely met."

Oh Lord, this was a temptation that vibrated through his body and between his legs.

"I am afraid I will be very busy during this trip," he said. "I have a full week of work, reports to prepare. If I fail . . ."

". . . to go through all the compartments and find what you are looking for," she said, reaching over to touch his hand and lean within a foot of his face.

He could smell her essence.

"No, I cannot. And I do not know where you got the idea that I am looking —"

"You examined the luggage," she reminded him.

"I was humoring you," he said. "I did not want to be impolite to a woman."

"And would you have humored me had I been old and ugly?"

"I must go now," he said, getting up, his nose almost brushing hers.

"Perhaps we can sit together at dinner tonight," she said. "Perhaps we could discuss putting your work aside for a bit and pursuing our new friendship."

"I have already agreed to dine with a French couple," he said, moving to the door.

Her eyes met his and held. He closed his eyes and said, "I must go."

When he was gone, the woman sat back down. Her smile disappeared. She had learned what was necessary and now she was prepared to act. There were risks involved, risks that might end her career, but the chance of success would be worth the risks.

Tonight she would have a long talk with the plumber and the handsome young man who called himself Roman.

The watcher had listened to Pavel Cherkasov tell his jokes at the breakfast table, had heard him give the name David Drovny, had watched him eat.

Cherkasov was a remarkably capable courier. He did not hide. He played the role of glutton and near-buffoon to perfection because his persona was both true gluttony and buffoonery. That Pavel Cherkasov was well-armed there was no doubt. That Pavel Cherkasov would be cautious with his mission was equally certain. The watcher knew that the courier was a professional, an illusionist, a magician who could improvise brilliantly and execute his plans without error.

The watcher had been informed that there were two policemen on the train. There had been no problem spotting them. They matched their descriptions. Rostnikov was a difficult man to hide.

The important thing was that Rostnikov and his assistant not know that they were in a game, that they continue to believe and pursue their difficult task and not think there was another player. The presence of the two detectives gave the watcher an advantage, a backup plan.

If the attempt to make the transfer was observed, even anticipated, the watcher could act swiftly, beat the policeman to the prize. It was what the watcher expected. But there could be mistakes. Chance could intervene. Rostnikov might make the interception, capture the prize.

And then, unaware of the game, the prize could be taken from the policeman. It was really only a matter of who had to be killed. Pavel Cherkasov? The two policemen? The watcher would have preferred simply killing Pavel, but the difference was not great.

The watcher had ample weaponry and could improvise. Sometimes improvisation proved to be the best procedure, especially if it resulted in the conclusion that the necessary death had been an accident.

The watcher had pushed a woman in front of a bus in Rome, lifted a lean, surprised man over a low wall along a tower walkway of the Cathedral of Notre Dame in Paris, dropped a heavy steel loading-ramp door on an American in Budapest, and worked variations ranging from overdoses of drugs to quite accidental drownings.

The watcher had not kept count. Numbers did not matter. If murder was a sin and there was a God to punish, then ten or twenty meant no more than the first. The same would be true if the watcher were eventually caught, which was always a possibility, a slight possibility but a possibility nonetheless.

It had been a long career, a highly successful career, and there was no reason to stop. Assassination was the watcher's life. There were no hobbies or interests beyond a professional interest in the tools of destruction and the game, which included planning, tracking, and execution.

Money meant little. In the beginning it had seemed important, but it no longer was, though the fees for such services were high.

The train rattled on. A stop in twelve minutes. Shar'ya. It was time to move, find the courier, stay with him, not be spotted.

The watcher did not have a sense of humor, but there was something that approached amusement in the fact that four people were now looking forward to the inevitable transaction.

There was a good chance that Rostnikov did not yet know who the courier was. The fact that his assistant was still going from compartment to compartment in search of the suitcase supported that conclusion, but it was sometimes dangerous to make assumptions even though they seemed obvious. It was far better to act solely on the facts and be prepared for the human factor, the variants that could neither be controlled nor anticipated.

Chapter Four

Through the train the four winds blow
The arctic and the sirocco
Stalactite and stalagmite
Stalag camp and satellite
Pass the captives on death row
The gulag archipelago
The skulls of reindeer in the snow
The longboat drifts, the dead sea floats

"*Kher s nim,* I don't give a damn," Misha Lovski tried to shout, but it came out as a faint dry croak.

He no longer had any sense of how much time had passed. Was it a day? A week? A month? The lights had remained on except when they came in to take his bowls, empty of food and water, and his bowl filled with excrement.

The music was ceaseless. His own voice. His own band. The words lost their meaning. He could not see the speaker. They were watching him. He knew it, felt it. And so he sat on his mattress folded over to cover his legs. He was feeling a definite chill. He was coming down with something. Maybe they had been putting something in his food. What the hell did they want? He wanted to *dat'pisdy*, kick ass, bash a head in with his guitar.

"I will not die," he croaked. "I will not cry. I am a cossack, a free man, an adventurer, a *kazak*. I live at war. I am the cossack Illya of Murom of the *bylina*, the heroic poem, the best."

I am a cossack, he told himself, a warrior of the Dnieper and the Don.

"We are a community of Russians, Tartars, Germans, Serbs, Georgians, Greeks, and Turks. Warriors. I know what you are doing. You are testing me to see if I am a real cossack, if I am worthy to meet the challenge, be a worthy warrior."

He received no answer but the sound of his own voice and the shock of metal vibrations from the music.

"I am going to go to a cossack camp," he said. "I am going to learn to fight with my fists, with the *shasqua*, saber, and the *kinjal*, lance."

The music seemed to get louder.

"I will ride bareback, learn to fire guns, cross rushing rivers, sing cossack songs, embrace Christianity, and wear a true cossack uniform. You know why I am the Naked Cossack?"

The music grew even louder. Misha was talking to himself.

"Because I am not yet worthy of the uniform," he said so softly that even he could not hear himself.

He tore at the corner of the mattress. Frenzy. Another idea. There was padding inside. Some material. Cotton, wool. He rolled two balls of the material and stuffed them in his ears. He did it openly, not trying to hide. He wanted whoever was watching to see this as an act of ingenuity and not as an indication that their torture was working. He folded his arms, crossed his legs, and stared at the door.

The sound was muted but not stilled. The music continued. He dozed in exhaustion and then awoke. His plan had to take place soon or it would be too late. He would be too tired or too crazy.

He had to be ready to move quickly, silently.

Misha had noticed something. Not for the first ten or fifteen times, but after that, when the lights suddenly went off and the music stopped while his bowls were taken and relatively clean ones placed in front of his bars. Whoever made the exchange always reached over and checked the door to his cell with a quick pull to be certain that it was still firmly locked.

Misha had tried it. The cell door was surely locked and he had no tools to work on it. It could not be long now. Someone would come. The ritual would be repeated. He would be ready. He had actually practiced walking barefoot, silent, learning the exact number of steps from the wall to the bars of the cell so that he could move across the floor in total darkness.

While he was going over his plan again, the lights went out. The music stopped. He had placed his bowls very close to the bars. Whoever came would have to move close. He could hear the door beyond his cell open, hear the footsteps, sense when the person was about to reach down. Misha got to his feet, moved quickly, feeling his testicles beating against his thighs.

Hand through the bar, ready. The sound of his jailer reaching for the door.

Misha struck, reached through the bar, grabbed the wrist. The wrist was not thick, but he could not hold it as the jailer pulled away with a grunt and gasp, dropping metal bowls that clattered to the floor.

The jailer said something through clenched teeth. "*Propezdoloch*, clever bastard."

Misha thought he recognized the voice. He croaked defiantly, "I am going to get out."

And the voice of his jailer came back, "*Ni khuya,* no way."

The jailer moved quickly to the door at the end of the room, not stopping to pick up what had been dropped, not wanting to put a hand into or touch the toilet bowl.

The outer door opened and closed and Misha was alone again, but this time he had something to work with. He had recognized the voice of his jailer. He would not utter the name. He would pretend that he did not know. The darkness of the visits was still his protection.

They would keep it dark when they entered for only two reasons: to help drive him mad or to protect themselves from Misha identifying them when he was free. Which meant that Misha had a chance of being free. It was slim hope, but he clung to it, and the knowledge that he knew who his captors were.

The lights came on. The music did not. Misha looked at the mess outside his cell. One bowl, the one which had held water, was on its side against the far wall. The food bowl was overturned within his reach. Miraculously, his toilet bowl had not been moved.

In addition, there were three fresh bowls within reach just beyond the bars. Misha reached through the bars and worked the food and drink inside.

He was hungry now, thirsty too. There was much to think about. He could fashion new earplugs while he considered his plight.

He was not being tested by cossacks, but he would behave as if he were a cossack. He would imagine himself in full blue uniform and long blue coat, leather boots, and a fur hat.

Misha felt a chill. He coughed once, took a drink of water, and retreated to the wall and mattress. He had much to do.

"Your name is Anatoly Zagrenov," said Karpo, looking down at the sheet on the badly scarred wooden table.

"People call me Bottle Kaps," the young man said. "I call myself Bottle Kaps."

They were in a small room in a local precinct police station. There was nothing in the room but a table and two chairs. A single window, quite small and quite dirty, about seven feet up on one wall let in a little light. The walls were a thin brown with spots and smears of dirt. The floor was rough, cracked gray concrete. There was no two-way mirror. There was but one door and any police officer passing the room ignored whatever sounds, pain, anguish, pleading, or cries seeped into the dark corridor.

The young man who wanted to be called Bottle Kaps had moved to the chair to sit. Karpo motioned to him to remain on his feet. The detective also remained standing on the opposite side of the table with the sheet of paper before him.

"You are nineteen years old," Karpo went on. "Your mother is dead. Your father lost his job two years ago as a janitor in a plastic factory."

"He is a drunk," the young man said. "A parasite."

"In contrast to you," said Karpo.

"I work."

"At what?"

"Things," the young man said. "I know cars. I can fix things. But only for the right people."

The young man rubbed the top of his head. He hadn't shaved in about a day. Prickly small hairs were starting to grow.

"You are going back in the *obyezannik*, the monkey cage with the drunks and thieves," said Karpo. "With Sergei."

"Sergei?"

"Sergei Topoy, Heinrich," said Karpo.

"Sergei Topoy," the young man repeated with a smile.

"You will remain in the cage until you answer my questions and I believe your answers, Anatoly," said Karpo.

Anatoly cocked his head to one side, spread his legs slightly, and clasped his wrist behind his back, a posture meant to show that he had no intention of cooperating.

"What happened to Misha Lovski?"

"I told you. We went out into the street. He just went his way."

"You are lying," Karpo said calmly.

"You may think what you like," said Anatoly.

"A boy was murdered near the Mahezh Shopping Center yesterday, a rapper," said Karpo.

The Mahezh was an underground mall off of Red Square where Russian rappers in loose-fitting parkas and baggy pants gathered.

"So?"

"You killed him," said Karpo.

"I . . . I was nowhere near there yesterday. I have never killed anyone. I was with Heinrich and friends all day. We . . ."

"But you killed the boy," said Karpo.

"No."

"I have a policeman who will testify that he saw you do it," said Karpo.

"I did not kill anyone," Anatoly said. "Ask Heinrich. Ask . . ."

Karpo moved to the door and opened it. A young uniformed policeman stepped inside.

Karpo nodded toward Bottle Kaps and said, "Is that him?"

The young policeman looked at Anatoly and said, "Yes."

"You are certain?" asked Karpo.

"Certain," said the policeman, who turned to leave.

"Wait," cried Anatoly. "You . . . it must have been someone else. We look alike."

The policeman was gone. Karpo had asked him to step in and identify the young man Karpo had brought into the precinct two hours earlier. Karpo had said nothing about a murder and, as far as Karpo knew, there had been no murder.

"I did not kill anyone," Anatoly insisted, his arms now in front of him. "That cop is . . . I understand."

Karpo said nothing.

"You are bluffing just to get me to tell you what happened to the Naked Cossack."

"One minute," said Karpo. "I give you one minute. Tell me what happened or you go back in the cage and I give Sergei the opportunity to tell me and walk out the door while you remain to be tried for murder."

"You are bluffing," said Anatoly with mock confidence.

"You are running out of seconds," said Karpo.

The young man looked at the pale unsmiling figure in black. He knew the police had taken others off the streets, put them in jail for crimes they had not committed, found witnesses, usually the police themselves, to testify to their guilt. Anatoly had heard such stories. Such arrests accomplished two things. They officially solved a crime and they put someone in jail the police wanted off the streets.

"Your time is up," Karpo said, gathering his papers.

"No, wait."

"Your time is up," Karpo repeated, turning toward the door.

"I will tell you, but you do not let Sergei or anyone else know I told you," the young man said in near panic.

Karpo started to open the door.

"Please," called Anatoly. "It was the girl, the red-haired girl, the crazy one who calls herself Anarchista. The one in Naked Cossack's band. She paid us. Told us the Naked Cossack was a Jew. She gave him something in his drink at Loni's and we put him in a car. He was unconscious. She drove away. That is all I know."

"She paid you?" Karpo said, looking back.

"Cash and . . . and a quick fuck for both of us behind Loni's."

Karpo closed the door and turned to face the young man, who was bouncing on his heels nervously.

"What did she say she was going to do with him?"

"I do not know."

"Kill him?"

"She did not say. She was high on something. Happy. It was a game. The sex, everything. A game. I do not know where she took him."

It was getting worse all the time. No foundation. Creatures like this roamed the streets and alleys. Democracy had not brought democracy. It had brought chaos and anarchy. The girl had aptly named herself. There was no dignity, no sense of mission in catching her, in freeing Misha Lovski if he was still alive. There was only the task.

"If he dies or is dead, you are an accomplice to murder."

"But I told you what happened," Anatoly whined. "You owe me for that."

"And for many things," said Karpo. "Many things."

The open-air stalls in Gorbushka market were closed. Snow was more than a foot deep and the temperature was below freezing with an occasional sweep of cold wind bending the branches of the surrounding trees. The only real activity was in the dingy concrete building at the edge of the market.

The interior of the building was packed with people, almost all younger than thirty, laughing, haggling, swearing. Music screamed, a hundred different sounds, voices in a dozen languages, instruments knifing through the bodies.

Karpo and Zelach walked through the crowd, drawing stares, glares, and occasional comments, though no one was quite up to facing the pale man in black.

"Vampire in the daytime," said one boy, head shaven, teeth bad.

Some assumed the two men were older sympathizers, last-generation pavers of the way. There were a few holdovers. Maybe these two were here to buy or sell. Maybe.

The huge open space was warm with bodies and rank with sweat and the oil on leather jackets decorated with skulls, swastikas, church towers, bottles marked *poison*, daggers, guns. A fat man in a black sweat shirt stood behind a table covered with German World War II medals, all imitation. He held up a watch and shouted, "The real thing. The real thing. Look at it."

At another table were books and pamphlets with titles like *Defending Russian Purity* and

International Skinhead Bulletin.

Karpo and Zelach moved on, scanning the crowd, looking for the girl. There were many girls with bright-red hair, most of them blocked by larger young men and boys.

Another table was doing a brisk business in Confederate flags and hats, white hoods advertised as genuine Ku Klux Klan antiques.

More tables. Boots, boots, boots, German army T-shirts and uniforms.

Noise. Stares.

Earlier, Karpo and Zelach had gone back to the apartment of Misha Lovski. The door they had broken had been repaired. They knocked and a voice had answered, "What?"

"Police," Karpo had said.

"Shit, not again. Do not break the door. I am coming."

A few seconds later the door had opened to reveal Valery Postnov, the frail blond boy who called himself Pure Knuckles. There seemed nothing pure about him, and his knuckles, both detectives knew, were bony and thin. One good punch and the boy's hand would be broken.

"What?" he asked dreamily, wearing only soiled white briefs, scratching his hairless chest. "You find the Cossack?"

The room had not been cleaned or cleared or touched since their last visit.

"Nina Aronskaya," Karpo said. "Where is she?"

"Anarchista?"

"Yes."

"Why?"

"Because I ask," said Karpo, staring down at the boy who tried to hold his ground.

"I do not know where she is," he said.

"You will come with us," said Karpo. "Put on some clothes."

"Where are we going?" the boy asked, looking at Zelach, who blinked behind his glasses.

"Somewhere where you will be very uncomfortable," said Karpo. "Somewhere where you will remember where Nina Aronskaya is. Somewhere where you will remember perhaps where Misha Lovski is."

"I do not know where the Cossack is," the boy said. "He is . . . this is no big thing. He just wandered for a few days. He will come back."

"Put on your pants," said Karpo. "You have one minute. It is cold outside today. One minute or we take you as you are."

The boy looked at Zelach, who continued to do his best to look impassive. He wanted to tell the boy to do what Karpo wanted, that Karpo had been behaving even more strangely than usual, that the boy would be very sorry if he did not cooperate. Zelach willed the boy not to show any disrespect. Karpo was never in the mood for disrespect for the law. Today would be a particularly bad day to test him.

"She went with Acid," the boy said.

"Yakov Mitsin," said Karpo.

"Yes," the boy said. "To the Gorbushka. They are looking for new clothes, giving us a new look in case the Cossack does not come back."

"You just told us you were sure he would be back," said Karpo.

"I know, but Anarchista said we should not count on it. She is getting a little . . . forget it."

"A little what?" asked Karpo.

"She said the Cossack is a Jew, that his father is rich," the boy said. "She has been talking crazy like that. They got new clothes for the band and when the Cossack comes back he will be pissed."

Karpo stared into the eyes of the boy, who tried to meet the look but gave up.

"Does Mitsin have a cell phone? The girl?"

"No," said the boy.

"If you are lying and you call them, we will return for you," said Karpo.

"I will not be here," the boy said. "This is getting too . . . I am getting out."

"No," said Karpo. "You will stay here. If you leave, we will find you and you will not be pleased when we do. You understand?"

"I will be here," the boy said with a sigh.

Then the policemen had headed for the market.

It was Zelach who spotted the girl, not because his eyes were more keen than Karpo's. They were not. Not because he was looking more closely. He was not. It was a sense he could not explain, a sense his mother had taught him to accept. One moment he was looking at random faces and the next he felt that he should turn left and look all the way across the room. The crowd parted for a fraction of an instant and he saw her.

"There," he said to Karpo.

Karpo turned his eyes toward where Zelach was looking. He was tall enough to see over most of the people who shuffled and stomped down the aisles, and he caught a glimpse of scarlet hair.

It was pointless for Emil Karpo to try to hide in the crowd, in any crowd. People parted when he approached, even people inside this concrete shrine to hatred.

"Go to the door," he told Zelach. "She does not get out."

"Yes," said Zelach.

"You understand?"

"Yes," he said.

"If you must shoot her or anyone who attempts to stop you, do so, but try not to kill them."

Zelach did not say yes. He did not nod. Karpo was already beyond him, making his way toward the girl with the flaming-red hair. Zelach looked toward the girl, who did not seem to have noticed the two policemen. He made his way as quickly as he could back to the main entrance. People did not part for him as they had when he was at Karpo's side. He was jostled, given nasty looks. He heard a few muttered insults and some not so muttered. Alone he looked less formidable and more like a storekeeper or office worker who had made the wrong turn into a bad neighborhood at lunchtime.

It took him almost a full minute to get back to the front entrance. He patted his jacket with the inside of his right arm and felt his gun resting in the holster. He was almost certain that he would be unable to shoot the girl or anyone else unless they were armed and directly threatening him. He would brandish his gun, which might bring the crowd down on him but might succeed in stopping the girl. He could fire into the ceiling, which might bring the crowd down on him and might stop the girl. Or he could try to subdue her and hold her till Karpo came to his aid.

Zelach was not weak. He did not have

nearly the strength of Porfiry Petrovich Rostnikov or Iosef Rostnikov or Emil Karpo, but he was not without his reserves.

That was what he would do.

Zelach was now convinced that something had happened to Karpo, that he would have to tell someone about the strange things he was doing, but who? Porfiry Petrovich was the logical choice, but he was on a train heading into Siberia. Zelach had no desire to come face to face with Director Igor Yaklovev, who might not believe him or might not care. He had the distinct feeling — no, the certainty — that Yaklovev considered Zelach a fool to be suffered because Chief Inspector Rostnikov wanted him.

Emil Karpo was the senior inspector in the Office of Special Investigation in Porfiry Petrovich's absence. Zelach decided to do what he always did in difficult situations. He would ask his mother.

Positioned next to the door, trying not to draw attention to himself and failing miserably, Zelach adjusted his glasses, leaned back against the wall, and plunged his hands into his pockets.

Across the room in the vicinity of where he had seen the girl, Zelach could make out the spear-straight figure of Emil Karpo. He wished he could hear what was being said. He had the distinct feeling that it was not going well.

Had he been close to Karpo and privy to the conversation, he would have seen and heard what follows:

Neither the girl nor Yakov Mitsin at her side noticed Karpo approaching. They were haggling over the cost of studded-denim and leather jackets, caps, and belts with a thin man wearing a black overcoat.

"Nina Aronskaya," Karpo said.

The girl froze in mid-sentence. She had met Karpo but once. She would never forget his voice and knew what she would see when she turned.

Mitsin turned first and faced him. Then she turned.

Karpo said nothing. He ignored the young man and looked at the girl. She was overly made-up, her artificially powdered face even whiter than Karpo's own. Her lips were a bright artificial red that matched her short hair. She wore a ring through her nose, which she had not borne when Karpo had seen her naked in Misha Lovski's apartment.

The look of fear was there and gone almost before it came into existence, but Karpo recognized it. Now would come the bluff, the lies. They would come if Karpo did not stop them. People around them were watching them now, sensing a confrontation.

"Misha Lovski," answered Karpo.

"How did you find us?" Yakov Mitsin asked.

Karpo ignored him.

"You found him?" the girl asked.

"If we had, I would not be here."

"What do you want?" asked Mitsin, looking at the watching circle of faces.

Karpo continued to ignore him.

Mitsin was wearing a leather jacket covered with patches displaying weapons. The girl wore an almost-matching jacket, but hers bore painted images of naked males and females, some pressing together facing each other or with the male figure behind.

"Where is Misha Lovski?" Karpo asked the girl.

"I do not know," she said. "How should I know? I am not his mother."

"That is Anarchista," a male voice came from behind Karpo.

"And that is Acid," came a female voice. "It is Acid."

"You drugged him, had Heinrich and Bottle Kaps put him in a car, and you took him somewhere," Karpo said. "You will tell me here and now where he is. Then you will go with me to find him or his body."

"You are crazy," said Mitsin, getting between Karpo and the girl, putting his face up inches before the taller detective, playing to the crowd.

"You will step out of the way," Karpo said, so quietly that Mitsin could barely hear him. "Or I will shoot you in the left leg just above the knee. The pain will be unbearable and you will be fortunate to walk normally again."

Mitsin's smirk faded. In the eyes of the tall ghost he could see truth. He stepped out of the way and said, "We are not going with you."

"No," agreed the crowd, which pressed forward slightly.

More and more people in the concrete block were now aware that something was happening. Fights were not uncommon here. Murder was not unheard of just outside the doors.

Karpo showed not the slightest fear or concern, and in fact he felt none. He was calm, ready, and very determined. For an instant he considered that he might welcome an attack from the crowd.

The girl seemed uncertain. She looked at Mitsin, who avoided her eyes.

"What happens if I tell you?"

"That depends on where he is, if he is alive and well, and why you did it," said Karpo.

"Do not talk to him," called a burly skinhead in the front of the small circle.

"He is alive," she said. "I think he is alive. It was just a joke. He is alive. Someone wants to teach him a lesson, that is all."

"Someone paid you," said Karpo. "Who?"

The burly skinhead pushed ahead of the crowd. Karpo barely glanced at him. The detective's hand went inside his jacket and came out with a gun pointed directly at the skinhead, who suddenly stopped.

"Who paid you?" asked Karpo.

The girl hesitated, her eyes moving around, considering a run for the exit, hoping the crowd would protect her. Her thoughts went no further than that.

"It would be a very bad idea," Karpo said, seeming to read her thoughts.

The girl who called herself Anarchista gulped nervously and Karpo could see tears forming in her eyes. He could also see two men moving quickly through the crowd, two men who fit into the scene even less than Karpo and Zelach.

The men were wearing identical dark suits with white shirts and ties. They had the look of athletes. Both were no more than forty.

"Where is he?" asked Karpo as the two men moved behind the girl and Mitsin.

Suddenly both men had weapons in their hands. One of the two, the larger, had a small machine gun, which he had pulled from under his coat. Karpo turned his gun on the two men. The crowd began to back away in panic. People screamed and fell. Tables toppled.

Each of the men in suits grabbed an arm of the girl and began to back away with her. Mitsin moved with them. They were all facing Karpo, who was certain he could shoot the man with the automatic weapon through his forehead before he could fire. It was unlikely that he would get off a shot at the second man before he himself was killed.

The quartet backed away toward the entrance, toward Zelach, who had his weapon in two hands aimed at the backs of the two men.

Zelach fired.

The man not holding the machine gun fell to his knees but did not scream. The crowd was screaming louder, making for the exit, blocking Zelach's vision. He could not fire again without the risk of hitting someone innocent or, given the nature of those in the building, someone who was at least innocent of what was taking place at the moment.

The man behind Nina Aronskaya ducked with her as cover and kept backing away, leaving his partner on his knees. Karpo could shoot the girl or Mitsin, but there was no point to it.

The man with the gun, Mitsin, and the girl

joined the fleeing crowd and swept past Zelach through the doors and into the cold day.

Karpo followed, nodding to Zelach to deal with the fallen man. In the street, Karpo saw Mitsin entering the back seat of a black car with heavily tinted windows. The door closed and the car pulled away. Karpo hurried back into the building, where Zelach stood over the fallen man. The man's weapon had been kicked professionally out of reach.

"He needs a doctor," Zelach said.

The wounded man, now in a sitting position on the concrete floor, turned his head toward Karpo. Zelach's bullet had entered his right thigh. Blood was oozing out. The pain must have been great, but the man did not show it. He calmly removed his belt and began to use it as a tourniquet around the top of his thigh.

"Get an ambulance," Karpo said to Zelach.

Zelach said nothing. He holstered his gun and looked around for a phone. The hall was clear of people now and he saw no phone. But he did see a glass door in one corner that might well lead to an office. He hurried toward it, half expecting to hear a gunshot, half expecting to turn and see the wounded gunman on his back, dead or dying.

But there was no shot. Emil Karpo had already decided what to do with the wounded man.

Chapter Five

Frightened wolves, nowhere to go
Find winding cloths of sleet and snow
The sleeping kings of long ago
Deep beneath Ben Bulben grow
Drifts are shifted by the plough
Like waves that break against the prow
How do you like your blue-eyed boy now
Mr. Death?

Porfiry Petrovich Rostnikov was seated in the dining car, his notebook in his lap, a mechanical pencil in one hand, a cup of tea before him. It was just before dawn and he had the car to himself except for a train attendant who sat in the rear, his head against the window, his mouth open, his eyes closed.

For some reason, probably the jostling of the train, Rostnikov found it difficult to sleep. What remained of his left leg kept waking him with a vibration he was sure no one with full limbs would understand.

Added to that he had a nightmare. No, that

is not exactly right. He was filled with neither fear, horror, nor repulsion during the dream, only a morbid curiosity.

In the dream, he had opened his eyes and found himself on an operating table. Paulinin stood over him, a bloody saw in his hand. Behind Paulinin, blazing down on the helpless Rostnikov, were the bright lights of an operating room. Paulinin nodded his head to the right. Rostnikov turned his eyes in that direction and saw what certainly was his severed left leg a few feet away. There was something sad about the leg. Rostnikov felt like weeping. He turned back to look at Paulinin but the scientist was gone. Rostnikov found himself staring directly into the sun. He felt heat, thought he would go blind, and then a warmth came over him. That was when he awoke in darkness to the clanking of steel wheels. The others in his cabin were quiet except for one of the old Americans, who snored gently. Rostnikov had risen, dressed quietly, found his notebook, and gone to the dining car after picking up a cup of tea using an English tea bag and the steaming water from the samovar in the corridor.

Now Rostnikov drew the nearby mountains, very roughly, and tried to suggest the first rays of sunlight coming over them. He was dissatisfied. He tried traditional rays, almost like the paintings of a child, erased them and tried an indistinct, faint arch between two ridges. He moved up an inch and drew an even-less-distinct arch. Then, to show the contrast between light and dark, he shaded in the foreground, trees, mountains. He would have liked to suggest something dark and wild in the early shadows but he was not a good enough artist for that.

It was just after five in the morning, according to Rostnikov's wristwatch. He knew the train would pass through many time zones before Vladivostok. He did not try to keep track by changing his watch, though he was aware of when the train would reach each stop.

While he worked on the rising sun, someone approached down the aisle. He did not look up. He did not have to. He recognized the slight perfume of the woman who had called herself Svetlana Britchevna. She sat across from him.

"You are also an artist," she said. "A plumber and an artist. Interesting combination. There is a depth to you, Ivan Pavlov."

Rostnikov raised his eyes but not his head. She was wearing a loose, light-blue sweater and a darker skirt. She had a cup in her hand. Rostnikov could smell the coffee.

"And to you, Svetlana Britchevna," he said,

putting the finishing touches to his drawing.

"May I ask what you are drawing?"

"The sun," he said. "For reasons I cannot explain, I have been dreaming of the sun, the fragile sun."

"The sun is fragile?" she asked, amused.

"All life is fragile," he said.

"And the sun is alive?"

"Sometimes I think all life is the sun. Perhaps I should consider becoming a pagan, a sun worshiper."

"And," she said, taking a sip of coffee, "spending hours in the nude in worship."

"It would not be a sight that would delight the sun god," said Rostnikov. "He might be so offended that he would strike me with skin cancer."

"From the metaphysical to the pragmatic," she said. "We can add poetry to your list of accomplishments, Porfiry Petrovich Rostnikov."

Rostnikov showed no reaction to her having used his name. Instead, he clicked his pencil, put it in his shirt pocket, closed his notebook, put it next to him, and drank the last of his tea. Then he looked at her.

"I did not expect to surprise you," she said. "You knew something of who I was last night."

"Your approach was designed to alert me,"

he said, folding his hands. "I wonder only at why you want me to know."

"I work for the ministry," she said. "Not high on the ladder, but not at the bottom either. My mission on this train is to watch a certain Pavel Cherkasov. We try to keep track of certain figures who do not like to walk in your sun."

"Pavel Cherkasov," Rostnikov repeated.

"My mission is considered by my superiors to be very low priority, routine. Others could have been selected ahead of me but none particularly wanted to ride the Trans-Siberian Express."

"Why?"

"They find the trip boring and the assignment the same," she said.

"But you do not," said Rostnikov.

"I do not," she said. "I have some information which the ministry provided for me and some I have picked up through my own connections and bribes from my own pocket."

"You are ambitious," Rostnikov said.

"Very," she answered, her smile broadening. "One of the bribes I paid was to place you in Pavel Cherkasov's compartment."

"Drovny, the man with the jokes," said Rostnikov. Rostnikov looked out the window, his eyes ahead, searching for the first light of the sun, but it was still too early, though perhaps he sensed the faintest hint of morning light. "And our discussion last night?" he asked.

"To test you," she said.

"Did I pass your test?"

"Yes. And so did your assistant, Tkach. I tried to seduce him. I am very good at it and my information was that he was very susceptible. He did not succumb."

"I am pleased to hear that," said Rostnikov. "You are out of coffee. Shall I get you more?"

"No, thank you," she said. "I have a proposal for you."

Rostnikov sat attentively.

"I have told you who you are looking for. I can tell you where his transaction will take place. You will tell me what his mission is, and if we succeed in catching him in the act, I get credit for his apprehension."

"And what do I get?" asked Rostnikov.

"Whatever it is Cherkasov is planning to get or give or both. We each have information the other needs. I see no point in our doing battle. Time is running short."

"There is a long way to go," said Rostnikov.

"Not for Cherkasov. I know about you, Rostnikov. I am willing to trust you. Tell me we have an agreement and I will tell you where and when and with whom he plans to make whatever transaction he has planned."

"Why not simply seduce Cherkasov?" Rostnikov asked.

"He is not interested in women. His passion is bad jokes, expensive food, and high living. Well?"

Rostnikov fleetingly considered asking the
woman for identification but it would be
meaningless. Anything could be forged. Even
if he did not believe her, he did not see that he
had anything to lose. The Yak wanted the
money and whatever it was Cherkasov was
exchanging it for. The woman, if she was to
be believed, wanted Cherkasov and the person he was dealing with. She would need
something to prove her case. That could be
arranged.

"We are in a temporary alliance," he said.

"Ekaterinburg," she said.

Fitting, thought Rostnikov. Ekaterinburg,
which had been Sverdlovsk during the Soviet
era, was where the Bolsheviks had taken the
family of Czar Nicholas II in 1918 and killed
them in a small, dank stone basement.
Sverdlovsk was the name of the Bolshevik
who had planned and carried out the execution of the royal Romanov family. It was also,
Rostnikov knew, the birthplace of Boris
Yeltsin.

"What do you know about Ekaterinburg?"
she asked.

"It is on the Iset River, about a million and a half people, the capital of the Sverdlovsk Oblast region. Steelmaking, the Pittsburgh of Siberia. Industrial, turbines, ball bearings, other things. I believe there are even gold mines nearby."

"And copper," she said. "Titanium. It is what the Americans call a boom town since the end of the Soviet Union. America is the region's number-one investor with one-hundred-and-fourteen million dollars. Coca-Cola, Pepsi, US West, Ford, IBM, Procter & Gamble. Three Lufthansa flights a day to Frankfurt."

"Impressive," said Rostnikov.

"It is also the murder capital of the region, possibly of all Russia, possibly the world. The Uralmash Mafia controls the city. The heads of the Ministry of Justice and the director of the Federal Security Service visited Ekaterinburg to investigate corruption, and a commission from the Ministry of Internal Affairs of the Russian Federation convened there for almost two weeks to investigate charges that the head of the regional military, Lieutenant General Kraev, was connected to the Mafia."

"And they discovered?"

"That he was innocent, of course. The commission did not address the contract killings."

Rostnikov was aware that the region was a center of gang activity.

"More than one thousand twenty-five killings for the Sverdlovsk Oblast region, the most criminal region in all of Russia," she said. "Almost ninety-six thousand major crimes. Examples: There was a contract killing last year of a thirty-year-old gang member named Lebedev. Shot ten times by an automatic pistol in the courtyard of his home on Frezerovschikov Street, eleven in the morning. Three days later there was a car bombing in a parking garage on Pekhotinstev Street. Five cars blown up. No one killed. Two days later, near the Svetly health center, a Mercedes-230 belonging to Anatoly Dmitriev, the center's director, was blown up. He escaped."

"Interesting," said Rostnikov.

"More than interesting," she said. "Crucial. One of the Uralmash killers is on this train. I believe he is following Pavel. I believe he plans to get to him before we do. We must not allow that to happen."

"Pavel Cherkasov is a very popular man," said Rostnikov.

"Not a result of his sense of humor," she said.

"Who is this Uralmash killer?"

"Ah," she said, sitting back. "I have a name, from the same source that provided me with the information about the location of the transaction. Our killer's name is Vladimir Golk."

"And our next big stop is . . ." Rostnikov began.

"Ekaterinburg," she said. "This afternoon."

"Of course," said Rostnikov. "The sun is beginning to rise."

She turned to look out the window. "Impressive," she said.

"I think we can order breakfast now. Shall we wake Sasha and have something to eat?"

"I am suddenly quite hungry," she said, rising.

Rostnikov tucked his notebook in his pocket and rose with difficulty. There was no cloud cover. The sun would be bright, the train windows frosted. It was the promise of a good day, but Rostnikov had learned from experience that the sun was indifferent to the petty crimes of man.

Sasha had staggered into the dining car, looking for Rostnikov, who had not been in his cabin or in the lounge. He found him seated at a table with Svetlana Britchevna, having coffee, their breakfast plates pushed to the side.

Rostnikov motioned to him.

The car was not crowded. This was the first call to breakfast, but there were early risers, most of them with the tired morning look of insomnia or disorientation. Most looked at newspapers. A few sat trying to wake up.

The Trans-Siberian Express was an adventure but, after two days, the train like almost any other became a soporific cradle. Sleep always seemed to beckon. Avid conversations ended in closed eyes and books on laps.

Games of cards had already begun in the lounge car and some of the compartments Sasha had passed. He had seen nothing that resembled the suitcase for which they searched.

Sasha sat next to Rostnikov and looked at the woman. She seemed awake, alert, and glowing with energy which Sasha could not meet. He had not slept well, not well at all.

"You have met Miss Britchevna," Rostnikov said, motioning to the waiter and indicating through simple mime that another cup was needed for coffee.

"Yes," said Sasha cautiously.

"She tells me you behaved like a gentleman in spite of her charms and advances."

Sasha said nothing as the waiter approached and poured a cup of coffee. Sasha ordered yoghurt, black bread, and an orange.

"We have entered an unholy alliance with Miss Britchevna," said Rostnikov. "She has told me where the transfer will take place and the name of the man we are seeking, but there are complications."

Rostnikov explained the situation. Svetlana Britchevna listened, drank coffee, and added nothing.

"And so," said Rostnikov. "We have several hours. All we need do is watch our Pavel Cherkasov, be alert for the assassin, and step forward at the moment of interception."

"That is all," said Sasha with a sigh, indicating that the task promised to be far from easy.

"You and Svetlana . . . may I use your first name?" Rostnikov asked.

"You both may," she said, looking from one man to the other.

"You will jointly watch our Pavel every moment from the time we leave this table. Find him and watch him."

"We can play the role of lovers," the woman said. "Since I know I cannot corrupt you, you will have to be a good actor. Are you a good actor, Sasha Tkach?"

In spite of what he knew about the woman, Sasha was stirred. Her eyes met his. She made it clear with a smile that she recognized the ripple of desire she was causing. Svetlana Britchevna was pleased. She had perhaps six or seven more years, perhaps more if she were fortunate and took care of herself, to have this effect on men, an effect that could be turned and tuned to her ambition. And her ambition was considerable. She intended to become the highest-ranking female member of the ministry. If she did not move too quickly and used the skills of men like Rostnikov, she might even rise to the very top. She did not say this aloud to anyone. There was no point to it and no one close enough to her with whom she wished to share her ambition. Besides, she would have been considered seriously deluded for believing that she could penetrate the all-male power structure.

"I have played many roles," Sasha said as his black bread and yoghurt were brought to the table.

"Settled," said Rostnikov. "I have some news for you, Sasha. Svetlana has allowed me to use her little cell phone to call Moscow. Anna Timofeyeva has checked on Matvei Labroadovnik."

"How is he involved?" Svetlana asked.

"In our enterprise? Not at all. In Sasha's life, monumentally. The man is, indeed, an artist of some secondary repute. He is, indeed, working in Istra on the Cathedral of the Resurrection."

Sasha wanted to feel relieved. The prospect of his mother actually removing her shadow from his family promised a new start for Sasha and Maya, but he could tell from Porfiry Petrovich's voice that there was more coming. And it came.

"Matvei Labroadovnik has won awards," Rostnikov said. "He has had some government and private commissions, but, according to Anna Timofeyeva, he is now considered somewhat of a relic, a hopelessly old-fashioned artist whose time has long come and gone, been revived, faltered. This is Anna Timofeyeva's conclusion. She has also concluded with certainty through confidential sources that Matvei Labroadovnik is down to his last few thousand rubles and has already spent the advance he received for his work on the cathedral."

Sasha nodded. He felt an odd mixture of vindication and disappointment.

"Thank you," he said. "I will address this when we return to Moscow."

"My guess, Sasha," Rostnikov said, reaching down to scratch just above his left knee, "is that Matvei may already have told Lydia that he is without money. If he is reasonably clever, he would realize that she might have resources for finding out his financial status."

"Then there would be nothing I could do," said Sasha.

"You could consider that he is sincere,"

said Rostnikov. "You could wait and see what develops. You could pay him a friendly visit. You could make plans for attending your mother's wedding, should it prove inevitable."

"If he is seeking my mother's money," said Sasha, "he will learn that there is a steep price to pay for it."

"You could break his fingers," the woman said with interest. "He is an artist."

"No," said Sasha, "the price he would pay would be in having to live with my mother. She is no fool. She will not part with a single ruble easily unless it is for me or my family, and when she does, there is always an unspoken demand for respect and compliance. The artist will pay dearly and probably wind up with very little for his efforts."

"I agree," said Rostnikov. "A question."

Svetlana and Sasha looked at him.

"If all the oil in the world comes from fossil fuels, there must have been billions of dinosaurs. And those dinosaurs must have died suddenly and been buried instantly. If they died naturally or from predators, there would have been nothing remaining except bones, nothing to turn to oil. Out that window."

Rostnikov looked out at a vast plain of small trees.

"Out that window thousands of dinosaurs

must have roamed, fought for food, grown enormous. Either the oil we have does not come from fossils, the oil out there below this very ground, or some cataclysm engulfed the earth. What happened?"

Neither Svetlana nor Sasha answered. She was thinking about Pavel Cherkasov. He was thinking about his mother.

"The sun," said Rostnikov. "The source of life. Something happened to the sun. It ceased to burn or something came between it and the earth. Something sudden."

Svetlana wondered for an instant if Rostnikov might be just a bit mad. Sasha had heard such musings on a variety of subjects many times before. He knew Porfiry Petrovich Rostnikov was a man with unfathomable imagination.

"It could happen again," said Rostnikov. "In the next few seconds. That which we think is important, whatever it might be, would be meaningless. Life would have to begin again. Perhaps the cockroaches would not even survive this time."

"Perhaps," said Sasha, glancing at the woman, whose eyes were fixed upon him.

"It is sometimes good to remember that the things we believe are important have little ultimate meaning," said Rostnikov.

"One might be depressed," said Svetlana.

"One might," Rostnikov agreed. "But one might also be relieved. Like the Hindus we are free, if we choose, of earthly connection. There is the immediate moment, the likely short-term present, and the distant possible future. And in the immediate moment, it would be a good idea to find Pavel Cherkasov."

Sasha had finished his breakfast. Svetlana Britchevna rose. So did he. They left Rostnikov sitting at the table.

At the end of the car she turned to Sasha and said, "Does he often talk like that?"

"Often," he said.

She took his hand. He considered pulling away but did not.

"We are lovers, remember," she said, turning her face to his.

Sasha would find it difficult to forget.

Pavel Cherkasov was awake and dressed. He had several jokes he wanted to try out on whoever might be fortunate enough to be seated with him for breakfast.

Pavel had a well-honed sense of imagined smell. He considered food first as a remembered savory odor, followed by recalled taste. Confirmation came in seeing the food, and taste was an ecstasy that surpassed sex.

He was alone. The old Americans and the one-legged Russian were gone. The old men,

Pavel knew, needed little sleep at night and many naps during the day. Perhaps they had all gone to lunch early and saved him a seat at their table. He would listen patiently to their stories of a war long past, eat modestly in anticipation of a very important day, and try out his jokes. He had retrieved his suitcase and would keep it at his side until the moment came to exchange it for the smaller package on the railway platform. He would explain, if anyone asked, that he carried the duffel bag because he had papers inside it he would be needing, that he would be spending much of the day working. They would not question him. The bag was not large. The bills were packed tightly. People, Pavel knew, displayed little curiosity about such things.

Satisfied that he was properly dressed for the day, he stood up and looked out of the window. In the vast plain, he did not imagine wandering dinosaurs or a dying sun.

Soon, he thought, I can head back to civilization. Soon I can be on an airplane heading for Paris or Vienna or New York. Soon.

The compartment door opened. Pavel turned from the window and smiled. "I was just heading for the dining car," he said, duffel bag in hand.

The watcher stepped forward, covered Pavel's mouth with one hand, and plunged the long pointed awl deep into his heart. Pavel tasted the moist unpleasantness of the watcher's hand. Gone was the imagined odor of food. His final taste was of dirt and human flesh.

There must be a joke to fit such an occasion, but Pavel could think of none. The pain was brief and then Pavel was dead. He sank to the floor.

The watcher picked up the duffel bag, leaving the awl where it was.

A man and woman carrying their suitcases and arguing in Russian, their son of no more than eight or nine trailing behind them, wedged past Sasha and Svetlana. They were the family Sasha and Porfiry Petrovich had gotten onto the train behind.

"It is too soon," the woman said.

"It is better to be first in line to get off," the man said. "How many times are we going to talk about this? We are getting to the door. We can sit on the bags."

"For two hours?" the woman asked.

The little boy dragged a bag, listening to his parents. He looked up at Sasha and Svetlana apologetically, embarrassed by his parents.

"You fight with your wife like that?" Svetlana said as they moved forward. She held his hand.

"Not like that," Sasha said.

"But you fight," she said.

"All couples fight," he said. "Porfiry Petrovich says it goes in cycles. Honeymoon, fights, truce, shorter honeymoon, fights, truce, crisis, tentative peace agreement, followed by comfort and only minor conflict."

"Always?" she asked, playing with his hand.

"No, not always," said Sasha.

"My vision is different," she said. "Brief honeymoon and it is over. Next honeymoon. Stop before the first fight."

"The relationship never gets, what is the word? . . ."

"Deeper?" she supplied. "No, depth requires commitment and effort. My need for male contact, sexual and romantic, is very much alive, but I reserve my depth for myself, my work, my ambition."

They were glancing into compartments now just in case Pavel Cherkasov might be inside of one, though they both knew that his own compartment was in the next car.

"You feel the need to confess all this to me?" he asked.

"It is not a confession," she said, turning to him. "It is a proposal which may or may not come to fruition. Consider it."

"I think not," he said.

"I think you will," she said. "But when and

where will depend on what takes place in the next two hours or so."

What took place next put Svetlana's proposition far from either of their minds. They reached the compartment of Pavel Cherkasov. The door was closed, the curtains drawn.

Svetlana did not hesitate. Sasha had known her for only a few hours but he was sure she would have a bold and plausible excuse if someone was inside. She slid open the door.

The bloody body of Pavel Cherkasov lay on the floor, the long awl protruding from his chest. That he was dead was without doubt. His eyes were closed. His mouth was open. His face was white and his shirt and jacket a deep, dark, and bloody red.

Sasha closed the door. Svetlana began a quick search. It took moments.

"No money," she said.

Neither expected to find it.

"I'll stay here," she said. "You get Rostnikov."

Sasha said nothing. He went through the door and heard her lock it behind him. What she would say to the old Americans if they returned would, he was sure, be most inventive and bold.

Rostnikov was seated in the lounge, talking, in fact, to the two old Americans.

"Yes," the tall one, Allberry, was saying.

"We were First Army. You lost your leg on this side of the front. I lost the hearing in my left ear on the other, and Jack lost his mind for two years."

"Three years," the other old man, Susman, said. "Don't even remember what it was I saw that put me into cuckoo land, but I spent almost three years in a basket. Hell of a war."

"Yes," said Rostnikov in English, looking up to see Sasha motioning to him. "Hell of a war. Please excuse me. I have to tend to my leg. You understand."

"Perfectly," said Jack.

Rostnikov rose and the two men continued to talk.

"He is dead," Sasha whispered when Rostnikov was at his side. "Cherkasov."

Sasha led the way through the cars. People passed. They stepped around the luggage of the man, woman, and child Svetlana and Sasha had encountered minutes earlier. The family was at the end of a car in the small alcove near the door. They were not speaking. The man was eating a piece of cheese. The woman sat sullenly. The little boy dozed.

When they reached the car, Sasha knocked and said, "It is us."

The door slid open. They moved in and Svetlana slid it closed and locked it.

"The Americans are in the lounge car," Sasha said.

She nodded and said, "He has been dead no more than ten minutes."

It was awkward for Rostnikov to kneel. He did not try. He accepted her word. Rostnikov eased himself down into a seat. Svetlana and Sasha stood, waiting, swaying with the movement of the train.

Rostnikov was taken by the fact that the sunlight cast a broad bright beam across the dead man. Rostnikov imagined the sun intensifying, an amazing heat that touched only what fell within the beam, consuming the body without smoke or fire, absorbing it, taking it, making it a part of timelessness. But the body did not disappear.

"Why did he kill him before he made the exchange in Ekaterinburg?" he asked himself aloud.

"Panic. Perhaps he just wanted the money," answered Sasha.

"Our assassin is a professional," Svetlana said. "He would not panic."

"Then he has a plan," said Rostnikov.

No one spoke for a moment. Then Rostnikov looked up at them. Svetlana understood immediately. It took Sasha a beat longer and he said, "He is going to take Cherkasov's place. He is going to make the transaction. The person he is to make the exchange with does not know Cherkasov."

"But he knows something that will identify him," Svetlana said.

"The bag," said Rostnikov. "Whoever is carrying the bag with the money when we reach the station is our assassin."

"What is he doing?" asked Sasha. "He is not going to turn over the money."

"He wants the person with the valuable prize to identify himself," said Svetlana. "Then he will take whatever it is he has and keep the money."

"Kill him on the train or the platform?" asked Sasha.

"Possibly," she said. "Maybe he will wait, follow him. Once he knows who the bearer is by sight . . . but he will probably kill him or her immediately."

"Why?" asked Sasha.

"Because of him," said Rostnikov, looking at the dead man. "The train will be in a panic when the body is discovered. He will want to get everything done quickly. At least that is what I would do."

"And I," agreed Svetlana.

"So, what do we do?" asked Rostnikov.

"Watch to see who gets off with the suitcase," said Sasha. "Stop him."

"Armed killer on a train platform," said

Rostnikov. "I think it would be better to catch him before we get to the station."

"How?" asked Svetlana. "We are not even sure what the suitcase looks like."

Rostnikov looked down at the body again. It showed no sign of becoming one with the universe. He got back up slowly.

"So how do we find him?" asked Sasha.

"We get the suitcase, inform him that we have it, and wait here for him to come and claim it," Rostnikov answered.

"And where is it?" Svetlana asked.

"A little boy is sitting on it at the end of the last car we came through," said Rostnikov.

Sasha and Svetlana looked at each other.

"The duffel bag the little boy is sitting on belonged to Cherkasov. It was on that shelf," said Rostnikov. "Cherkasov took a pair of pajamas and a robe out of it. My guess is that under the pajamas and robe was and still is a great deal of money. He was hiding it in plain sight. Our killer took it and has persuaded or paid the boy's parents to take it off the train when we stop. Your killer will get off carrying nothing, drawing no suspicion. He will pick up the bag from the little boy and wait for the person he intends to get the package from."

"You cannot be sure of this," Svetlana said.

"I cannot," Rostnikov agreed. "But that family had no duffel bag when we saw them board the train. In any case, it is easy to find out. I will go talk to the happy family. You two wait here."

Rostnikov left the compartment and slowly made his way through the car and into the next one where the three people sat.

"My name is Porfiry Petrovich Rostnikov," he said to the man and woman. He had his wallet out and showed them his identification card. "Someone has asked your boy to carry that bag off the train."

The couple said nothing.

"He told you not to tell anyone. I understand. He paid you already?"

"Yes," the woman said.

"Olga," the husband warned.

"I do not want trouble with the police," the woman said. "Do we have to give you the money he paid us?"

"No," said Rostnikov. "Keep what he gave you. In fact, I will add this to it."

He took several bills from his pocket and handed them to the woman, who gave them to the man.

"I take the bag and you go find the man who gave it to you. Find him and tell him that it was taken by the man with the bad leg."

"And we are in no trouble?" the man asked warily.

"None," said Rostnikov. "You are heroes

of the new Russian Confederacy. If you wish to give me your address, I will send you a medal."

"I have four medals," the man said. "Worthless. Bata," he said to the boy. "Go find the man. Tell him the man with the bad leg took the bag."

The boy got quickly to his feet, not sure of which direction to go.

"That way," said Rostnikov, pointing, and the boy hurried away.

Rostnikov picked up the duffel bag and moved back to the car where one dead person and two live ones waited for him.

Chapter Six

Before the crocus cloaked the steppe
Before the tadpoles and the nests
Jack Frost screamed, his voice so hoarse
The signalmen were blown off course
They passed Attila on his horse
Passed the Visigoths and the Norse
Villages with Viking forts
And knew not where they were

The Kolomenskaya, Kashirskaya, and Kantemirovskaya stops were in a row on the Gorkovsko-Zamoskvoretskaya Line, the green line. Iosef had spent the first two hours of his morning moving from one of these stations to the other, getting off, standing on the platform, pretending to be absorbed in a report in his hands. The report was a six-page memo from the Yak's sweaty assistant, Pankov, on proper procedures and terminology for filling out case reports.

Iosef had chosen his attire carefully, duplicating, as best he could, what Toomas Vana had been wearing when he was murdered. Iosef even carried Toomas Vana's briefcase. At each stop he positioned himself near a post or pillar in the same position witnesses had said Vana had been standing.

The odds of the woman's next attack coming at one of these three K stations were, according to Paulinin, three to one against. However, if she were to appear, he was making himself the ideal target.

Now he stood against a post at the Kashirskaya station. Nine o'clock in the morning. Traffic moderate at this station outside the central ring of the Koltsyevaya line. No one appeared to notice him. No woman fitting the description appeared.

Elena had agreed to the plan on one condition, that she accompany Iosef to each stop at a discreet distance and watch the crowd for anyone who might be the woman they sought. They had been at this for two hours and had not once made eye contact with each other.

A number of women in the crowds rushing to work or shopping or who-knows-where generally fit the description, but the only one who had come very close to Iosef had been wearing thick glasses and appeared to be searching for someone in the crowd. She was also carrying a heavy black-plastic shopping bag in her right hand, the hand Paulinin said had been seriously sprained or possibly broken.

Elena, hands plunged into the pockets of her coat, kept checking her watch to give the impression that she was in a hurry. The act had begun to bore her, but she kept it up, watching Iosef without staring.

He really did look the part: tall, good-looking, wearing his best suit, his only suit other than the one in which he sometimes worked. Over his suit he wore a serious black coat he had borrowed from a friend. All of the previous victims had been about ten years older than Iosef. So Iosef had touched his temples with gray and brushed his hair straight back.

Their discussion early in the morning over coffee and rolls had been a reprise of their discussions of the day before.

"We cannot be sure we will see her in time if she moves quickly," Elena had said.

"We will both be watching," he said.

"But . . ."

"Her right hand is probably useless," he said. "She will have to attack with her left. She should not be difficult to stop and, unlike the others, remember, I will be ready."

"Porfiry Petrovich would not approve if he were here," she said.

"We can ask him what he would have done

when he returns," said Iosef, "but we may be able to save a life or two before we wait for my father's opinion."

He was determined, stubborn. She knew that, had known it from the first time they had met. She too was stubborn. Kindred diverse spirits on this issue and many more positive ones.

She watched. People passed. Trains roared in, stopped, doors slid open, people moved in and out. The smell of bodies, food. Coughing, talking, echoes in the tunnels off of the ceiling.

Everyone could not be watched.

They kept it up for almost forty minutes. Iosef appeared to be just as absorbed in the report as he had for the past several hours. Elena, however, thought it might be time to move on, not that any other metro platform was more promising but simply because she was both bored and concerned.

They were dealing with a madwoman. Maybe this time she would have a gun. Maybe this time, left hand or not, she would plunge the blade of her knife into his stomach, between his ribs, into his neck or eye before he could react.

Enough. Elena slowly made her way across the platform and stepped directly in front of Iosef, who lowered the report. He smiled. She was breaking his cover.

"Can I help you?" he asked, as if they were strangers.

"Enough, Iosef," she said.

He let the smile go and nodded.

"Perhaps it was not such a very good idea," he said.

"It was not bad. We had nothing better. Now . . ."

"Now," he said, "we wait till we catch her in the act or right after she attacks her next victim or the one after that or the one . . ."

He shrugged and picked up the briefcase, clicking it open so he could drop the report into it. "You know, according to Pankov, Form four five three four is supposed to be done with five printed copies and a computer-disk copy."

"Fascinating," she said. "Let us go."

Inna Dalipovna saw the man and woman talking. At first it looked as if they were strangers, but the conversation kept going and for some reason the man had put away the papers he was reading.

Inna moved forward. She could see the woman's face now from an angle.

The need surged through her, but it was different this time. The betrayal was before her eyes. She would have her moment. She would prove her love and hate. She would make him suffer. Eventually he would repent, look at her as if she were a worthwhile human being and not a pitiful overgrown child-servant. Perhaps that moment would be now.

She felt the knife in the lefthand pocket of her coat. Her fingers were wrapped tightly around the handle. Her throbbing, tightly wrapped right hand was tucked in her right pocket.

Inna was close now. The two did not seem to notice her any more than the others had noticed her. Her father, Viktor, never noticed her. She had to use her knife to get his attention, to show her love and hate.

She wanted to scream but knew she was too timid.

"Father," she wanted to shout, "look at me. Listen to me. Help me live. Help me be a person."

It was Iosef who saw her first. She was not a particularly interesting figure — plain, cloth coat, pale face — but there was a determination in her eyes that made him feel that she might be the one. The sighting and the realization came in a fraction of a moment. The woman had only been truly visible to him when she was four or five feet away.

The knife came out. Elena's back was turned. Iosef pushed Elena to the side and lifted the briefcase to ward off the blow he knew was coming. He was ready but not for what took place.

The woman came in a quick rush and thrust the long blade into the shoulder of Elena Timofeyeva.

"*Maht'*, Mother," the woman wept. "Stay away from him."

Inna Dalipovna raised her hand to strike again, but Iosef reached out and grabbed her wrist. The woman tried to wrench free. She was remarkably strong, but she had only the one arm to use. Iosef brought the briefcase down hard on the woman's left wrist.

Inna whimpered and tried to hold on to the knife. She looked down at Elena, who had slumped to the platform.

Iosef wrenched the knife from Inna's hand and turned her around, pulling a pair of hand-cuffs from his pocket. The crowd was beginning to gather.

"What is happening?" asked a man.

"Cops," said a woman. "Beating up a gypsy beggar."

"Good," came an old woman's voice. "Good. The gypsies should all be sent to Roumania."

"One of the gypsies is hurt," said a young woman. "Look."

"Elena," Iosef said, holding on to the handcuffed hands of Inna Dalipovna.

"I am not hurt badly," she said. "I do not think . . ."

She started to get up and found herself on her knees, looking down at the blood dripping onto the platform from her wound. She did not want to be seen like this, on her knees, about to pass out, pathetic. If there was one thing she wanted never to be, it was pathetic.

She looked up at the woman Iosef was holding, the woman who had attacked her, called her "Mother." She looked up at the face of the woman and sensed that she was feeling the same thing, the same desire to be viewed as something other than pathetic.

After five hours of working with the small piece of metal he had pried off the handle of his chamber pot, Misha Lovski got the door to his cage open at precisely two minutes after nine in the morning. He had no way of knowing that. For him it could have been night or day. In spite of the constant sound — the speakers were now blaring his own song, "Guts in the Snow" — and ever-burning light, he was fairly certain that his jailer, his keeper, would not be coming back for some time, perhaps hours. It was difficult to be sure, but he felt that he did have time.

He pushed the cage door open slowly, listening for an alarm that would give away his escape. He heard nothing, but that proved nothing. The alarm might be two rooms or miles away. The alarm might be a silent flashing light.

Misha the Naked Cossack would write a song about his experience. It would be true. He would tell his audiences that it had happened to him. He would make them believe. They would shout, faces red in praise at his triumph. The song, which he had already been writing in his head, would be called "Cossack in a Cage."

He recited lines softly, ignoring his own voice, his own music being piped in around him. He tiptoed in his bare feet in the direction of the door, carrying the heaviest pot, the one they gave him to use as a toilet. It was empty. His mind was full.

"Prisoner in the light," he said, reaching for the wall to his right. "Looking for a night. Searching for the dark. Cursing at electric sun. Weapon in my hand. I should have saved the shit I made to throw right in their face. Fuck the human race."

He inched his way along slowly.

"Face them in sun," he whispered. "Have a little fun. Put them in the cage. Misfits in a rage. They tried to stop the Cossack, tried to make him weep, tried to make him go insane, tried to hide the truth, now they are in the booth. Strip them of their clothes. Let them hold their nose when you give them neither pot nor food, water nor repose. Play ninety decibels high. Beat out their eardrums. Watch out, Jews and Gypsies, here the Cossack comes."

He was next to the door now. He could easily reach out and grab the knob with his left hand. Instead he simply stood. In his right he held the pot tightly. He stepped back behind the door, waiting. He could wait forever. The Naked Cossack could wait forever. And then the lights would go out and the music stop and his jailer would enter and the Cossack would strike and strike and strike. Let him die. He wanted the jailer. It was the warden he wanted more. He would find a better weapon, a more deadly weapon, and then he would kill the warden, for he knew without doubt who the warden was.

"Find the warden in his den," he recited. "Drag his writhing carcass to the pen. Russias come and Russias go. Friends to no one. Cossack foes. What will happen no one knows, but the Cossack will survive. The Cossack like others who passed before will be there to settle the ancient score."

He heard something. Outside the door. Soft under the music. He lifted the pot high.

Lights went out. Music died. And the door slowly opened.

The name of the wounded gunman was Raoul Bronborg, a Swedish citizen. Karpo had the printout from Interpol on the desk before him along with Bronborg's fingerprints, which had led to the message from Interpol.

Bronborg was thirty-six years old, a mercenary who had worked as a private bodyguard in Brazil, Norway, France, and Bahrain. He spoke many languages and had many names, including Antonio Barleon, Sven Istermann, and Stephan Pomier. His current name was unknown and he had given Karpo none before he went into surgery and when he emerged after it.

Bronborg answered no questions. He met Karpo's eyes and spoke, but answered no questions. He had been given, at his own insistence, only a local anesthetic. It was clear that he wanted no drug or medication to interfere with his thoughts. Pain was preferable. Karpo understood.

"I will answer no questions," he said in nearly perfect Russian.

"Then," said Karpo, "I shall ask you none. I will tell you that we know who you are."

"Interpol?"

"Yes," said Karpo. "Interpol. You are not wanted anywhere."

"I know," said the man in the hospital bed.

He was the embodiment of a mercenary or bodyguard, powerful arms and chest, a determined, hard dark face of no particular ethnic distinction. He had a white scar high on his forehead, and up close Karpo could see that the man had lost just a small piece of the tip of his left earlobe.

"I know who you work for," Karpo said.

The man in the bed looked at the policeman with his deep-brown and unemotional eyes and said, "I believe you."

"You tried to kill a police officer," Karpo said.

"I did not know you were a police officer," the man said. "I thought you were an assassin or kidnapper."

"So you and your friend were there to protect a pair of minor musicians."

"That is a question?"

"Let us call it a statement."

"My companion, whose name I do not know, and I saw you and assumed the worst. You are not exactly a reassuring figure. And people do lie about being policemen."

"And about being protectors of musicians."

"You have my file. I work for whomever pays me. It is what I do. I cannot tell you more. In my work, my reputation for confidentiality is essential. I am sure you understand."

"I understand," said Karpo.

"So, if you plan to torture or drug me, please proceed. It will not be the first time. I will not speak."

"You will be neither drugged nor tortured," said Karpo. "I know who your current employer is. It is in your file."

"Then I would like to rest," said the man, closing his eyes. "We can resume our conversation later."

"You will be charged."

"You will do what you must," the man said.

With that the man was asleep. Karpo was certain the Swede was not pretending. It was not just the aftermath of surgery. The man had learned the art of sleeping when one could and, Karpo was certain, the art of awakening fully prepared when one had to do so.

And now Emil Karpo sat behind his desk, Akardy Zelach sitting across from him, trying to hide his feeling, something between fear and concern. He was sure Karpo could read him clearly, knew what he was thinking, while he had no idea what was on Karpo's mind. He never knew what Karpo was thinking even when the man was his usual self, which he had definitely not been for several days.

"How is he?" Zelach asked. "The man I shot?"

"He will recover."

"That is good."

"Perhaps," said Karpo as he closed the folder and rose. Zelach rose with him. Karpo moved out of the cubicle with Zelach behind him. Zelach wanted to ask where they were going, but he said nothing.

Karpo did not tell him that they were going to confront a kidnapper.

Misha Lovski, the Naked Cossack, did not think he had killed his jailer. He had gone into the next room, found a light switch, and turned it on. When he went back to examine the jailer, he thought he detected breathing. Blood flowed thick and dark from the matted hair of the man.

Misha dragged the unconscious man to the cell, stripped off his clothes, and put them on. They fit well. He knew they would. He left the cage and locked the door. The jailer had carried a small revolver, not terribly impressive, but the man was not in a business that normally required him to carry a weapon. For that matter, neither was Misha, who had never fired a weapon in his life. The gun in his hand felt remarkably light as he moved back to the door to the room and opened it. If he encountered anyone, he would pull the trigger and hope it would fire.

He was well aware that his confinement, the light and darkness, the blaring music, his humiliating nakedness, which he believed he had turned to cossack strength, had altered him. That he might be a bit mad was a distinct possibility. But that would pass or, if not, he would make use of it. It had already helped him compose new songs. His mind was racing with words and driving, hammering music demanding to be set free. He wanted a guitar, not a gun, but he would use the instrument in his hand first.

The room into which he stepped, about the size of the room in which he had been imprisoned, was simply furnished, with concrete floor and walls. It looked like a space into or out of which someone was just moving, with a large, modern, modular metal computer desk against one wall with a large-screen computer on top of it. A chair stood in front of the computer. There was another table, same material, with three chairs, metal arms and legs, seat and back of tan material. A chair which matched those at the table stood in one corner, not far from the door to his former prison. It was meant to be a comfortable version of the others, with a small footrest. Next to that chair was a side table with an open book on top of it.

Misha moved to the book and picked it up. It had something to do with communications technology. He put it back and moved to another door quite different from the one to his prison. This door had a button, a round white button, next to it. He pressed the button, gun in hand, ready to kill.

The door opened almost instantly. There was no one before him. He stepped forward and the door closed behind him.

Karpo in front, Zelach behind, moved in front of the person waiting behind the window. They stopped and Karpo said only, "We will see him now."

It was not a request. It was an order. Zelach had no idea how his order would be taken. He took a deep breath as quietly as he could and looked around at the armed men around them. This was not a terribly good idea, but he did not know what to say or how he might put into words what he was feeling. He tried to remember his mother's advice, but it was too late for that. He was with Emil Karpo. He would do his duty even if Karpo had begun to . . . He did not want to finish his thought.

There was a long beat and Zelach would not have been surprised if Karpo had pulled out his gun and fired.

Instead, the person Karpo was addressing looked into his eyes and saw much of what Zelach had become well aware. The person nodded.

Misha Lovski stood, eyes forward, weapon ready. His hands were moist and he felt his heart beating quickly. He recited a mantra aloud though he did not call it that.

"The Cossack will have revenge. The Cossack will emerge stronger than ever. The Cossack will have revenge. The Cossack will emerge stronger. The Cossack will have revenge. The Cossack will emerge stronger."

The door opened. Misha Lovski stepped out, weapon raised, and aimed at the man behind the desk across the room. Two men stood before the desk. Misha did not recognize them. One was rather soft-looking, with large glasses, a bookkeeper. The other was dressed in black with the pallor of a zombie.

The man behind the desk was Misha's father. He looked up at his son calmly, hand flat on his desk.

"Whoever moves dies," Misha said.

His father smiled and then the smile faded.

"You did not? . . ." he said.

"My brother is in the cage where you put me. I think he is alive. I do not care. You can care for another minute. Then I will kill you."

Misha moved forward.

"You cannot go back to your skinhead anti-Semitic friends," Nikoli said. "They know you are a Jew. Sit down. We will talk. First, I want to get medical attention for your brother. Then, I consider that you think about this offer. I will send you to South America. We have holdings, a television station in Buenos Aires. That is what I have planned for you. I can see no choice, Misha."

"You are wrong," Misha shouted. "There is no Misha Lovski. There is only the Naked Cossack."

The gun was leveled at the man behind the desk now, and Misha had closed the distance to no more than ten feet. It was at this point that Emil Karpo stepped between father and son.

"I will shoot you too," said Misha. "Get out of the way."

From behind the ghost before him, Nikoli Lovski said, "In a very odd way, I am proud of you, Misha. I did not think escape was possible. There is hope for you. You still have a brain."

"With no thanks to you, Popchick," Misha said with venom. "Now, out of the way, you."

"You have never fired a gun before," said Karpo.

There was something hollow in the man's

voice, something hollow, unafraid, something almost dead.

"I have," said Misha.

"I am a policeman," Karpo said. "You may put the gun away and we will accompany you out of here. If not, you will have to shoot me and you will have failed in your resolve. My partner will kill you before you have a chance to shoot your father, who will fall to the floor behind his desk as soon as you shoot me."

Zelach felt a quiver run down his back. He was not at all certain he could accomplish this mission, could shoot his second man the same day, but he did not fail to notice that Karpo had called him "partner" and not "associate."

"We shall see," Misha shouted.

"Live to fight another day," said Zelach. "When death is near don't run away, but hide until the strength is yours, the true cossack always endures."

Misha turned to look at the odd rumpled man in glasses who was reciting Misha's own words, words from one of his distinctly lesser-known songs from a compact disk that had sold but a few thousand copies.

"You know my work?" Misha said.

Zelach nodded and said, "I would not like to shoot you. I do not know much about

South America, but I believe you could begin a new career anywhere. You have something new to say now."

Misha looked at the rumpled man whose brow was definitely moist. And then he looked at the ghost before him.

Zelach willed neither Nikoli Lovski nor Emil Karpo to speak. He did not know where his own words had come from but he feared that either of the other two might, for very different reasons, say something that would cause Misha to pull the trigger.

"He deserves to die," Misha said.

"We all deserve to die," said Karpo.

Zelach cringed.

"I need revenge," said Misha angrily. "I need revenge. Do you not understand? That is the cossack way. I cannot let this pass. I cannot live with this."

Zelach was at a loss. This conversation was beyond him. He needed Porfiry Petrovich or even the old Emil Karpo, not the one standing there asking to be shot, but neither was present.

"There are many ways to get revenge," Zelach said. "Do not be what others demand. Listen to your own command. Follow the path you wish to choose. Leave the bloodsuckers behind to live and lose."

"Apache Cannibals?" Misha asked.

"No," said Zelach. "The Finnish band Living Dead."

"I do not know them," said Misha. "They are good?"

"I like them," said Zelach.

Karpo stepped forward, his chest inches from the barrel of the gun in Misha's hand.

"Leave the bloodsuckers behind to live and lose," Misha repeated to himself.

Karpo reached out and took the weapon from the young man's hand.

Misha Lovski, the Naked Cossack, crumpled to his knees. Zelach moved forward quickly and grabbed the young man before he passed out. Karpo had stepped to one side.

The last image Misha had before he closed his eyes was of his father behind the desk, looking at his son with eyes distinctly moist.

The last sound he heard before fainting was of his father on the phone, saying to someone, "Get to the cell. My son is in there. Get him to a hospital."

Chapter Seven

The world is long, there is no consolation
For those who join at the end of the line
The skeletons were at the feast

"We get snow. Don't get me wrong. We get snow in Cincinnati, but look at that. Look out that window."

The old American, Susman, was seated at a table near the rear of the dining car, an empty seat beside him.

Rostnikov had paused next to the little bald man who now said, "Have a seat?"

With his usual difficulty Rostnikov sat next to the old man, checking his watch quickly. In less than an hour they would be arriving at the Sverdlovsk-Pass station, Ekaterinburg.

"You a religious man?" asked Susman, looking out the window again.

"I have a respect for the mystical," said Rostnikov. "The wonders of existence."

"Me, too," said the American. "But can't say I understand it. Life. Hell, I'm feeling small today. You know what I mean?"

"I do," said Rostnikov.

"Overcast," said the American. "Sometimes I wonder . . ."

"The sun," said Rostnikov.

The man turned to the Russian with a smile. "Yes, the sun. It looks big to us but it's just a pip-squeak of a star."

"You are intrigued by the heavens?" Rostnikov asked.

"I'm an astronomer," said the American. "Retired. Professor emeritus, Ohio State University."

Rostnikov nodded and they went silent for a moment before the detective asked, "Is the sun shrinking?"

The American smiled and said, "Follow this. The solar radius is four hundred and forty-one thousand miles and is ninety-three million miles away. It subtends an angle of thirty arc minutes at this distance, so . . . you're not following?"

"No."

"The sun's not shrinking. If the sun were shrinking by three percent it would be a two-hundred-mile-a-year loss. If it were shrinking at one hundred times smaller than this, astronomers would have noticed a long time ago. The size of the sun hasn't changed over the last one hundred million years. If it had changed, even a minute part of a fraction, we would have gone into a global heat wave or ice age. In fact, the sun is expanding."

"Expanding?"

"In five or six billion years, the sun will become a red giant star, swell to be the size of the entire orbit of the earth," Susman said with enthusiasm, turning fully to face Rostnikov. "In a few hundred million years, there won't be much life on earth, maybe thermophilic bacteria that can live in nearly boiling water."

"I see," said Rostnikov.

"I'm sorry. This kind of information seems to scare lay people."

"It has implications," said Rostnikov.

"Yes," said the American, sitting back. "But, hell, within a few-dozen centuries, we should have the technology to pack everyone up and move them to another galaxy. No more America," said Susman.

"No more Russia," said Rostnikov.

"We'll probably start the battle for new nations the day the first colonists reach a reasonably inhabitable planet near Alpha Centuri," said Susman.

Rostnikov sat silently for a beat and looked past Susman at the sky before asking, "How long have you known Mr. Allberry?"

"Bob? Met him in the railroad station in

Moscow. Came right up and introduced himself, said he'd been told there was a fellow American in his compartment. We hit it off right away. Never know where or when you'll make friends."

"Yes," said Rostnikov. "Do you know where Mr. Allberry is now?"

"Back in the compartment, I'd guess."

"No, I just came from there. I was looking for him."

Susman looked at Rostnikov with curiosity.

"I was in Rostov during the war," Rostnikov said. "The same area where Mr. Allberry was an intelligence liaison."

"That where? . . ."

"I lost my leg, yes."

"You're too young," said Susman.

"Some of us were as young as nine years old," Rostnikov said.

Susman shook his head.

"Nine years old," he said. "Some of the German soldier kids I saw in Italy, dead ones, live ones, weren't much older than that."

Rostnikov rose with minimal awkwardness.

"Perhaps he is in one of the cars farther back," said Rostnikov. "I will look."

"See you back in the compartment," Susman said, his attention now fully focused outside.

Rostnikov started, bracing himself on the

seats and the walls of the car, heading back. Eventually he would meet with Allberry.

Eventually came very quickly. When he got to the end of the next car, the door of the WC shot open and Allberry stepped out.

"You looking for me?" he asked.

"Yes," said Rostnikov. "If I am not mistaken, you invited me to find you."

"You are not mistaken," Allberry said in perfect Russian. "Which of my invitations did you accept?"

A woman inched past them, a scowl on her face, and entered the WC, slamming the door behind her.

"You mentioned a dish you had when you were working with Russian intelligence near Rostov during the war," said Rostnikov. "You knew I had been in Rostov. You knew that I would know that a delicacy with three different meats would not have been available, not even to a general. Even the officers were chewing on leather, drinking snow, and nearly starving."

"And you said nothing when I mentioned this meal," Allberry said.

"You could have simply been lying about your past, bragging about being in the intelligence service, about being in Russia."

"So, you filed my error away and . . ."

"You killed Pavel Cherkasov, and I saw the

boy with a large bag. You transferred the money to that bag and gave it to the boy's family to carry off for you for a few rubles. That family had only two cases. Now they have three. So, I am here."

"You know there is a gun in my pocket," Allberry said.

"It would make sense."

"We go into the WC when the woman comes out," Allberry said. "We both go in. We lock the door and wait till we get to the station. At the last possible moment, I get out and jam the door, leaving you inside. I will get what it is that the late comedian had come for."

"And?"

"And I will eliminate the person who bears the gift. It is what I do. So, you will go quietly into the rest room."

"Or . . ."

"Or I shoot you now, here," the old man said. "No one is looking. I start shouting that you have fallen, had a heart attack. I will look confused, dazed, call for help, a confused old man."

"Risky," said Rostnikov.

Allberry shrugged. "I have taken greater risks," he said. "It really is not that difficult. Forty years of this teaches one a great deal about human reaction."

"Including the conviction that I will simply enter the rest room with you and be shot."

"You do not believe that I will let you live?"

"No," said Rostnikov.

"Then I shall have to shoot you now," the old man said, looking beyond Rostnikov and starting to remove his gun from his pocket.

Allberry was an assassin, a confident, experienced one, but an old one with slower reflexes. He was overconfident. Rostnikov threw himself at the old man, his entire weight behind the move, all of his strength coming off his good leg. They fell to the floor, Rostnikov on top, the air going out of the old man. Rostnikov thought he heard something break in the man under him.

The door to the rest room came open and the scowling woman looked down at the fallen men.

"I think he has had a heart attack," Rostnikov said. "I am a police officer. I am giving him artificial respiration. Quick, go to compartment two-fourteen, two cars that way. There is a doctor in there. Dr. Tkach. Tell him Inspector Rostnikov needs him."

Allberry gasped beneath the weight of the policeman, trying to catch his breath.

The woman stood with her mouth open. People in the car heard the commotion and were emptying into the corridor.

"Run, hurry," said Rostnikov to the woman. "Seconds count. Run. You do not want to be responsible for the death of this man, do you?"

The woman came out of her momentary stupor and hurried in the direction Rostnikov had indicated.

Twenty minutes later the Trans-Siberian Express pulled into the station and the doors opened. First those departing or getting off the train to stretch their legs, take in the frigid air, or buy trinkets and snacks got off. The platform was crowded. Many of the bundled people selling furiously had an Asian look. Cacophony reigned.

Through the crowd a boy no more than twelve years old made his way, hands deep in his coat pockets. He had already developed signs of the regional face: flat, rugged, serious. He was looking for someone in the crowd, someone who had stepped off of the train. He saw the person he was looking for or thought he was looking for. He was carrying a blue bulging duffel bag.

The boy pushed his way through the crowd toward the man who was standing still, waiting patiently.

He approached the man and began to remove his right hand from his pocket.

"For you," he said nervously, looking at the nearby faces and handing the man a folded sheet of paper.

Rostnikov unfolded the sheet and looked at the boy, who was already elbowing his way quickly through the crowd.

Sasha Tkach and Svetlana Britchevna suddenly appeared at Rostnikov's side.

"Shall I catch him?" Sasha asked.

"No," said Rostnikov. "It is a brief stop. Sasha, please hurry and remove our bags from the train before it resumes its journey."

Sasha moved quickly toward the train.

As Svetlana turned toward the train, Rostnikov put out his arm to stop her.

"You have the money," Rostnikov said. "You have the assassin. It is here we say good-bye."

Svetlana held up her hands. "You have not made your exchange," she said. "Our courier has panicked."

Rostnikov shrugged. "Sasha and I will try to pick up the trail. If not . . ."

"I had better arrange for the removal of our assassin and the body," she said. "As you say, there is not much time."

Sasha was back at their side, a suitcase in each hand.

"Good-bye, Sasha Tkach," she said. "Perhaps I will look you up in Moscow."

"It would be better if you did not," Sasha said.

"For whom?" she asked, picking up her suitcases. Then she turned to Rostnikov and added, "If you find the package, will you open it? To satisfy your curiosity?"

"My orders are to turn it over to my director without examining the contents."

"And," she said, "you always do what your director says?"

"Except when I feel that to obey an order might compromise me or one of my associates."

She nodded in understanding. "Wish me good fortune, Porfiry Petrovich Rostnikov."

"I do," he said. "May I provide some small advice?"

"Of course," she said.

"Be wary of your own ambition," he said. "Temper your vision with an understanding of the value of survival."

"Philosophy," she said, stepping back.

"I read it somewhere," he said. "Something like that. Take care of yourself, Svetlana Britchevna."

"And you too, Porfiry Petrovich Rostnikov."

She moved between a small man moving from foot to foot and bargaining with a very fat woman over a heavy-looking necklace of thick white beads. Before she faded into the crowd, Svetlana gave Sasha a long, lingering smile.

When she had disappeared, Rostnikov said, "Beautiful woman."

"Yes," said Sasha.

"Very clever too."

"Yes," said Sasha.

"And? . . ."

Rostnikov handed the sheet of paper the boy had given him to Sasha. On it, in neat letters, were the words "Sverdlovsk statue. Come alone."

"We may or may not be watched," said Rostnikov. "Our courier is being very cautious. I will find a taxi and go to the Sverdlovsk statue, wherever it may be. You take the suitcases and come in another taxi. Simply tell the driver to take you to the statue. Be ready. I shall . . ."

"Cold," came a voice from behind Rostnikov, who watched Sasha move toward the station in search of a taxi.

"Cold, like heat, is relative," Rostnikov said, as Jim Susman moved to his side swathed in a thick down parka and a hat with flaps that covered his ears. "We are not really into winter yet."

"Cold enough for me," said the little man. "You seen Bob?"

"A while ago," said Rostnikov. "I think he said something about getting off the train here for a few days."

The little man looked around. "Off, here? Why?"

"Interesting things to see," said Rostnikov. "Churches, museum, countryside, mountains. Industrial. Very much like your Pittsburgh."

"He didn't say anything to me."

"Sudden impulse," said Rostnikov. "I am debarking here also. Business."

"Guess it'll be just me and the comic with the appetite," said Susman, rocking from one foot to the other. "Tell you the truth, I don't care much for his jokes."

"If you are fortunate, you will not have to hear any more of them. Perhaps he too is getting off here. The regional food is unusual and Mr. Drovny has expressed a keen interest in fine cuisine."

"I should be so lucky," said Susman. "Say, listen, I'm getting back on the train."

"One last question," said Rostnikov.

Susman looked at the detective.

"Does the sun make a sound?"

"As a matter of fact," Susman said, "it does."

"I would like to hear that sound."

"You can if you have an internet connection. Search for the Michelson Doppler Imager. There are sound files in something called AU format. The sun rings like a bell in a lot of frequencies and with distinct harmonics. Music."

The little man took off his right glove with his teeth and extended his hand to Rostnikov, who took it.

"Good to meet you," the American said through clenched teeth.

"And you," said Rostnikov. "Enjoy your trip."

Susman put the glove back on and looked up. "Sun's coming back out."

Rostnikov looked up at the huge glowing orange sphere and nodded. Yes, there it was.

Holding the blue bag in front of him, Rostnikov made his way to the front of the train station, pushing through the crowd. Almost half the faces were Asian.

There was no real taxi line, just a scattering of cars facing in various directions with cabs of different drab greens and browns inching their way, miraculously avoiding a collision of fenders.

Sasha was nowhere in sight. Rostnikov did not bother to try to discover if he was being watched. He found a particularly faded brown cab with the virtue of being empty and opened the door.

"Hotel?" asked the driver, a short, bulldog-faced man wearing a Cleveland Indians baseball cap. The cartoon Indian on the cap grinned at the chief inspector.

"The Sverdlovsk statue," Rostnikov said, shoving the duffel into the back seat and carefully getting in next to it.

"You do not want a hotel?" the driver said, looking back at his passenger.

"No, I wish to see the sights of your wondrous city."

The driver gave him a look that conveyed serious doubts about his passenger's intelligence or sanity.

"We can drive past the statue," the driver tried. "Then out to the memorial, the one over the cellar where the czar and his family were murdered. Nice little wooden church-like thing. For very little I can sell you a complete list of the items taken from the royal family before they were killed. Long list. I can, for a small extra charge, get you an exact copy of the crucifix one of the daughters wore around her neck. And if . . ."

A car horn was blaring behind the cab, demanding that he move.

"Sverdlovsk statue," said Rostnikov.

The driver shrugged, turned around, adjusted his baseball cap, and began to make his way skillfully through the morass of vehicles.

"You like American baseball?" asked Rostnikov as they broke through the jam and onto a wide street.

"No," said the driver. "Why? Oh, the hat? An American gave this to me last year. I drove him to the airport. Spoke terrible Russian but he was happy. He had just made a big deal and was going back to this Clevylund place where they have laughing Indians. He gave me a good tip and the hat. Why don't I just drive around the statue and take you to . . ."

"The statue," Rostnikov said.

That ended conversation. The ride through the town, which seemed to be engulfed in a low fog, took more than fifteen minutes. Rostnikov had once been to Frankfurt, Germany. Ekaterinburg reminded him of Frankfurt. Large office buildings of no distinction, apartment buildings huddled close together. Beyond the city, through the patches of fog or smog, he could see distant mountains and the hint of the sun.

"There it is," said the driver, pulling into a large square.

The dark figure of a man stood atop what looked like a boulder mounted on a pedestal. Across the square stood an old, official-looking two-story building with a row of pillars before its entrance. There were people hurrying through the square, their breath clear as they moved, their hands plunged into their pockets, their heads and sometimes faces covered.

"Winter coming," said the driver.

"Wait for me," Rostnikov said, opening the door.

"Do not try to run away," the driver said. "I will be watching."

"I have one leg," said Rostnikov. "Running for me is a distant childhood memory."

"I will be watching," said the driver, adjusting his cap.

Rostnikov made his way out of the cab and slowly, duffel in hand, moved toward the statue.

It was not that the chief inspector was impervious to the weather, but only the most extreme of temperatures, hot or cold, seemed to affect him. He did not see Sasha but he was sure he was somewhere nearby, watching.

Rostnikov moved toward the statue. A vendor's cart stood before the looming form of the assassin. Rostnikov moved to it and ordered a slice of pizza. The bearded man behind the cart, only his eyes showing behind his scarf, nodded, opened a metal lid, and came up with a round piece of baked dough covered with a thin layer of white cheese.

Rostnikov put the duffel between his legs

and said, "Can you bring a slice to the cab driver over there?"

"*Da,*" said the man.

Rostnikov paid him and began to eat as he watched the man hurriedly shuffle, small pizza in hand on a sheet of brown paper, toward the cab.

The pizza was tasteless and barely warm, but Rostnikov found himself hungry. He ate slowly as he moved back from the statue and looked up.

"History is made by the innocent and the guilty," a woman's voice said behind him.

"Guilt and innocence change with history," said Rostnikov, finishing his pizza. He did not turn around.

"I'll take the bag," the woman said.

"And you have something for me," the man said.

"First you," she said.

He turned and found himself facing a slight, reasonably pretty young woman with pink cheeks and no makeup. Her coat was dark fur but quite old.

He handed her the bag. "Now, . . ." he said.

"First I check to be sure you have what you have promised," she said, starting to unzip the bag she had been handed.

"Clothes," the man said.

The woman looked up at him. Fury, anger, and then fear.

"I have given you a better gift than money. I have saved your life," he said. "That is what I have for you."

"You have? . . ."

"The man who was to give you the money was going to kill you as soon as you handed him what you are carrying. If I had not taken care of him, you would be lying on the ice here now, and he would be walking off with the money and your gift."

"You are lying," she said, starting to back away.

Rostnikov limped a step toward her.

The young woman turned to run and found her way blocked by Sasha Tkach. The woman tried to dart past the young man but Sasha reached out and grabbed the woman's wrist with one hand as he reached into her coat pocket with the other to remove a wrapped package about the size of a paperback novel.

When he had placed it in his pocket, the young woman was released.

"I want my money," she said, turning to Rostnikov.

"We can arrest you," he said. "We can also let you walk away. We give you the choice."

The young woman looked at the two who had stopped her, bumped into a woman carrying a bulging shopping bag, and ran away.

"We got it," Sasha said, handing the package to Rostnikov. "What do you think it is?"

Rostnikov unzipped the duffel bag and placed the package inside.

"There are questions to which it is best we not know the answer. I have a cab waiting."

They moved to the cab and got in.

"Extra for a second passenger," said the cabbie.

"We are policemen from Moscow," said Rostnikov. "Consider the pizza your extra fare."

"Where do you want to go now?"

"The airport," said Rostnikov.

"You just got here," said the cabbie. "You came all the way from Moscow to look at a statue?"

"We collected a souvenir," said Rostnikov.

It took them a little over an hour to arrange for a military plane at Koltsovo Airport to take them to Moscow. A call to the Yak had been needed. Their conversation had been brief.

DIRECTOR YAKLOVEV: You have it?

ROSTNIKOV: Yes.

YAKLOVEV: In what form is it?

ROSTNIKOV: A package about the size of a paper-covered copy of *Diary of a Madman*.

YAKLOVEV: You have not opened it?

ROSTNIKOV: No.

YAKLOVEV: The money?

ROSTNIKOV: It is in the possession of another branch of the government which provided us with assistance essential to secure the package.

YAKLOVEV: The money is of little importance. The courier?

ROSTNIKOV: Dead.

YAKLOVEV: You had to kill him?

ROSTNIKOV: No. He was assassinated by an old man who is now in the custody of the other branch which I mentioned. We are at the airport in Ekaterinburg.

YAKLOVEV: I know the commanding officer of military security in Ekaterinburg. He owes me a favor. Go to the ticket counter. There will be two tickets on the next plane to Moscow.

ROSTNIKOV: We are on the way.

YAKLOVEV: Come to my office directly when you arrive. A car will be waiting for you at the airport.

With that, the Yak hung up the phone.

The flight back was uneventful. It was a small business-flight plane with a handful of men in business suits. One of the businessmen, clutching a briefcase in his lap, his eyes closed, sat alone in the rear of the plane. His face was rigid. A brief burst of minimal turbulence made the man quiver in fear.

"Porfiry Petrovich," Sasha said. "Maya will be home when we get to Moscow. Maya and the children."

Since he knew this, Rostnikov said nothing.

Sasha continued. "That woman."

"Svetlana Britchevna."

"Yes. She . . ."

"I know," said Rostnikov. "A beautiful woman, very skilled."

"I have been tempted by those less beautiful than she," Sasha said.

"You have no choice," said Rostnikov. "None of us do. Temptation is . . . let us leave it at that. Temptation *is*. You make choices. Give in to it or do not because of the consequences."

"It is a weakness in me," Sasha said.

"Obviously," said Rostnikov. "But it is not one which you need indulge. These things are indeed obvious, Sasha Tkach. I am giving you no great words of wisdom. Now, if you will please, I will remove this leg, this enemy with which I have a truce, place it on the floor, and indulge myself in some self-indulgent scratching."

Chapter Eight

Before the dreams of ancient Greece
Before the shaman and the priest
Jason and the Golden Fleece
Before the Dead Sea Scrolls released
Their meaning or the experts pieced together
The epic of Gilgamesh
Trans-Siberian Express

The car was waiting for them at the Star City military runway just outside of Moscow. It was night.

Rostnikov was surprised to see Akardy Zelach seated next to the driver. However, he was grateful that Zelach was not driving. He was, Porfiry Petrovich knew from experience, a threat to mankind behind the wheel.

"To what do we owe the pleasure of your coming to greet us, Akardy Zelach?" asked Rostnikov.

"I must talk to you," Zelach said, his voice less than steady.

Rostnikov did not bother to ask if the subject of Zelach's concern was urgent. If it were not, the slouching and obviously uncomfortable detective in the front seat would not have had the courage to impose himself on the scene.

"Can it wait till we get to Petrovka?" Rostnikov asked.

"Yes," said Zelach, who turned his head forward, adjusted his glasses, and closed his eyes, trying to remember approximately how he and his mother had worked out what he would say to the chief inspector.

They drove straight to Petrovka, Rostnikov breaking his usual rule of sitting next to the driver so that he would be at the side of the silent Sasha. The snow was falling softly, crystals glittering in the headlights, streetlights, and the eyes of men and women.

"You did well," Rostnikov said.

Sasha nodded and said, "Maya is back."

"Yes."

"Maybe I should wait till tomorrow to go home."

"Maybe you should take three days off. Be with your family. Find your mother's artist friend. Be a husband and father. Play with your wife and children in the snow. Let us make that an order. You are to take three days off."

Sasha nodded and said no more.

When they pulled up in front of Petrovka's gates Rostnikov got out, being careful to hold on to the door of the Lada to keep from slipping. Zelach was standing on the sidewalk, waiting.

"The driver will take you home," Rostnikov said. "Give my love to Maya and kiss the children for me. And one more thing."

"Yes?"

"Brush your teeth before you go to bed with your wife tonight," said Rostnikov, closing the door and waving the driver into the night.

"Now," said Rostnikov as he joined Zelach on the sidewalk in front of the iron gate, "do you want to go to my office and talk for a few minutes or wait for me there while I report to the director?"

"I would like to speak here. I will be brief," said Zelach, looking around as if he expected someone to intrude on their conversation. "It is about Inspector Karpo."

"Karpo," Rostnikov repeated when Zelach paused, considering whether he could go on.

"I think . . . I know it is not my place, but I am concerned about him. And about me. My mother is concerned. She agreed that I should tell you."

The night was cold and the hour late. Rostnikov stood patiently, waiting for the tortured man before him to provide some clarity.

"I think Inspector Karpo is behaving very unlike himself."

"In what way?" asked Rostnikov.

"I think he might be doing things that are not . . . I am not doing this well."

"Things that are? . . ." Rostnikov prompted patiently.

"Things that could get him hurt or killed. And me too. I mean they could get me hurt and killed too, not that I am doing such things. I mean, Inspector Karpo is the senior detective and I do whatever he orders, but . . ."

"You think he is behaving suicidally?"

"Sui— I don't know. I am just concerned. I thought, my mother thought, you should know."

"Have you told Inspector Karpo about your concerns?"

"Yes."

"And?"

"He never really answered me."

"Be calm, Akardy," Rostnikov said, starting to feel the cold creep into his half leg. If he stood out here long enough, he would have definite difficulty walking. "Tell me what has brought you to this conclusion about Inspector Karpo. Talk slowly."

Zelach sighed, a cloud of cold steam billowing from his mouth, and began to speak.

When Zelach had finished, Rostnikov said,

putting his right hand on the man's shoulder, "You were right to tell me, Akardy. Now, go home. I will see you in the morning."

Five minutes later, Porfiry Petrovich Rostnikov was ushered into the office of Director Yaklovev by Pankov, who trotted ahead of the chief inspector like a puppy in urgent need of a fire hydrant.

The Yak was seated behind his desk, hands folded, making no pretense of doing anything but waiting for the arrival of his chief inspector. He motioned Rostnikov toward one of the two chairs across from the desk and as soon as the detective was seated, the Yak held out his right hand.

Rostnikov, still wearing his coat, reached into his pocket, pulled out the package he carried, and handed it across the table. The Yak placed it in front of him and patted it once.

"I will write a full report in the morning unless you need it immediately," Rostnikov said.

"There will be no need for a report," said the Yak.

Rostnikov nodded. "Then I may —"

"A moment," said the Yak, tapping the package before him. "There were developments while you were away. The missing son of Nikoli Lovski has been located and returned to his father. Zelach shot the kidnapper. He will explain it to you, I am sure.

Inspector Karpo has already submitted a report about the incident, which I have edited somewhat."

"The kidnapper?"

"A foreigner," said the Yak. "Appears to have some influential connections. He was released an hour ago. No matter. The affair is settled to my satisfaction and that of Nikoli Lovski."

"You said *developments?*" Rostnikov said.

"Your son and Elena Timofeyeva have apprehended the subway attacker," said the Yak. "We are being given full credit. Unfortunately, Detective Timofeyeva was slightly injured during the apprehension, but she is resting at home. I have recommended her for a medal."

"Now may I —"

"Rostnikov," the Yak said, sitting back. "You are to forget the existence of this package."

"I shall direct my curiosity in other directions."

"Not toward the Lovski case," said the Yak.

"Then, with my limited options, I shall go to see Elena Timofeyeva."

"We understand each other," the Yak said, rising.

Rostnikov rose too. "I believe we do," said the policeman.

The Yak seated himself again while Rostnikov crossed the room and paused at the door, where he turned and said, "I have given Sasha Tkach three days' leave."

The Yak nodded.

"I should like to also remove Inspector Karpo from the regular case rotation."

This time the Yak paused and cocked his head to one side.

"Special assignment until further notice with your approval," Rostnikov went on.

"Reason?"

"His skills, I believe, will be better utilized in other areas. And I believe there is a fatigue factor involved."

"Fatigue?"

"Inspector Karpo has worked tirelessly for two decades, tirelessly and, I believe, at great cost to his emotional well-being."

"Signs of emotion in Inspector Karpo have evaded my observation," said the Yak.

"And his," said Rostnikov.

"Your request is granted. However, this must be temporary."

"Six months should be sufficient," said Rostnikov.

"Six months, then. You will not forget to keep me informed of his assignments," said the Yak.

"I forget only what you order me to forget," said Rostnikov.

Unspoken was the quid pro quo. Neither man smiled. Rostnikov limped from the room, closing the door slowly behind him.

Rostnikov had opened the package and examined its contents. Of this Igor Yaklovev was reasonably certain. Even without certainty, however, he had to assume that the chief inspector had done so. Survival depended on assuming worst-case scenarios. Rostnikov's requests for leave for Sasha Tkach and an assignment change for Emil Karpo suggested that Rostnikov had something with which to bargain, something unspoken. That did not, ultimately, matter. The director and his chief inspector had an unspoken agreement. Their relationship was nearly perfect. Since it was based on long-term mutual benefit and not transient loyalty, they both seemed comfortable in the pragmatic relationship. The Yak had kept his part of the agreement and would continue to do so. Igor Yaklovev would contrive, blackmail, instigate, and further his own ambitions, but he would never betray one of his people. The Yak's loyalty was well established. It was his principal currency among those who worked for him. Igor Yaklovev's word was good, though his methods were without scruples.

He rose, moved to the door, locked it, and

returned to the chair behind his desk. Then he opened the package before him. There was a leather string around a thick, brown-paper wrapping. He untied the string, carefully opened the paper, and found a neatly folded stack of papers pressed into a metal box about an inch deep.

The first sheet of paper was brown, cracks intruding at the places where it had been folded. Beneath the first sheet were newer sheets.

Yaklovev gently unfolded the first sheet. It was a short letter, written in a fine hand in firm strokes of black ink. In the righthand corner of the sheet was the date: January 6, 1894.

The note was in German. The Yak had more than a reasonable command of written German. He read:

Dear Baron Von Vogler,

You have certainly noted that enclosed in this sealed pouch delivered into your hands by Colonel Maxim Verobyanov of the Royal Guard is a gem of considerable worth. I believe you will recognize it and know its monetary value and its value as a national treasure. I have been informed that it is the largest and most nearly perfect in the world. I have had it replaced in the collection of my jewelry with a fine copy. My beloved Nich-

olas, I am certain, will never notice.

From time to time I hope to send you more such treasures. Out of your loyalty to my father I trust you to keep them safe in the event that my children and I may someday need them.

There are signs of unrest, to which my husband does not give value. There are concessions to the forces which threaten us, the forces of a conspiring military and the horrid prospect of discontented masses. Need I say more? Of all this I have been advised by many.

I am uncertain about the effect this new railroad will have on the czar's power and position. The cost is great, the treasury of our nation threatened, and problems continue to plague its construction. Yet my husband is confident that the railroad will open new Vistas and stand as a memorial to our entire family and a rallying force for all the Russian people under the royal family of Romanov.

May it be so. But if it is not, I trust in you, dear friend, to be prepared to receive those of us who may need a safe haven in the world.

As you called me in childhood and as I remain to you —

Alix

There was no ruby in the package. This did

not surprise Yaklovev, though it did provide him with a dilemma. If he took credit for recovering this historic document in the hand of the Czarina Alexandra, there might well be those who wondered if he had also recovered the gem.

It was obvious that the gem and the letter had never reached the German baron, and after more than a century it was pointless to speculate on what had happened to the ruby. He could certainly argue that point, but there were potential enemies, rivals who might raise the question. Tempting as it was to take credit for this discovery, it was far more prudent to put it away safely, perhaps to use another day.

The letter had been a bonus and not necessarily a welcome one. The real treasure he had sought now lay before him in the form of neatly folded sheets of names, dates, transactions, agreements, and documents.

Igor Yaklovev slowly examined the list on top of the pile, a list of some of the most prominent men in government and public life, not only in Russia but in various states of the former Soviet Union.

Before him was clear evidence of payoffs to these men from the Ural Mafia in return for protection and favors. There were even documents making clear that some of the most influential of these men were aware of killings that had taken place.

These documents were the real treasure.

Director Yaklovev returned the papers to the package, rewrapped it, and stood. He placed the package in his briefcase, lifted his phone, and pushed the button to connect him with Pankov, who answered instantly. The Yak ordered a car and hung up.

In his apartment, he would make copies of everything in his briefcase on the machine he kept in the alcove of his bedroom. The Yak lived modestly. His goal was not luxury but power. His physical needs were simple. His ambition was great but well calculated for his own protection. He did not aspire to the highest offices of Russia. He aspired to gently dictate policy to those who held such offices.

Documents like the one in his briefcase, tapes he had been collecting along with favors granted, would soon put him in position for a major move. He would savor his power like a secret collector of great art who kept his treasures for his own eyes and information and the simple, pure satisfaction of having them.

Once home and having made the copies, he would follow his long-established pattern of protecting his acquisitions by making copies in triplicate and securing them where they could not be found.

He retrieved his coat from the small closet behind his desk and reflected on what had been a very good day. Earlier, the unspoken agreement with Nikoli Lovski had gone smoothly. The Yak had arranged for the release of the man Akardy Zelach had shot and had assured Lovski that there would be no further inquiry into the situation regarding his son. In fact, there would be no report on the incident. It was a family matter. Lovski had made it clear that he fully understood and appreciated what the director of the Office of Special Investigation was doing.

As a test of their new understanding, the Yak had said to Lovski that he would very much appreciate it if Lovski's media "gave proper credit to the heroes who had, at the risk of their own lives, made Moscow safe from the subway killer."

Lovski had said that he would see to it that Iosef Rostnikov and Elena Timofeyeva were treated as heroes and their positions with the Office of Special Investigation made quite clear.

"And, of course, we will see to it that you too are given full credit."

"I would prefer it if my name and contribution were not mentioned," the Yak had said.

"Then they will not be," Lovski had readily agreed. "There may be one problem, which I leave fully to your discretion. Your man, Karpo. He is a bit . . ."

"He will be no problem," the Yak had said reassuringly.

And that had ended the conversation. It had been a good day. The car was waiting for him when he stepped beyond the gates of Petrovka. The snow was deep now. The sky dark. The air cold, a brisk, satisfying cold. Yes, it had been a good day.

It had not been a particularly good day for Elena Timofeyeva. If one discounted the pain and the twenty stitches in her shoulder, however, it could have been much worse.

There was one small lamp on the table next to the bed and it was turned on the lowest of its three-way bulb.

"I can stay but a minute," Porfiry Petrovich said, standing over her at the bed in her aunt's tiny bedroom. "You are all right?"

"Some pain, tired, but all right," she said with what she hoped was a smile.

She looked very pale, and Rostnikov suspected that she had a fever. He reached down and touched her forehead. She was decidedly warm but not hot.

"I'm taking pills," she said. "Anna is doing her best to play nurse. She is not very good at it, but she tries."

"I will let you sleep," he said. "I will come back tomorrow."

"You look tired," she said.

"I am," he said, touching her hand.

She gripped the hand and said, "Has Iosef told you?"

His son was in the next room, the only other room of the tiny apartment, with Anna Timofeyeva.

"What?"

"We have decided to marry as soon as I am out of this bed," she said. "He asked me to tell you."

"You have told me and I am pleased," Rostnikov said.

"I do not intend to leave my job," she said.

"I would not wish you to," said Rostnikov. "Recover. Sarah and I will plan a wedding."

"Small," she said. "Talk to Iosef. A small party. No religious wedding. A simple state wedding."

"May I ask you a question?" Rostnikov said.

"Yes."

"If it is an intrusion? . . ."

"You want to know if we plan on children."

"Yes."

"At some point. We have talked. At some point."

"Good. Now sleep."

She closed her eyes and smiled.

"Shall I turn off the light?"

"No," she said. "I prefer it on, at least for tonight."

Rostnikov nodded and left the bedroom.

Anna Timofeyeva sat in her chair near the window with her cat, Baku, on her lap. Iosef stood, a cup in his hand.

"Coffee or tea, Porfiry Petrovich?" she asked.

"Coffee, perhaps."

Iosef moved to the small stove near the door to the apartment to get the cup of coffee for his father.

"You look tired, Porfiry Petrovich," Anna said.

"I am," he replied, taking the cup from his son. He took a sip. The coffee was tepid but strong. "And you, Anna Timofeyeva? How are you?"

"Angry," she said with resignation. "But I have been told it is bad for my heart to be angry, so I try to convince myself that the anger is something I can put into an imaginary box and hide in the cabinet with the soup cans."

"And does it work?"

"Of course not," she said. "But I am trying. I read about it in a book Elena and Iosef gave me. Mysticism."

Her reaction to the word *mysticism* was a

nod of resignation. She was a pragmatist, always had been. She had been quite comfortable in the Communist Soviet Union, though she acknowledged its defects. Authority had been clear. The world had been solid and tangible. You worked. You died. Now her niece and the man she was going to marry gave her books about achieving tranquility. Anna was willing to exert her considerable will on being calm. She needed and wanted no books. One could rely on one's mind if not one's body.

"She will be all right?" Rostnikov asked.

"She will be fine," said Iosef glumly.

"He thinks it is his fault," said Anna, stroking the cat, whose eyes were shut in contentment.

"Of course it was my fault," Iosef said, looking into his empty cup. "I should have seen, been more prepared. She could have been killed because I was not alert."

"One cannot anticipate all contingencies," said Anna Timofeyeva. "You deal with crime and criminals, sometimes lunatics. You are a policeman, not a bricklayer."

"I know," said Iosef. "But . . ."

"If you spend your life going over each act that you did not and could not anticipate," said Anna, "you will fail to address the present."

"Anna Timofeyeva does not believe in the

past," Rostnikov explained, gulping down the last of his coffee. "And she does not believe in God."

"There is no past," she said. "It is gone. There is now. There may be tomorrow. That is what you address. That is where you live, right where you stand."

"You have turned to philosophy," Rostnikov said.

"I have time for reflection and the reading of mystical books which, thankfully, tend to be very short, though obscure."

"I must go home. I called Sarah from Petrovka. She wanted to come but I told her to stay, that I would be home soon. She is waiting up for me. Iosef?"

"Anna Timofeyeva has invited me to stay here tonight," Iosef said.

"In Lydia Tkach's apartment," Anna said. "Lydia is thankfully away somewhere, looking at religious paintings with her artist. She left me the key. She will not mind."

Rostnikov looked at his son and touched the younger man's cheek. "Elena said you will be married when she is well," he said. "We will have a party. Who shall we invite?"

"I . . . just a few friends," said Iosef.

Rostnikov nodded and moved to the door. Perhaps he would include the Yak and Pankov on the guest list. It would be interesting to see them attempting to be sociable. He doubted if either would come but the possibility intrigued him.

"Perhaps a surprise or two," said Rostnikov.

"I can do without surprises for a while," said Iosef.

Rostnikov nodded to Anna, touched his son's arm, and left the apartment.

Twenty minutes later, Rostnikov entered the apartment on Krasnikov Street as quietly as he could in the hope of not waking the two girls and their grandmother, who slept in the front room. One more week and grandmother and grandchildren would have their own apartment, only a single room, but a large one on the floor above. But for now they were here. Rostnikov moved slowly and as quietly as his mechanical leg would allow.

He made it to the bedroom without awakening the sleeping trio, opened the door, and found Sarah sitting up in the bed, a book in her lap, a pillow behind her back. The only light in the room came from a small reading lamp on the table next to the bed. He closed the door behind him and stood for a moment looking at her.

She was pale, a paleness that contrasted with the darkening red of her hair, which had grown back since her operation. She wore the blue nightgown he had bought for her when she got out of the hospital. Sarah Rostnikov was still a lovely woman. She smiled and patted the right side of the bed next to her, his side.

He moved to her and sat.

"How is Elena?"

"She will be well. They want to marry soon. Perhaps next week."

Sarah nodded.

"I told them we would have a party."

"Of course," she said.

"You can? . . ."

"Galina and the girls will help me. It will be fine, Porfiry Petrovich. Hungry?"

"No. Tired."

"Take off your clothes and Lenin, shave, shower, and come to bed."

"Lenin?"

"I have decided," she said, "to call your alien leg Lenin. You should have something to call it."

"Why Lenin?" he asked, starting to undress.

"You can engage in secret political discussion and seek cooperation to your mutual satisfaction," she said. "And no one will know but the two of you."

"Then Lenin it is," he said, looking at her.

"The Korcescus on the second floor are having trouble with their toilet again," she said.

"I will deal with that challenge tomorrow night."

"Porfiry Petrovich," she said. "How long has it been since we made love?"

He thought for a moment.

"You have not been . . ."

"I am well," she said. "If you are too tired . . ."

"I am definitely not too tired," he said.

"There is one condition."

"What is that?"

"Lenin goes under the bed where he belongs," she said.

Rostnikov laughed. He rarely laughed. The world was often amusing, tragic, dangerous, and touched with individual sadness, but not funny. He could not remember the last time he had laughed. Granted, this had been a brief laugh but it was a real one.

"I'll shower first," he said.

"Shower later," Sarah said.

Chapter Nine

Don't cry for me I never cried for you
Just left without the name
Of the place I'm going to
Left without so much as a whisper to
  remind you
I'm traveling to forget you
And to find you

In the morning the sun was shining and the snow had stopped falling. For today at least there would be a clean, soft white blanket covering Moscow. People would be polite. Some might even smile. This was Moscow weather. If there were no rain the snow would slowly take on a fragile crackling crust of gray, and if it did not melt it would begin to break out in irregular pocks of dirt and city grime. Smiles, always held dear and protected by seriousness, would fade. All would wait for, hope for, discuss the winter, the expectation of a fresh snow.

"It will snow tomorrow," said Maya in a

whisper, lying next to her husband on the mattress laid out on the floor. "The television said so."

Sasha faced her, his head propped on two pillows.

"Yes," he said.

They said nothing. Her left breast was exposed under her nightgown. When he had gotten home, the children had been asleep in the bedroom. His knees had threatened to give way under him when Sasha opened the apartment door.

Would she be dressed in a business suit, arms folded before her, ready for no-nonsense discussion, a laying-out of the ground rules of their fragile reconciliation?

Maya had been sitting on the sofa in her nightgown.

She had said nothing, simply stood, looking quite beautiful, her dark hair pulled back, her face clear and clean, her full lips in a welcoming smile which, Sasha was certain, carried with it a touch of caution.

Maya had come to him, moved into his arms. He had pulled her close, gently, his knees still shaking, and then he had wept.

Now, with the sun coming through the window, he knew it was time to talk, talk about more than the winter and the snow, about more than the Trans-Siberian Express.

"Your mother is coming back tomorrow," said Maya, who still had the distinct lilt of the Ukraine in her voice. "She called. She is bringing her artist."

"Good," said Sasha.

Silence again.

"Maya, I . . . I will do better. I must do better. Just stay."

She took his right hand and placed it on her exposed breast.

"I am here, Sasha," she said. "The children are here."

They had made love when he came home. He had shaved and washed on the plane wanting to look as good as possible when she saw him. They had made love. He had been afraid that he would be too tired or too frightened or that she would reject him, but they had made love and it had been good, and strong and long, and she had been satisfied.

"A new beginning," she said as the baby began to make small whimpering sounds in the bedroom behind them.

He kissed her, remembering her smell, a special smell, not sweet but distinct. Each woman had a smell, her own smell, that came not from perfumes or perspiration but from her essence. Maya's smell was gentle, the hint of some forgotten forest and a spice which eluded him. He put his face to her neck, pulling in her smell, savoring it.

"The baby is up," said Pulcharia from the doorway of the bedroom.

Sasha turned on the mattress to face his daughter. She was going to be four years old in less than a month. She had been gone for more than two months. Pulcharia was the same child and yet a different one. She wore a large white T-shirt that came down to her ankles. Her hair had grown longer and was unbrushed and tumbling into her eyes. She stood looking at her father.

She is her mother's child, he thought.

"Pulcharia," he said.

She rubbed her eyes and took a step forward, a slow tentative step, and then padded across the floor and into his arms. The baby was crying with conviction now.

"I will get him," Maya said, getting up.

"Kiev looks like Moscow, only different," Pulcharia told her father. "Why do you have tears?"

"I am crying for joy," Sasha said. "I am crying because you are all back."

"Are you hungry?" the child asked.

"Very," he said. "Let us find something to eat."

In the morning the sun was shining and the snow had stopped falling. Vendors, packed in layers of clothes, looking like ragged Marioshki dolls, set up their tables near the metro stations selling *kvas,* chestnuts, crinkly cellophane packages of American corn chips. People passed. The world was white. The ponds in the parks would be almost frozen by now.

There was a wariness held in deep check, the recollection of a bombing that kept some of the vendors out of the underground pedestrian tunnels that carried swarms of shuffling people under the broad streets. After the bomb, people had braved the dangers of reckless drivers rather than go where they might be trapped by explosion. Now, more were going through the echoing tunnels.

Viktor Dalipovna had called in to his office and said he would not be coming in that day and possibly the next and possibly the one after that.

He had taken the metro, gone through a pedestrian tunnel, and walked many blocks. He could have gotten closer, but he wanted time to think, the cold air, the tingle that should slap at his cheeks and make him truly understand the reality of what had happened to his daughter.

They had given him an address, actually a street where a neighborhood police station was tucked between an old gray five-story office building and a garage. The station was on a small side street. Viktor had lived all of his fifty-five years in Moscow but remembered no police station here.

There were many things he had not noticed in his lifetime.

The station was dark. Uniformed young men who did not look old enough to shave stood inside the doors with automatic weapons. People, mostly policemen talking to each other, moved by him, ignoring him.

Viktor moved to an old desk behind which sat a man with pockmarked face, a heavy man with gray-black hair and a uniform with a collar so tight it turned his exposed neck into a line of taut ridges. The man's face was red and he wheezed slightly when he spoke.

"My name is Viktor Dalipovna," he said. "My daughter is here. I was told I could come."

The man behind the desk looked up at him with disapproval and then down at a list on the desk. Viktor could see names, some of them lined out, some open, others underlined in red.

"Room seven," the man at the desk said, filling out a small rectangular form and handing it to him. "That way."

Viktor took the sheet and moved past the flow of policemen. The station smelled of age and decay. He found room seven, knocked, and a voice called, "Enter."

Viktor opened the door and found himself in a very small, dirty white room with a wooden table. On the other side of the table his daughter Inna sat, her hands handcuffed together awkwardly because of the white cast on her right wrist. Next to her sat a man who looked at Viktor and pointed to a wooden bench facing himself and Inna.

Viktor sat, keeping his eyes on his daughter.

"I am Inspector Iosef Rostnikov of the Office of Special Investigation," Iosef said.

"Yes," said Viktor, hardly glancing at the tired-looking young man. "You were on the television. The policewoman. The one Inna . . . is she? . . ."

"She will be well," said Iosef.

Inna looked at her father. He saw nothing in her eyes, no emotion, no fear, anger. Perhaps a quiet resignation.

"You have ten minutes," Iosef said.

"Can we be alone?" Viktor asked.

"No," said Iosef. "I am sorry."

Viktor turned to his daughter and reached out to touch her manacled hands. She neither responded nor pulled away. Her hands were cold. Or perhaps it was his hands which were cold.

"Inna," he said. "Do you really hate me so much?"

"I do not hate you, Poppa," the woman said flatly.

At that moment, and just for a moment, Inna reminded Viktor of his dead wife, Inna's mother at the very end when she had decided to ignore what remained of her life and those who had been a part of it.

"Then why?" he asked.

"I love you, Poppa," she said. "And I hate you. I want to kill you, to make you see me as a person, not as a pathetic child, a sick child. But I do not want you to die. You want to know why?"

"Yes," he said.

"Because I am afraid of being alone. I am afraid you will go with my mother and leave me alone. I hate you for that and I hate her because she might come and take you. I am afraid and I hate her and you."

"Have I been that bad to you?"

"You have not been anything to me at all," she said. "I am your burden. I clean and cook and shop and I do not exist."

"We talk," he said.

"You talk," she said. "I pretend to listen."

"But to kill people, Inna?"

She looked away and said, "They say I am crazy. I hear them. The doctor last night. She said I was crazy, but she did not use that word. They are going to put me in a crazy house, Poppa. Who will make your meals, do your shopping?"

"That is not important, Inna," he said.

She pulled her hands away from his touch.

"Not important? It has been the only meaning my life has had and now you say it is not important?" she said, showing not anger but pain.

"I did not mean —" he tried.

She started to rise but the young inspector put his hand gently on her arm and guided her back into her chair. Inna closed her eyes.

"I will get a lawyer," Viktor said. "Kolya in my office, who handles our contracts. He knows lawyers."

"You will be alone now, Poppa," she said, so softly that he was not sure if she had spoken or he had only imagined her voice.

"Inna —" he started.

"I want to go back now," she said, turning to Iosef.

Iosef nodded and rose. Inna Dalipovna rose too and looked at her father. He sat, unable to rise, frozen by the look on the face of his daughter. She was smiling, not the smile of happiness or the calm smile of feeling alive, but a smile of satisfaction.

★ ★ ★

In the morning the sun was shining and the snow had stopped falling, but he no longer cared. The Naked Cossack would have cared, but he was no longer the Cossack. His father had taken care of that. He was no longer Misha Lovski. He had renounced that. He was no one.

He had been informed that his brother had been treated by a doctor and would be well. He did not care. Songs did not run through his mind. There were no causes. There was just his father, who sat there.

He sat across the breakfast table in the dacha, cleaned and scrubbed, in new casual clothes, a plate of food before him which he did not look at.

"You feeling better, Misha?" Nikoli Lovski asked.

"Better than what?"

"Better than you did yesterday, Misha," Nikoli said, working on his coffee.

"Better? Of course. You locked me in a cage, tried to drive me insane, took away my identity. How could I not be better?"

"Misha . . ." Nikoli Lovski began calmly.

"Do not call me that," he said.

"What shall I call you?"

"Nothing," he said. "Call me nothing."

"You are not nothing," said his father with

a sigh, putting down his coffee cup. "You are an educated young man, a Jew, a member of my family, an important family. You can have a great deal, be someone important."

"Nothing," the young man said. "I want nothing. I am nothing."

"Would you like to go to South America?" Nikoli said.

"I embarrass you here," was the reply.

"Yes, you do, but that is not the reason I want you to go to Chile. You can start your life again. We have a television station there. You can work, be something."

"I was a cossack," he said angrily.

"You were never a cossack," his father answered. "You are a Jew. The cossacks would stomp on you with their boots and leave you with your insides steaming on the street without giving it a thought."

"And so I am nothing," he answered.

"You are going to South America," his father repeated.

"And if I do not choose to go?"

"You will do what? Go in the streets? Hide from your former friends? A new life is better."

"And I have no choice?"

"None," Nikoli said.

"The law . . ."

". . . will not interfere with our family. I am

not your enemy, Misha. Give yourself a new name. It will not change who you are. I am not trying to hurt you."

"Just control me."

"There is nothing more to say," Nikoli said, wiping his face with a napkin and dropping the napkin on the table. "You will be treated well. You will work. I see no point in our talking again before you leave. I am sure our conversation would get no further than it is at this moment."

"And . . ."

"I will come to Chile in six or seven months," Nikoli said. "We will see what changes have taken place in you. I will have someone there to teach you Spanish."

"Everything is planned," the young man said with as much sarcasm as he could muster.

"Everything is never fully planned," his father said. "But plans are necessary if we are not to be completely surprised by life."

"I will remember that," the young man said.

"Then we are already making progress."

In the morning the sun was shining and the snow had stopped falling. It was not spring that held out the hope of a new beginning to Moscovites. It was winter. The cold wrapped them in a protective embrace. The snow provided a fortress of respite. From what? From crime which prowled under the sun and struck under the moon. From madness in the streets born of despair. From the restless and the overworked and those who did not work and took to the streets to escape the bleakness of small apartments with restless cats and dogs and television screens that had long since failed to provide more than a temporary narcotic.

Crime went down in the winter. Tempers cooled in the cold. Bodies moved more slowly and were less likely to collide or, if they did, were less likely to take umbrage at the crash. Automobile accidents, which in other cold countries went up in the winter, fell in Russia with the coming of snow and cold. Yes, there were exceptions, usually caused by vodka, but drivers moved more slowly, coaxing their vehicles, talking gently to them, urging them to live through one more winter under the promise of pampering.

Porfiry Petrovich Rostnikov and Emil Karpo sat in a café, drinking coffee. They could not talk outside walking in the cold. Lenin would rebel. They could not talk in the offices in Petrovka. The Yak would listen. And so the moment Emil Karpo had entered his cubicle in the morning he had been greeted by the chief inspector.

Karpo was generally the first one in the office. This morning had been no different. He had simply followed Rostnikov back onto Petrovka Street and walked at his side silently till they reached the café where people were packed in at the counter or the small tables along the wall, drinking hurriedly, checking their watches.

Karpo, as always, was dressed in black. His leather coat was black. Even his scarf and fur hat were black. Rostnikov thought that clothes reflected the people who wore them. Rostnikov himself dressed neatly, conservatively, in old comfortable suits and ties Sarah had bought for him at market stalls. As for Karpo's choice of black, Rostnikov was not given to simple judgment. He himself was rather fond of black, which was either the absence of color or the totality of color. There was a statement in black, he thought. Black said, You cannot penetrate my being by looking at my exterior. I am a dark cipher.

"The report on the Lovski case is on your desk," Karpo said.

"Good," replied Rostnikov, who was munching on a brown flat piece of cake that tasted too little of chocolate and was too hard. It dipped well in his coffee.

"We will, I think, want to change the report

before presenting it to the director," he said.

"And why is that?" asked Karpo, who had not touched his coffee.

"Because it contains the truth. Misha Lovski was kidnapped by his own father. Two mercenaries hired by Nikoli Lovski took two witnesses, conspirators in the kidnapping. Both witnesses, a boy and a girl, may well be dead now. Misha Lovski is now in his father's hands. The mercenary Zelach shot has been released from custody."

"And? What is in error?"

"Nothing. The report is, I am certain, complete and accurate."

"But it must be changed?"

The chocolate brick softened only minimally with its dipping into the now-warm coffee, but it was edible. At first Rostnikov did not answer. He sat upright. A portly little man with large glasses carrying a cup of coffee almost collided with Karpo. The little man began an apology but cut it short when he looked into Karpo's eyes.

"I believe Director Yaklovev has taken advantage of the situation to fortify himself with political currency to further his own ambition," said Karpo. "I believe the concept of justice has not been served. We exist to serve the goals of a man in a system which is no longer interested in justice."

"And this is something new?" asked Rostnikov.

"No, but it has become something petty
and without meaning. It has no foundation."

"We still do our work, take criminals off the
street, neutralize them," said the chief inspector. "Elena and Iosef did that. We do it every
day."

"Except when there is a prize to be won by
the director. Before . . ."

"During the Soviet Socialist Union," said
Rostnikov.

"Yes, during," said Karpo. "One could
hold on to the precepts, the hope of Communism. The people who were in power
were corrupt, but there always existed a
hope."

"And now you see no hope?" said Rostnikov.

"The only justice that will prevail is justice
taken by those who are willing to take responsibility for their convictions," said Karpo.

"You mean bypass the law?"

Karpo looked directly at his superior and
did not answer.

"I admit it is tempting to know one is right,
face a thief, a murderer, a rapist, a corruptor
of children, and simply shoot him," said
Rostnikov. "But what of those who are not
able to discern who the thief, murderer, rap-

ist, and child corruptor is, those who are not certain?"

"I know when I am facing evil," said Karpo. "You know. I cannot speak for others. If we do not act, then too often there will be no action. Those with money and means will prevail."

"As it has always been," Rostnikov agreed. "Do you realize, Emil Karpo, this is the longest conversation we have ever had?"

Karpo said nothing.

"And so you want to start shooting criminals?"

"Yes," said Karpo. "But I will not do so."

"No," said Rostnikov, "you will do the opposite. You will justify your ethics by martyring yourself."

"I do not believe in martyrs," said Karpo.

"You believe in? . . ."

"The small evil. The larger ones are beyond us."

"I see," said Rostnikov. "Do you think much about Mathilde?"

"She is dead," said Karpo. "Killed without meaning. Her killers, if they have not yet been gunned down by rival Mafias, still swagger in clubs and drive in expensive cars."

"Emil Karpo, you are bitter."

Karpo did not answer.

"I think that is a good start," said

Rostnikov. "*Bitter* is a sharp edge of emotion. It cuts deeply. You are going to have a new assignment for the indefinite future."

Karpo registered nothing, asked no questions.

"You have your files of dead cases," Rostnikov said. "Your black books filled with crimes which have never been solved, which you work on when you have time. And there are more pages and more books all the time."

"The point of this, Chief Inspector?"

"You are to work on your dead cases," said Rostnikov. "Choose whichever ones you wish, go back as far as suits you. Take the time you need on each one. No pressure for success. Simply keep me informed. No written reports unless you successfully conclude a dead case. You understand?"

"Your words are clear."

"And no killing," said Rostnikov. "Justice, Emil Karpo. Avoid, if you can, cases with political implication, cases which might have in them the possibility for exploitation. And do not take unnecessary risks. You understand?"

"Perfectly. When do I begin?"

"When we finish our coffee. Oh yes, Elena and Iosef are to be married as soon as she is up and well. You will of course attend the wedding and the party."

"If I am invited."

"You are. Now, questions?"

"No."

"I have one. What are your thoughts about the sun?"

"It is the source of energy and life on earth," said Karpo. "It is a star that will some-day die."

"Nothing else?"

Again, Karpo did not answer.

"I have brought you something," Rost-nikov said. "I would like you to read it."

He reached awkwardly into his coat pocket and came up with a ragged paperback book. He handed it to Karpo.

"Poetry," Rostnikov said. "Russian poetry. Yevtushenko. Have you ever read poetry?"

"No. It serves no function other than feed-ing delusion and fantasy."

"Humor me, Emil," said Rostnikov, start-ing to rise. "Humor me. Perhaps you will find that you have undervalued the function of de-lusion and fantasy. What takes place in our imagination is as real as that which exists out-side our body."

"I have not found it so," said Karpo, also rising.

"One can but hope," said Rostnikov.

Epilogue

Siberia: 1912

Boris Antonovich Dermanski adjusted the straps on the pack he carried on his back and tried to get his bearings. It had been nineteen years since he had been here. The train tracks were there, two sets of them now, but there was no train at rest to tell him which way to go.

He knew that the rock where he had hidden the package was north of the tracks and no more than a few hundred yards from them. That reduced the search area to several million acres. He also knew that the rock was somewhere between Beloyarskiy and Sverdlovsk-Pass.

Boris had survived the search and killing two decades earlier. He had been tortured, lost a small finger, but played the fool and survived. Lieutenant Smolkov had not been so lucky. Boris had continued to work on the tracks, had hidden the package deep into his thoughts, covered it with a gentle fog, waited, fearing that there might be those who still watched, still combed the area where the box might be hidden.

He had left the railroad and with the little money he had saved opened a small shoe-repair shop on Gogol Street in Ekaterinburg with the thought that someday, a day when he was absolutely certain it would be safe, he would return for the package he had hidden. Boris had married, had a son, survived with food on the table, just short of prospering.

When fifteen years had passed he had taken up hiking, always alone, staying out in the forest for days at a time, professing a love of nature which he did not feel. He had walked along the tracks, marking off the areas, probing into the forest through the aspen and birch, once fighting off a pack of six wolves, once getting lost for almost a week.

What he searched for was some sign, some landmark he might recognize, but it all looked the same.

This day, however, was different. There was something familiar about the woods to his right and the mountains far beyond. He had felt this before, had been wrong, but this time felt different. It was a visual memory brought back from the protective fog.

He plunged into the forest. It did not feel the same as it had when he and the others had come in to drop the dead, and yet he was almost certain that he was right. He had gone more than a hundred yards farther than he was sure the rocks had been. He turned around, moved to his left about twenty-five yards, and started back. His plan was to continue this pattern, back and forth, till he found the rocks or was certain that he had to move on.

It was not the rocks he spotted first. It was the bones, and he almost missed them. A single bone stuck up from the earth, pointing toward the sun. Boris almost tripped over it because his eyes were scanning the trees before him in search of the rock.

It was a human bone, probably from an arm. He got on his hands and knees and clawed at the tundra with his calloused hands and fingers. In half an hour he had found a skull, probably the remains of one of the dead he had helped carry and whose remains had been dragged here and eaten. He threw the skull away and began to circle, using the skull and bone as his center point. Just as the sun was going down he saw the rocks.

His heart was beating fast, too fast. He ran through the trees toward the rocks and when he reached them was surprised that they seemed so much smaller than he had remembered. His wife's reading aloud of the Bible had colored his memory. He had been searching for a large altar, a rock worthy of Abraham's planned sacrifice of his son Isaac.

Instead he had found a grouping of small rocks, gray and black, covered in green patches of moss, unworthy of the dreams he had hidden from his wife and son.

The niche was there, just as it had been, but what of the package? Almost twenty years.

It was there, the leather peeling, the cord still tied. He had not been told by the long-dead lieutenant what the package had contained, but he knew it had to be valuable.

He looked around the forest for signs, feeling watched. The sun was almost down now but he opened the package and found a metal box, a gold box. Inside the box, which opened easily, Boris found the ruby, huge, bright red, catching the last beams of the sun through the branches of the nearby birch trees. He clutched the ruby in his right hand, clutched it so tightly that his palm began to bleed.

There was a sheet of paper inside the box with handwriting. Boris could not read. He cared nothing about pieces of paper. He put paper and ruby back in the gold box and stuffed them in his backpack.

He should stay here for the night. He knew that, but he felt the presence of ghosts, perhaps the men whose corpses they had dropped. More likely it was his imagination. But he did not remain there. Moving to the south with the last of the twilight, he went to the tracks and began to follow them toward Ekaterinburg.

Back in town four days later, Boris hid the leather pouch and gold box with the letter inside them. He carefully approached the town's most successful and corrupt government official, Arvidis Sujnesk, who had been a customer in Boris's shoe-repair shop for a decade.

When he was confident of the level of Sujnesk's corruptibility, he entered into a partnership. The details had to be worked out carefully to protect Boris, but Boris had spent almost twenty years perfecting his plan for this very event.

It took more than a year to find the right intermediary to handle the sale of the ruby. Sujnesk and Boris not only shared the considerable wealth, they used their money carefully, covertly, to corrupt and infiltrate the government and the managers of the nearby mines.

Within two years, the men had successfully established a criminal operation that made them powerful and wealthy. Boris was in his office when the news of the revolution came. The day the czar and his family were brought to Ekaterinburg on the train line Boris had helped to build, Boris and his son were on the road in their carriage heading for their dacha. The truck carrying the last of the Romanovs drove past them. They watched the royal family ramble down a country road in an open-backed truck. One of the princesses looked out at Boris and met his eyes.

There was a history of sorrow and resignation in that look that Boris never forgot. He instructed his son to keep a record of everyone their organization dealt with, to keep evidence that might be used in case someone came to take his family away in an open-backed truck.

When Boris died, his son took over the business with sons of Sujnesk. The revolution came to Ekaterinburg but business continued, prospered. Hundreds died when the famine came. Stalin's fist pounded on Siberia. The town became a city of exiles who poured in by train, hungering for work, willing to kill for bread.

The son of Boris Antonovich Dermanski kept records faithfully and secretly, and when his wife bore him a daughter and no son, he gave her the golden box with the ancient letter and told her where to hide it and what records she should keep.

She did so faithfully, and when her father

died he passed the gift to her. When she too had a daughter and the Mafia had risen and taken over the underworld, she had turned the gift over to her daughter, who dutifully maintained the family tradition.

It was only when the husband of the great-granddaughter of Boris Antonovich died that the young woman living now as a clerk for an electrician contacted one of the few members of the Mafia she felt she could trust, a man whose loyalty was purchased uncertainly for several nights of passionless sex and the gift of the gold box passed down to her by her father. The Mafia member had risked his life and eventually lost it by contacting a cousin in Moscow.

Two months later, the great-granddaughter of Boris Antonovich Dermanski had lost the precious, carefully compiled contents of her package to the man with the limp, and escaped with the gift of her own life.

Now she sat as the winter wind hummed down the street outside the building where she shared a room with a friend. She looked out the frosted window and saw snow dancing madly in thin waves down the street.

She watched for hours, finally falling asleep in her chair, covered by a blanket. She dreamed of her father and mother, of the limping man at the train station, of her dead husband, and of a dark formless mass streaming toward her from under the door.

She awoke with a gasp to the sound of the Trans-Siberian Express roaring to a stop at the train station less than a mile away. She awoke to the sound and a warm light.

Outside the window, the sun was shining brightly.

The employees of Thorndike Press hope you have enjoyed this Large Print book. All our Large Print titles are designed for easy reading, and all our books are made to last. Other Thorndike Press Large Print books are available at your library, through selected bookstores, or directly from the publishers.

For more information about titles, please call:

(800) 223-1244
(800) 223-6121

To share your comments, please write:

Publisher
Thorndike Press
295 Kennedy Memorial Drive
Waterville, ME 04901